Preparations for the first Grand Jubilee in five hundred years were in full swing on Ozark. Grannys, Magicians, and a delegation from each of the Twelve Families had gathered, eager for the festivities to begin. But Responsible of Brightwater was nervous.

Some Families were dead set against the Confederation of Continents, and this was the week it might go down for good. To make matters worse, handsome young Lewis Motley Wommack the 33rd had chosen this moment to arrive at Castle Brightwater, determined to use his amorous tricks to ferret out her Magic.

Responsible had cast Spells half the night, and still only gotten one answer. There was *trouble* ahead. And she was right smack in the middle of it...

Berkley Books by
Suzette Haden Elgin

TWELVE FAIR KINGDOMS
THE GRAND JUBILEE

SUZETTE HADEN ELGIN

THE GRAND JUBILEE

Book Two of the Ozark Fantasy Trilogy

BERKLEY BOOKS, NEW YORK

All of the characters in this book
are fictitious, and any resemblance
to actual persons, living or dead,
is purely coincidental.

This Berkley book contains the complete text of the original hardcover edition. It has been completely reset in a typeface designed for easy reading, and was printed from new film.

THE GRAND JUBILEE

A Berkley Book/published by arrangement with Doubleday & Company, Inc.

Printing History
Doubleday edition published 1981
Berkley edition/August 1983

Cover illustration by Frederic Marvin.

ISBN: 0-425-06045-4

A BERKLEY BOOK ® TM 757,375
Berkley Books are published by The Berkley Publishing Group, 200 Madison Avenue, New York, New York 10016.
The name "BERKLEY" and the stylized "B" with design are trademarks belonging to Berkley Publishing Corporation.
PRINTED IN THE UNITED STATES OF AMERICA

PROLOGUE

The Twelve Families left Earth on The Ship, disgusted and offended past all bearing, and settled the planet they named Ozark, determined that what had happened on Earth would never happen there. Because they blamed the outrages of Earth upon its governments, they fought doggedly against any attempt to centralize the government of Ozark. They settled its six continents as rapidly as possible, at great sacrifice for all, in order that there should be on Ozark none of the crowding that had contributed to the degradation of Earth; and they called their settlements Kingdoms, one to each Family. It was their goal to keep themselves to themselves, to respect the privacy of others—to be good boones.

In one thousand years they relented only to the point of establishing a shaky token organization called the Confederation of Continents, which sent small delegations to meet one month in four in Brightwater Kingdom, site of their original settlement on the planet. The delegates there discussed and debated and disputed; they had no authority to do anything more. And even this small concession was bitterly opposed by the anti-Confederationists, led by the isolationist Travellers of Tinaseeh, who saw it as the first step toward a strangling bureaucracy and the inexorable downhill path.

On Earth, they had seen what happened when science was the basis of all technology, and magic was a fringe activity despised by the powerful establishment. The Ozarkers turned this upside down, basing *their* technology on a rigorous and highly formal system of magic, maintaining only those few vestiges of science they felt were necessary to survival, and convinced that this separation of systems could be—must be—maintained.

Among the necessities they acknowledged were the comset networks, beamed out under the direction of the computers at Castle Brightwater, and gradually, over the centuries, coming to provide for Ozark almost everything that the mass media had provided on Earth. Basic supplies as well, grains and spices and herbs, lumber and ores and some essential manufactured goods, were carried by solar-powered transport ships from the central continents to those where the efforts of settlement and development were still primary.

But most of life on Ozark was firmly under the control of magic. The Grannys provided basic household and garden needs, healed simple illnesses, saw to the crucial work of Proper Names for girlbabies, and educated the little girls from age three to seven in the Granny Schools. The Magicians took care of sickness of moderate degree, saw to law enforcement and judicial affairs, regulated commerce and industry, provided Tutors for the little boys' education, and trained young men to carry on the profession of magic. The Magicians of Rank, only nine for all Ozark, had the really difficult task: control of those forces that had once struck humankind as catastrophes against which there was little defense. They dealt with weather, plagues and epidemics, intercontinental confrontations, truly serious diseases, fire, famine, and whatever else the universe saw fit to throw at them. Furthermore, they kept the Mules flying; no creature so bulky and so aerodynamically unsuitable as an Ozark Mule could be maintained as the dominant mode of personal transportation for a whole planet except by magic. And they had the power to overcome the Mules' regulated speed of sixty miles an hour in flight, and to take them almost instantaneously from place to place by the process called SNAPPING, which was useful in a crisis and in the absence of any other rapid transport.

As the five-hundred-year anniversary of the Confederation approached, Brightwater Kingdom invited all the continents to send special delegations, accompanied by their staffs and families, to a Grand Jubilee in celebration of the occasion. The anti-Confederationists cried "Waste!" and "Decadence!" and opposed the meeting, but this was to be expected, and was as necessary to the maintaining of their public image as the hosting of the Jubilee was to Brightwater's; it bothered no one. Even when things began to go awry with the system of magic at Brightwater, the Family took it lightly, considering it no more than mischief. Soured milk and shattered mirrors; scrambled signposts and Mules that flew just a tad erratically. Nothing that merited the dignity of attention, although it was annoying.

But then the anti-Confederationists went too far, kidnapping a baby right in the middle of a Brightwater church service and hanging him up in a cedar tree in a life-support bubble, where he could be seen and all his needs were attended to, but where no one dared interfere with the magic that held him there.

That was too much; it had ceased to be mere teasing and become open threat. The message being sent to the Twelve Families, loud and clear, was: "Better stay home from the Jubilee, because the magic at Brightwater isn't powerful enough to protect you and yours." A countermessage, and a forceful one, was required at once.

The Confederation could not be allowed to fall. It was not only that the frontier continents were far more dependent upon the services of Brightwater than they realized, making isolation a real danger for their people; that would have been problem enough. But beyond that, there were threats to the planet known only to a very few, and facing those threats demanded a united government, a united populace, and the strength that comes of long-established order.

And so Responsible of Brightwater, elder daughter at the Castle, set out upon a Solemn Quest, subject to all the ancient constraints upon such journeys, including the requirement that there be many adventures along the way to validate it. Its declared intent was to find the culprit tampering with Brightwater's magic; its real purposes were to demonstrate Brightwater's contempt for such petty tomfoolery, and to reassure the Families and guarantee their attendance at the Jubilee.

At each of the Castles she visited, Responsible of Brightwater became more aware of the troubles building on Ozark, and more convinced of the need for a strong intercontinental assembly to deal with them. She found Families afraid of other Families, and Families on the narrow edge of feud—this on a planet where the twin controls of religion and magic had made violence almost unknown. She found the beginnings of religious fanaticism; she found an unwholesome leaning away from systematic magic toward warped and random superstition; she found the first signs of ugly prejudice. At Castle Farson she was visited in the night by a representative of the Gentles, one of the three indigenous peoples of the planet, who complained to her that the Families of Arkansaw were violating the treaties signed between Gentles and Terrans all those hundreds of years before when the continent was first settled by the Ozarkers. And she found the criminal that had been using magic illegally—a weak and frightened woman egged on by a husband she loved to excess, and incapable of much more than mischief.

This last problem Responsible of Brightwater handled easily on the spot, setting a binding spell upon the woman that forbid her the use of any magic whatsoever, even the Housekeeping Spells. The other problems she carried home with her to be taken up later, hoping that out of the Jubilee would be forged a strong new governing body for the Confederation of Continents. If that could be achieved, and the assembly given sufficient status and authority, then perhaps some of her long list of problems needing attention could safely be attended to.

Once home at Castle Brightwater, Responsible was plunged into the frantic activity of preparation for the Jubilee. Food and accommodations had to be made ready for hundreds of guests, as well as all sorts of entertainments to occupy a large proportion of those hundreds while the delegations met for five successive days at Confederation Hall. With so much to be done and so little time to do it in, she had no choice but to set aside everything else, however trivial the organization of checkers tournaments seemed beside the urgent necessity for organization of a world government.

Now it is May, of the year 3012, and the Families and their staffs are arriving at Brightwater. And tomorrow the Grand Jubilee of the Confederation of Continents begins.

PART ONE

CHAPTER 1

"OH, GREAT GATES," said Jewel of Wommack. "I'll never manage it."

Her brother looked down at her and grinned.

"Afraid you'll fall in the water, are you?" he teased. "Tell you what, dear heart, I'll carry you down the landing ramp."

"You touch me, Lewis Motley Wommack," she said between her teeth, "and I'll scream you a scream they'll hear all the way to Castle Brightwater."

He leaned one elbow on the gunwale, set his chin in his hand, and looked at her sideways, considering. She had a scream that was deservedly famous, did Jewel, and the potential scene had a certain appeal for him. There they'd be, pulling up to the mooring, the great ship easy in the calm water of the harbor, and all the passengers crowding politely onto the ramp three abreast. And there'd be all the elegant citizens waiting on the landing in their Sundy best—*Jubilee* best!—standing under the ancient trees that shaded them and watching the delegations and their households disembark. And there *he'd* be, carrying his screaming squalling sister through all the decorous lines of pleasant people . . .

"Don't you think it," she said firmly. "Don't you even *think* it! You'll rue it, I swear you will."

"Will you set a Spell on me, little sister?" he asked, mock-terrified before her prowess, and then he gathered her against him and held her close to his side. It was a good deal like holding a sapling whipping in the wind, if you'll allow a sapling the skill to curse without ceasing; but she was no more trouble to him than the buttons on his cloak. He could have held half a dozen more like her, all screaming and spitting, and not begun to exert himself.

Jewel was fighting him only for the principle of the thing, having learned in the course of her twelve and a half years that it was a useless activity for any other purpose. She had seen her brother lift a full-grown man over his head and throw him into a tree, and he hadn't even been angry at the time, just slightly fussed. And then she had an idea.

The wicked point of the broochpin that she'd had at her throat took him right in the armpit, where there was little clothing and less muscle. The group behind them stepped back hastily at his roar of pain, and Jewel braced herself to be flung over the side. It would spoil her gown and her cloak and her fine new shoes, and she would lose her hat and her travelbag in the process. It would mean being hauled in dripping wet before the grave watching eyes of Silverweb of McDaniels, that she could see standing among those waiting on the Landing, and somebody near enough her age that she'd half hoped to have her for a friend. But it would be worth it all. She'd happily have swum ten miles before all the Grannys of Ozark assembled, in a full set of winter clothes and wrapped in a quilt to top it off, if it would of gained her one point against Lewis Motley Wommack the 33rd. For all that she worshipped the ground he walked on and the air he breathed.

"Well?"

"Well what, Jewel of Wommack?"

"Well, aren't you going to pitch me overboard?" She braced herself again, and then felt her cheeks flood crimson as he patted her on the bottom like a Mule colt, right in front of all those people.

"No, Little Wickedness, I'm not going to do any such thing," he said. "Smile pretty now, there comes the land—and I expect you to walk that ramp like a highborn lady, which you are, and if you *do* fall in and shame us all I'll put you over my knee right there under those trees soon as you're fished out. Provided I don't let you drown, that is."

The men had tied the lines, and the First Officer secured the gleaming ironwood steps that would allow the passengers to walk up to where the ramp met the gunwales instead of scrambling over on a rope ladder like the crew was used to doing. There were a few cheers from the younger children, hastily hushed by their elders, and Jewel heard the resounding smack of a sturdy hand against someone's backside. That, she thought, would be a Purdy female, and a Purdy child; neither Wommack nor Traveller would of laid hand to one of their offspring in public—or needed to.

"Why?" she demanded softly, still clutched to her brother's side—and then she realized that in the noise of the landing, everyone talking quietly but everyone talking at once, she didn't have to be quiet, and she shouted it at him. *"Why?"*

"Why what?"

She wiggled violently, and he set her aside with a courtly smile, not scrupling to tickle her ribs as he did so.

"Why aren't you going to throw me overboard?"

"One, it would give you far too much satisfaction," he said promptly. "Two, I've already told you—a dozen times, if I've told you once—I intend to be careful of the Wommack reputation at this Jubilee. I'm tired to death of being only one cut above the Purdys—they're stupid and we're cursed, that's a fine bedamned arrangement! And I'll not risk a scandal before ever we set foot to Brightwater land, Jewel of Wommack. Not if you run a sword through my armpit instead of a pin."

She would of liked to say she was sorry, but she didn't dare. If there was one thing that made her brother furiouser than somebody doing something outrageous, it was that somebody saying they were sorry, afterwards. She stood shaking in her finery and trying to get her breath back, and she held her tongue.

"All right now," he said, and gave her a gentle push toward the steps. "Here we are, and this is the famous Brightwater Landing, and I'm right behind you. No simpering, no giggling, no lollygagging, sister mine. Move!"

She moved. The press of people behind her would have moved her in any case. Up the nine shining steps; and then, with a hand from the First Mate to steady her against the gentle rocking of the ship, across the narrow space and her foot on the landing ramp that stretched out into the harbor. And down the ramp between the rows of flags brilliant in the May breeze, in front of all those staring people—not that they stared openly, but she knew they watched her, all the same. She turned an ankle once, but no one would of guessed; Lewis Motley was at her elbow and he steadied her instantly.

"It's *miles* long, this ramp!" she fretted. "Suppose that's to give the Brightwaters ample time to look everybody over as they land!"

"No," he told her, "it's so the ramp will reach out into the harbor far enough to let people land from an oceangoing ship with a deep draft. You have a mind, Jewel, and known to be spectacular; use it. Nobody's looking at you."

"They are!" she insisted.

She knew they were, in her bones. She was not quite sure when it had begun; one day she was a child, fresh out of Granny School and not caring if the whole world looked at her nor even thinking they might care to. And the next she knew herself the center of everyone's attention, at all times. For the women at Castle Wommack to tell her that this came of being twelve and would disappear with turning thirteen, approximately, was no help to her. Thirteen might as well of been ten years away as four months, for every day stretched out long and lanky before her full of ordeals. They had told her who knew how many times. Her nose was *not* too pointed; her freckles were *not* ugly; the copper-colored hair that fought its way instantly out of any attempt she made at bringing it to order was not untidy; her breasts and hips were not too big; her legs were not too long. It didn't help any. Her days were a misery and she endured them, that being a woman's place in this world; but she defied anyone to expect her to enjoy them.

"Jewel, sister Jewel," he said as they stepped off the ramp onto the stones of the Landing—sure enough, each one was a good four feet square, and blinding white, just as she'd been told!—"I am counting on you."

She would have clung to him in despair and hidden her face against his chest; but he knew that, of course, and he was gone in an instant. He disappeared into the clusters of talking people like thread into a needle's eye, and was out of her sight.

"Jewel." The voice at her elbow was like a blessing pronounced twice; she turned joyfully to greet it. There stood Gilead of Wommack, Jewel's niece despite her seventeen years; and Jacob Donahue Wommack the 23rd, Gilead's father and the Master of Castle Wommack; and there stood Grannys Copperdell and Goodweather, both bristling with impatience to get on with it, whatever it might be; and all the rest of her homefolks.

"Oh, I am so glad to see you!" she declared, doing her best to disappear into the middle of the group, and she meant it most fervently. Whatever it was that her beloved brother was "counting on" her for, she intended to postpone it as long as possible.

"Lewis Motley's upset her," said Gilead to the others. "I knew he would."

"She's no business letting him," snapped Granny Copperdell.

"Granny," objected Jacob Donahue, "the child's only twelve!"

"When I was twelve I had a babe at my breast," said the old lady, "and it would of been a cold day in a warm place before any nineteen-year-old lout such as that one would of upset *me*."

Jewel had no doubt that was true. Indomitable twelve year olds such as that make good Grannys, and Granny Copperdell was one of the finest.

"If I had a babe at *my* breast," said Jewel staunchly, "I'd have it hind-end to, and youall know it."

"Jewel of Wommack!" Gilead was shocked, and the Dozens only knew what the Attendant and the servingmaid bringing up the rear with the smaller children thought. But both Grannys cackled with appreciation, and Jewel saw that as a good sign and took up her position between them. She could think of few safer places to be than flanked on either side by a Granny in a good mood.

A Brightwater Attendant, splendid in his livery of emerald green piped with narrow silver braid, the crest on his shoulder looking to be embroidered only yesterday, stepped forward then to greet them, making his proper salutations with a flourish.

"If you'll follow me," he said pleasantly, "I'll take you to your lodgings at the Castle and see you settled in."

Lewis Motley, popping up as unexpectedly as he'd disappeared, spoke from the back of the cluster of Wommacks.

"All of us?" he asked.

"Beg your pardon, sir?"

"I said, all of us? That is, is there *room* for all of us?"

"At Castle Brightwater?" The Attendant was clearly flabbergasted.

Lewis Motley Wommack shrugged politely, and made it obvious that he was being too well-bred to mention the four hundred some odd rooms at Castle Wommack, or its vast acres of land.

"Ignore him," said Jacob Donahue immediately, "and accept my apologies. He has no manners whatsoever and never did have. And keep an eye on him while he's under your roof, because he can't be trusted. I've done my best with him, poor orphan that he is, but it's been a hopeless and a thankless task. He grows wickeder with every passing year."

Lewis Motley chuckled, and Jewel wondered grimly how he'd of been behaving if he *hadn't* been concerned for the Wommack reputation; and the Attendant, confused but doggedly set on his duties, explained that although Castle Brightwater was nothing like the size of Castle Wommack, it could surely manage to put up the delegations of the other eleven Families of Ozark without strain. Gilead moved forward smoothly to soothe the poor man with a steady flow of distracting questions, and Granny Goodweather leaned back and pinched the unruly younger brother's cheek—a Granny's privilege, however much it might hurt, and however much the red wheal it left might mar the effect of the young man's splendid beard.

They were handed into five of a long line of gleaming carriages, each with the Brightwater crest on its door and harnessed to a matched team of four Mules, and Jewel began to enjoy herself in spite of everything. It was one thing to watch the doings at Castle Brightwater on the comset while she sat at home at Castle Wommack, and it was quite another to actually be here. The carriages were a fine touch, and she could tell she wasn't the only one to think so. Lizzies would of taken them up to the Castle far more quickly, twelve at a time, but a lizzy had none of the elegance of a four-Mule carriage. They were speckledy Mules, a soft gray flecked all over with a darker shade of the same; their harness was gray leather with silver fittings; and their tails had been done in an intricate five-strand braid, not just looped up and fastened in the usual way. And their hoofs! Jewel had never seen Mules with their hoofs, that were naturally a kind of nothing clayey color, stained a jetty black. It was purely splendid, and polite of the Mules to allow it done.

And then there were the crests; a crest on the door of a lizzy would of been like a lace collar on a goat. It was well carried out, and a few points for the Family Brightwater.

Somewhere down the line the remark came—"Waste, waste, and never an end to it!"—and nobody had to look back to identify the source. That would be someone from the Traveller delegation, going through the obligatory rituals in his thrifty suit of coarse black cloth and his plain black coat. The Travellers considered *anything* either pleasant or attractive to be a "waste."

"*They* are going to be a nuisance," said Gilead, and her father nodded.

"Fiddle," said Granny Copperdell, "they just make for balance. Everybody else says 'how nice' and the Travellers come in all together with 'what a waste' and it evens it all out. Keeps us from getting carried away with delight and debauchery. Right useful of them, if you want my opinion on the matter."

"The eeeeequilibrium of the yuuuuuuuniverse is a fraaaaaail and—"

"Lewis Motley Wommack!" The Granny's voice whipped through the air in the open carriage, and Jewel tried not to wince. "You mock the Reverend, and on a Sundy at that, and I'll see you pay dearly for it!"

Jewel listened to the laughter in his voice, tucked under the charming apology that came properly and without a second's holdback, and wished she could stick him with her broochpin again. There was nothing in all the known universe that her brother feared, and nothing so far as she knew that had ever bested him—excepting perhaps Responsible of Brightwater, who'd run away from him and left him laughing till the tears poured down into his beard on the steps of Castle Wommack, and she hadn't the least idea what all *that* had been about . . . but his own brash fearnaught ways were no reason to risk bringing down the wrath of the Powers That Be on the heads of all the rest of the household.

At her side, Granny Copperdell touched her wrist. "You'll be having your hands full, child," she said. And Granny Goodweather on the other side, though she didn't leave off looking round her at the fields and farms of Brightwater, so much a park by comparison with the rough-hacked land at home on Kintucky, nodded a sturdy agreement.

"*My* hands full? Why? Of what?" Jewel's heart sank—here it came. Holiday or no holiday, Jubilee or no Jubilee, there'd be something; there always was. Botheration!

"Keeping Lewis Motley Wommack the Thirty-third in order, child," said the Granny solemnly. "Not a job *I'd* fancy."

Jewel was absolutely silent. Not a word entered her mind that she dared give voice to. But the Grannys went on, and spared her the trouble of trying to frame the questions without the broad words.

"You keep in mind, now," said Granny Copperdell, "you are the only woman in your brother's line. Your parents both dead since you were only babies, no other sisters, and him not married—that makes you responsible for his doings. You may well find out that you'd abeen better off with a half *dozen* babies, time this is over."

"It'll grow you up some," said Granny Goodweather calmly, and patted Jewel's knee. "And high time. You're near on marrying age, we can't have you shirking your duties and hiding in grannyskirts forever."

"It's not fair!" Jewel announced, her outrage sufficient at last to let her speak. "And I don't fancy it either!"

"Fair!" scoffed Granny Copperdell. "I ever tell you this world was fair, Jewel of Wommack?"

"No," she said, speaking sullen into her own collar. "No, I can't say as you ever did."

"Well, then," said both the Grannys together. And then the carriage pulled up at the gates of the Castle and everyone was suddenly moving about, gathering up what they'd laid down for the ride, and there was no more time for discussion.

Inside the Castle, Responsible of Brightwater sat at the desk in her bedroom, going over for the tenth time the welcoming speech that she would be giving to open the meeting tomorrow morning, including the elaborate agenda she was counting on to give her time to see how the wind blew. There must be no smallest niche of time left over tomorrow in the scheduled activities to allow the anti-Confederationists to begin their moves. She could count on their obsession with manners to keep them from tampering with that agenda on Opening Day; and good use she'd best make of it, seeing as she could count on nothing for the other four days. The only possibility she could safely exclude was murder—there hadn't been a murder on the continent of Marktwain in the entire one thousand years of its history—but that left a mighty long list of other kinds of disorder and disarray.

"Keep 'em busy!" she said out loud, and made herself jump.

She was nervous, that was for sure. Her mother had remarked on it. Her uncles and her uncles' wives and all the children, and even the Housekeeper, had remarked on it. Until Granny Hazelbide had told them all to leave her be, in no uncertain terms.

"She has enough to think of now," the Granny'd said, shaming them all—and they deserved it—"without you forever tormenting her. The Confederation of Continents might go down for good and all this week, after five hundred years of nursing it along, and she has *that* to think of. And if it doesn't fall, the Twelve Gates only knows what shape it'll be in after the Travellers get through chopping away at it. If she wasn't nervous I'd be calling in the Magician of Rank to see to her *head*, and I'll thank youall to *hush!*"

Responsible grinned, remembering. It was rare that a Granny, or anybody else, came to her defense. It had been a pleasant experience, and one she wouldn't mind repeating a time or two.

"You really worried, Responsible?" her grandfather had asked, sounding sorry for his teasing.

"Some," she'd said.

"They're not such fools as to think that without the Confederation things'd be even half proper—they'll just make the usual noises, and then back down like they always do. No need for you to fret."

She surely did hope he was right... And he ought to be. He ought to be!

On the wall before her hung a battered map of Ozark, the six continents set out in their oceans, and a pin stuck firmly at the site of each Castle. Black pins for those Families she knew to be dead set against the Confederation and ready to bring it down, come what may—Travellers, Guthries, and Farsons. And the Purdys thrown in, seeing as they'd not have the courage to stand against the other three. Red pins for those she knew to be loyal—Castle Airy, Castle Clark, Castle McDaniels, Castle Motley, Castle Lewis, and her own Brightwater. Green pins for those as might move either way, depending on what happened over the next few days—the Smiths, and the Wommacks. Six months ago the pin that marked Castle Smith had been a red one, but no longer. Their behavior had grown more and more odd, and the Attendant set to watch had told her half an hour ago that every one of the other Families was arrived and safely settled in the Castle, but no sign of the Smiths and no word from them. That did nothing to reassure her.

It looked, providing you were ignorant, as if things were fairly safe for the Confederation. Six for, only four against, and two undecided: sway those two and it would be eight to four and an easy sweep; lose them and it would be six to six, a standoff. But that would be your impression *only* if you were ignorant, and Responsible of Brightwater was not. Castles Lewis and Motley could be as loyal as they liked, there was little they could do to help. Two tiny kingdoms sharing one continent not much more than an oversized island, the total not much bigger than Brightwater Kingdom alone. The great bulk of Arkansaw loomed to their east, all of Kintucky to their west, and Tinaseeh—largest of the six continents and held by the Travellers—to their south. If the Confederation did not stand, the Lewises and the Motleys would be hard put to it to do more than make speeches. They could not survive without the help of their neighbors.

And yet, she could not bring herself to believe that there was really any danger beyond that of the anti-Confederationists wasting this precious week in stalling and wrangling so that none of the necessary work could get done. They had a lot to say about independence, but she was inclined to agree with her grandfather; they must have sense enough to know the terrible price of isolation.

Responsible sighed, and stamped her foot in frustration. She had cast Spells half the night, she'd done Formalisms & Transformations till her hands ached, and she'd gotten only one answer. An answer she could of gotten with Granny Magic alone, reading leaves in a teacup. *Trouble* ahead, she kept getting—as if she didn't know that! Something was wrong with her data, or something had been wrong with her methods, she had no least idea which; and there was no one she could ask for their opinion, seeing as how everything she was doing was illegal or worse. It fretted her, having no idea what *kind* of trouble.

There was a knock at her door, and she called "Come in!" expecting an Attendant telling her it was time for the banquet in the Castle Great Hall, but it was her own Granny Hazelbide.

"Granny!" she said, laying the thick sheets of paper down on the desk and resigning herself to the fact that there'd be no more reviewing of that speech. The Granny would of come to fuss at her about something, or perhaps a dozen somethings, then there would be the Banquet and the Dance, and then she must sleep or she'd not be fit to *give* the speech. She was so tired now that the words on the paper blurred when she looked at them.

"Responsible," said the Granny back at her.

"What can I do for you?"

"Do for me, indeed!"

"Well, then, what can you do for *me?"* asked Responsible patiently. "What is it, Granny Hazelbide? Has the Housekeeper run off? Is the food spoiled? Do we expect a hurricane off schedule?"

"Mercy, you're the cheery one," said Granny Hazelbide.

"If something weren't fretting you, you wouldn't be here, Granny, and we both know that. And if something's fretting you, then for me to be cheery would be foolishness. What's gone wrong?"

The Granny sat herself down in a rocker where Responsible would have to turn her chair around to look at her, and folded both arms across her narrow chest.

"For one thing," she said, cross as a patch, "the Castle's full of every kind of devilment ever invented."

"Granted," said Responsible. "And?"

"For another, it's so crowded you can't find a place to sit nor a place to stand, nor much air to breathe—and the Smiths aren't even here yet. And if I know *them,* they'll bring every piddling relation they can scrape from under a rock, and three dozen Attendants, and a servingmaid to every chick and child—a delegation of one hundred even, I'll wager you my smallest thimble and my oldest shammybag!"

"More nearly fifty, Granny," said Responsible. "You exaggerate."

"Still too many, *I* say!"

"Granted," said Responsible. "But it's their way, and none of our business to object to it."

"I-dislike-it-all," said Granny Hazelbide, each word separate and alone as it left her mouth, like a solemn pronouncement; and Responsible couldn't help but laugh.

"Granny," she chided, "you've known these last twelve months and more that this was coming. And you've known how it would be. We've gone over it and over it, and my mother has not held back *her* comments at any time. I don't know how it is her voice hasn't worn grooves in the floors by this time, complaining. There's been ample time to mope and moan and carry on over it, and we'd all come to an agreement that it was worth the trouble. Why are you bothering me about it now?"

"I have a funny feeling," muttered Granny Hazelbide, rocking slowly and staring at the floor.

"A funny feeling."

"That's what I said."

"What does your funny feeling tell you?"

"That there's trouble coming."

Responsible shrugged.

"And what were you expecting?" she asked patiently. This conversation was wearisome, and a waste of time as well, unless the Granny knew something that might be useful. If she did, she was going to make Responsible work for it.

"Know who's in the room next to yours?" asked the Granny suddenly.

"For sure," said Responsible, surprised at the question. "Anne of Brightwater, and her boring husband, Stewart Crain McDaniels the Sixth. And if I know Anne, and I do, they'll have the youngest tadling they brought along sleeping in their bed with them for safekeeping."

"Wrong," said the Granny.

"I arranged it myself."

"So you did, but it's been changed, and your uncles both approved it and remarked as how nobody should bother checking with you since you were so busy, bad cess to 'em both."

Responsible reached both arms above her head and stretched. Law, but she was tired! And asked the Granny, as politely as her strained tolerance would allow, to tell her what she'd come to tell.

"Who've they given me for nearest neighbor, dear Granny

Hazelbide?" she pleaded. "Leave off teasing, now, and tell me."

"Don't sass me, missy!"

"Granny, tell me!" said Responsible. "Or I'll go back to work on my speech. Notice that it's on *paper?* None of your pliofilm sheets for this ceremony—I'd put it on a set of stone tablets if I could carry them."

"Granny Leeward," said the old woman abruptly, and left it at that.

Responsible took a deep breath before she tried answering, and folded her hands in her lap where they wouldn't betray her. And then she said, casual as she could make it: "They've put Granny Leeward in the room beside mine?"

"That they have. It seems she wasn't comfortable where she was, and it seems the air is better on the side of the Castle nearest you, and it seems she can't abide the view where the rest of the Traveller delegation has their rooms because it reminds her of a tragic experience she had as a child, and it seems the beds in none of the other rooms will suit her back, which she declared to be frail, though the woman has pure steel for a backbone. But she faced me down and butter wouldn't of melted in her mouth—and the upshot is that you're one side of the wall and she's on the other."

Responsible thought about that for a while, and the Granny rocked.

And then she asked, "And what do you think it means?"

"Trouble." Granny Hazelbide's mouth was a little puckered line.

Responsible's mind, despite the control she tried for, took her back to the long table at Castle Traveller, and the black fan in Granny Leeward's hands, and then the jetty mushrooms, where the fan had been, rotting on the table.

"Responsible of Brightwater," demanded Granny Hazelbide sternly, "why are you shivering?"

"You said 'trouble' your own self, ma'am. And I respect your opinion."

"There's more to it than just mischief," said the Granny. "Like I said, I have a funny feeling."

"Think she'll strangle me in my bed?" ventured Responsible, her voice careful and light. It wouldn't do to have the Grannys feuding.

"I'll wager she could, without leaving her own."

"Ah, but she wouldn't! She's a Traveller born, Granny Hazelbide, and she'd be drawn and quartered naked before she'd use illegal magic."

"I'll grant you that much, but you mark my words—"

"Mark mine," put in Responsible. It wasn't polite to interrupt a Granny, but when Granny Hazelbide said to mark her words you were in for a good hour's worth to mark, and she just simply didn't have the strength.

"Mark mine," she said, "the woman's done it to torment me, purely because she delights in tormenting me. Nothing more. And I don't intend to let her have the satisfaction of thinking she's achieved her purpose."

"It's possible," said the Granny. "I suppose it's possible."

"And you, I'll thank you to help me rather than hinder me in this. All I need is that woman thinking she has *you* upset; it won't do, Granny! I need you serene, not all in a fidget."

Get in a staring match with a Granny, you can wear your eyes out, and Responsible's eyes already burned from no sleep and the hours poring over papers. But she held firm, and it was the old lady who gave way first.

CHAPTER 2

EVERY OZARK CHILD was familiar with the building called Confederation Hall, whether they lived five miles away or clear on the far side of the Ocean of Storms. Little girls in Granny School, and the boys under the instruction of their Tutors, became familiar with it whether they would or no, and at a very early age. They drew it on sheets of pliofilm and took the pictures home to be fastened up on the housewalls; they made lopsided models of it from Oklahomah's thick blue clay and gave them to their fathers for desk ornaments. The girls embroidered it on heavy canvas, with name and date beneath; the boys built it of scrap wood and carved their names with the points of their first good knives.

It was red brick, two stories high plus a tiny attic said to be haunted by a half dozen dead Grannys, with tall narrow arched windows framed in stone, and stone steps leading up to a central door. And the whole sitting square in the middle of a broad green lawn with a walk all around. A spanking-white bandstand stood in the left front corner of the lawn as you faced the Hall door, and the other corner had a statuary group lasered out of Tinaseeh ironwood. There on the pedestal block was First Granny, wading ashore with her skirts pulled up just high enough to show her shoetops; and there was Captain Aaron Dunn McDaniels, standing on the shore and reaching a hand to her; and there stood a miscellaneous child beside him looking very brave. The inscription across the base read: FIRST LANDING—MAY 8, 2021.

Confederation Hall was authentic Old Earth Primitive, right down to the solar collectors on its roof. And the children knew why. "Not *every* thing on Earth was bad," the Grannys and the Tutors told them. "When the Confederation of Continents was established in twenty-five twelve, meeting then just one week in the entire year, Confederation Hall was built as it was to *remind* us of that. It represents some of the good things."

Ordinarily it was a building empty enough to have an echo in its corridors. Even during the one month in four when the Confederation met, the delegations and their staffs weren't large enough to dent its emptiness, running as they did to two or three men and a single staff member. And the other eight months there was nobody at all there but an Attendant to show visitors around, one official to keep up the records and the archives, and a few servingmaids to see to the cleaning. The Travellers disapproved of that; if they'd had their way it would of been closed up tight except during meeting months. But the Traveller children were taught to make the embroidered pictures and the wooden models just like everybody else's.

Today it was a long way from empty. Responsible of Brightwater, standing at the speaker's podium in the Independence Room, ran her eyes over the crowd of delegates with satisfaction. Not one Family had boycotted the Jubilee, leaving the assembly without its full complement of votes; the message had come in that morning before breakfast, the Smiths were delayed but they would be there. Not every seat was filled—though every seat in the balcony was—and there were empty rows at the back. But it was a satisfying turnout, and when the Smiths did arrive they'd take up a goodly number of those empty spaces.

Twenty-eight of Ozark's twenty-nine Grannys, lacking only Granny Gableframe of Castle Smith, filled the first row of the balcony, a sight Responsible had never seen before and wasn't sure she could handle with a straight face. They looked like twenty-eight matched dolls up there, each with her hair knotted up high on top of her head as required, each with the same thin sharp nose and tight-puckered mouth, every last one of them in the same crackly gown and triangular shawl and high-topped shoes, and round eyeglasses perched halfway down their noses whether they needed them or not. Not to mention the twenty-eight sets of flying knitting needles. Responsible looked away from them hastily, feeling unseemly laughter tugging at her mouthcorners, and concentrated on the Travellers instead. That was dampening enough to end all hazard of either laughter or smile. And talk of waste! The Traveller delegation, by her rapid count, numbered twenty-four ebony-coated men. Quite a contrast with the grudging tokens they sent to regular meetings, and each and every one of them entitled to speak to any question raised, *plus* offer a rebuttal. They had men enough there to tie up the floor for hours at a time.

At her side, in the big square-cut chair reserved for the leader of the meetings, sat her uncle Donald Patrick Brightwater the 133rd, fidgeting. Since her father had been dead these seven years, it was Donald Patrick that would take over on behalf of Brightwater once she finished the welcoming speech. And he was itching to get at it, too, she could tell. It was made particularly clear when he grabbed her elbow and hissed at her under his breath to get started.

Responsible didn't intend to be hurried. There were still people moving into the balcony doors to stand and try to get a glimpse of the proceedings below, and the delegates hadn't yet left off rustling documents and muttering to one another. She'd not begin to speak till she had silence in the room, and she was not through looking her audience over. She'd had a bad moment when she saw who was included in the Wommack delegation, though she ought to of known Lewis Motley Wommack wouldn't let himself be left behind. A Grand Jubilee would come along only once every five hundred years; you miss your chance at one, you weren't likely to get a second try. She would have to deal with the problem he presented as it *was* presented.

"Responsible!" said her uncle, too cross now to be discreet. "*Will* you get on with it? At this rate it'll be noon and time for dinner before we get past your performance!"

He had been opposed to her making the speech at all.

"It's not appropriate," he'd complained, three Family meetings in a row, while his wife sat and lived up to her name and waited for him to exhaust himself. Patience of Clark wasted no words on her husband unless she was convinced he couldn't be relied on to talk himself into silence unassisted.

Donald Patrick had had arguments he considered potent. In the first place, he'd pointed out, women were not allowed in the business sessions of the regular Confederation meetings; therefore, a woman ought not to be allowed in this one. In the second place, if the excuse for having a woman present on the Hall floor was her social function as hostess of this to-do—*which* he could grudgingly see might be reasonable—then that welcoming speech should not be made by Responsible, it should be made by her mother, as Missus of this Castle. Thorn of Guthrie had raised her brows at that and allowed the ivory perfection of her face to be marred by a frown that was as downright ugly as any expression Responsible had ever seen her use, and had declared as how she'd have nothing to do with it; and no argument of Donald Patrick's would sway her.

"*Why* won't you do it?" he'd demanded, smacking his fist in the palm of his hand. "I will feel like a plain fool sitting there listening to a fourteen-year-old girl—"

"Going on fifteen," put in Granny Hazelbide.

"—a fourteen-year-old girl giving the welcoming speech on behalf of this Castle and this Kingdom. And so will every member of the Brightwater delegation. And so would *you,* Thorn of Guthrie, *and* you, Responsible, if you had any decency at all, or any respect for your father's memory, rest his soul!"

Thorn of Guthrie had looked at him and sighed, and then she turned to Responsible and said, "Well, Responsible, will you abide by my order and let your uncle do the honors?"

Responsible had said no, and Thorn of Guthrie had said "You see?" and Donald Patrick Brightwater had stomped out of the room in a black mood that had lasted well past suppertime.

Responsible had made an effort at calming him, in the few chinks of time available to her, promising that as soon as the speech was over she'd move to the balcony and mind her manners for the rest of the week. And Patience of Clark had put as much of her skill into soothing him as she'd considered reasonable.

But he sat beside her as unresigned and as infuriated as he'd been from the beginning. When Responsible began to speak, the silence having grown tangible enough to suit her, she felt almost obliged to be ready to leap aside at any moment and prevent him from snatching the sheets of paper out of her hands. He had his eyes fixed on the brilliant bunting that circled the room at the level of the balcony and ran across its front rail, with the crests of the Twelve Families hung in strict alphabetical rotation at each looped-up swath, and an expression of propriety slapped onto his face like a mask. But like all men, when sitting rankled him his thigh muscles kept tensing, and he would inch forward in the chair, and then recollect the situation and jerk suddenly bolt upright again. And then start it all over, tugging at his beard and then crossing his arms over his chest and then tugging at his beard again. He put Responsible in mind of a five year old too far from the bathroom, and she hoped his manners would last him till she finished.

She knew the words of the speech by heart, every one of them the perfect word. All about the solemnness of this occasion. Commemorating that great day five hundred years ago when after much struggle the Twelve Families had set aside their fears of anything remotely resembling a central government and allowed the Confederation of Continents to be formed. Commemorating the slow but steady progress as they moved from meeting one week in the year, a token foot in the waters, toward the present one month in four. A couple dozen sentences about the wickedness and corruption of Old Earth that had driven them away and into space, and the mirroring sentences that congratulated the Confederation for letting none of those varieties of wickedness arise here on Ozark. She rang the changes and pushed the buttons, and she could of done it all in her sleep, so far as the words went.

But the manner of *saying* those words—the modulation of her voice and the phrasing, the set of her features and the positions of her body—that was a very different matter. That demanded considerable fine-tuning, a constant eye on the men she faced, an adjustment for a frown here, a careful pacing of a phrase for a wandering expression there; it took her mind off both her uncle *and* Lewis Motley Wommack the 33rd.

If it hadn't been for that, she'd of been delighted to let Donald Patrick read the *words;* and if it hadn't been for that, and the fact that her mother knew full well she hadn't the skill to control this roomful of males, Thorn of Guthrie would of insisted on her right to read them and backed Donald Patrick in every objection he raised. Thorn had no reluctance for the limelight.

A thousand years had gone by here on Ozark, and who knew how many billions before that on Earth; and still men spoke solemnly of the power of logic, the force of facts and figures, and remained convinced that you persuaded others and won their allegiance by the words you said. It would of been funny if it hadn't been such pathetic ignorance, and there were times when Responsible wondered whether the males of other inhabited worlds suffered from the same ancient illusion.

It would for *sure* have been helpful if she could of known whether the members of the Out-Cabal shared the same faith in the power of the surface structure of language. In fact, it would of helped to know whether those three beings were males of their species, just for starters.

She put that thought out of her head instantly; it was distraction, and a sure certain way to lose her audience and run into objections to her plans for this day.

In the balcony the Grannys noted appreciatively the skill with which Responsible wooed her unruly crowd, and Granny Hazelbide felt she was justified in her pride at having brought the girl up. She stood up there, bold as brass before the restless males, and she played them as easily as a person that lived by fishing would play a little stippleperch in a creek. It looked easy when she did it, and Responsible looked cool and easy herself in her elegant gown of dark green with a pale green piping round its hem and collar. But Granny Hazelbide had held the girl's head all the night before while she'd first vomited everything she'd eaten and drunk at the Banquet and the Dance—which wasn't much—and then retched miserably on an empty stomach and cursed the weakness of her body. Not more than an hour's sleep all told had she had, Granny Hazelbide was certain of it, but none of that showed now. Not a tremble of her hands, brown hands that showed the hard work they did, against the creamy paper. Not a slightest hesitation of that voice, though her throat must of been raw. Smooth as satin, bold as brass, cool as springwater, that was her girl.

It wasn't working on the Brightwater men, naturally; they were used to Responsible and took her about as seriously as they did the servingmaids. And the Travellers were fighting it, staring up at the ceiling to break the hold of it upon them. Granny Hazelbide sincerely hoped they'd hear from their women later about their ill-bred behavior. But it was working on everybody else, they were just this side of trance, and the final paragraph would finish them off. Not a one had protested as Responsible read off the list of events that would fill Opening Day, and the comset screen on the front wall behind her spelled out the lengthy agenda in small bright lights.

There was to be a Memorial Address by the Reverend Terrence Patrick Lewis the 5th, head of the church of this Kingdom. There was a Commemoration Ceremony. There were three separate Awards Ceremonies for service to the Confederation, and at each of those there'd be awards speeches and acceptance speeches and folderols. There was a noon banquet, with two guest speakers. There was a reading of the Articles of the Confederation, with a commentary to follow from the senior Magician of Rank pointing out the satisfying parallels between the structure of the Articles and the notations of Formalisms & Transformations. When Responsible got through, there were not five unscheduled minutes available from the end of her welcoming speech to the Closing Prayer that would—so the lights recorded—be pronounced at six o'clock precisely that afternoon, just in time for supper. And Granny Hazelbide could tell by the backs of their necks and the set of their shoulders that the Traveller men were silently lamenting the loss of time before they could get on with what they'd be seeing as the real business of this Jubilee, and that the restraint was unsettling their stomachs. She wished she could of hoped they'd empty those stomachs as Responsible had hers, but it wasn't likely. No doubt the Travellers had to answer *some* calls of nature, but the idea that one of them might be so human as to vomit went beyond the bounds of imagination. That would, after all, be *waste*.

She felt the eyes of Granny Leeward on her then, her that was a Traveller born and bred, as Responsible had reminded her, and she didn't like it. The woman was uncanny, and she held some trump card—that much had been clear from the way Responsible went white when her name was mentioned, as well as from the arrogance of her behavior. She'd all but shoved the other Grannys aside taking the central place in the balcony row this morning, and she hadn't scrupled to do it without so much as a beg-your-pardon, either. Some trump card. Something that Granny Hazelbide had no clue to, but that came near unsettling *her* stomach.

Wickedness in a Granny was unthinkable; they were human like any other human, and they could make mistakes, but in everything moral they were above reproach. And it therefore made no sense that she should suspect Leeward of evil intent... but something there nagged at her.

Responsible had matters well in hand and needed no attention. She had turned the meeting over to her pettish uncle with casual ease and gone out into the hall to climb the stairs to the balcony. The men were still half stupored from the word patterns flowing over and around them, a situation Donald Patrick would no doubt put an end to in short order. He couldn't talk for beans, never had been able to. But it was his meeting now, and Granny Hazelbide could afford to give her mind over fully to the problem of Granny Leeward, where logic *did* apply.

No Granny could do deliberate evil, that was a given. It would turn inward and destroy her if she tried. She would sicken, and the evil would show plain in her eyes and in her flesh. Not Granny Leeward; the woman was rail-thin and had a nose like a fishhook, but she had the radiant bloom of health. It followed then, followed as the night the day (and praise be that had never failed yet), that Granny Leeward planned no wicked act toward Responsible of Brightwater or anybody else. She *could* not.

And yet, wherever Granny Leeward moved, the other Grannys pulled away from her, drew back their stiff skirts. The woman that sat at her right hand now, Granny Golightly of Castle Clark, was not overfastidious. She was famous for her mischief, and for a certain cavalier disregard of the consequences of that mischief. Still she was edged to the right in her seat in a way that crowded her next neighbor and could not be comfortable, but preserved her from any chance of touching Leeward—it kept a full two inches of space between them. That provided the second given: it was not just herself, Granny Hazelbide of Brightwater Castle, as looked at Leeward and saw darkness puddling round her skirt-hems; it was all the Grannys.

And that provided the third. Twenty-seven Grannys could not be wrong. She might be overly suspicious herself, because she had raised Responsible of Brightwater and knew the Travellers had set themselves to bring down the Confederation the girl was sworn to maintain. One or two others might have a hidden soft spot for Responsible, those as had known her well years ago, a child visiting the Castles of near kin. But every *one* of them, even those that scarcely knew the daughter of Brightwater, was pulling back from Granny Leeward like she was a source of polluted water. That many Grannys, all turning against one of their own—that had never happened before. Not ever. Generations ago, when the poor soul at Castle Wommack had nearly brought the whole system crashing down around their heads by giving a Wommack girlbaby an Improper Name, and the Twelve Gates knew there was cause and aplenty for resentment, no Granny had turned on the foolish one. And Granny Leeward had done nothing yet this day but sit there and watch the proceedings, knitting sedately on an unidentifiable strip of dark-gray work—probably underwear for the young girls of Traveller, scratchy to subdue the natural passions the Travellers feared inflamed them all—knitting and watching. And breathing. She'd done nothing more.

Granny Hazelbide saw Responsible come in at the side door and motioned to her to come take her seat; she'd had enough and then some, and she meant to head for home. It was all very well leaving matters to Responsible and mouthing platitudes about lying in beds once they were made, but she loved that child. She had a few tea leaves to brew, and a few Charms and Spells to try, and furthermore she intended to set strong wards in Responsible's bedroom, where she slept not twenty feet away from Granny Leeward's bed. And might could be she'd take a nap; she wasn't as young as she had been.

Responsible accepted the seat gratefully, however much it might annoy her uncle to look up and see her there among the Grannys instead of in the back row as he would consider fitting for her age and station. She was worn completely out; if there was a reserve of energy left in her someplace, she didn't know its location and hoped she wouldn't find herself obliged to seek it.

Here she could keep an eye on her uncle, and an eye on the delegations, and her presence would make it plain to Granny Leeward that she wasn't afraid of her. She *was* afraid of Lewis Motley Wommack the 33rd, but she was safe from him up here, and she intended to surround herself with respectable females of all ages and degrees until she was back in her room with her door barred against all untoward possibilities that might involve him.

There'd been a good deal of sympathy for the sister, young Jewel of Wommack, when the Attendants had brought the gossip back from the Landing. Two Grannys telling that child she had to keep her brother in order, more shame to them, and if they thought it was good for Jewel's character she hoped they both came down with pimples on their nosepoints. It wasn't fair to the girl, especially since she would surely believe them, and torture herself through the whole Jubilee—instead of enjoying herself as she ought to of been allowed to do—following that wicked young man around and worrying about how to see that he did no harm.

Personally, Responsible had no intention *what*soever of turning her safety from Wommack over to his sister. Jewel was beautiful, and it was said that she was astonishingly learned, and she had the awkward elegance that meant the beauty would be the lasting kind. But Responsible had looked her full in the eyes at last night's Dance, going down a Reel, and what she'd seen had been the clear innocent eyes of a child. A wise child, but a child all the same. Responsible of Brightwater was prepared to love the girl—she was irresistible—but she would take care of herself her *self*.

And she'd speak to the two Grannys. They'd no right to spoil the girl's entire holiday with their rearing practices—the Gates only knew when she'd get another one, stuck there on Kintucky. Let them bring her up properly when they had her home again at Castle Wommack; that struck Responsible as quite soon enough.

CHAPTER 3

SHE COULD NOT move, not even to shake one skinny finger at him; she couldn't talk except when it pleased him to permit her that privilege, which was rarely. But short of actually putting her into pseudocoma, there was no way that Lincoln Paradyne Smith the 39th could dull the red rage that glowed in the eyes of Granny Gableframe, and he didn't consider the coma justified by the situation. In fact, he found himself admiring the amount of hate the old lady managed to express without word or motion. There was an ancient saying—"If looks could kill . . ."—and it surely applied here. He'd seen some looks in his time, but this one was spectacular, even for a Granny.

"You might just as well stop glaring at me like that, my dear Granny Gableframe," he'd told her. From the very beginning. "I'm not impressed," he'd said, "not in any way, not to any degree. You may glare at me all day and all night—all you are going to get from it is a headache." It hadn't discouraged her any.

Lincoln Parradyne didn't mind, though he didn't look forward to the moment when he would have to turn her loose and put up with her tongue-lashing.

"How long can you keep her like that?"

Lincoln Parradyne glanced at the man that stood beside him, wondering if he could be serious, and sure enough he appeared to be, and so he shrugged his shoulders and raised his eyebrows and said, "Till she dies, if I like."

"Well, I don't want her dying," objected Delldon Mallard Smith the Second, "whether you like or not!" And all three of his brothers, standing round the Granny's bed, indicated that they strongly agreed with that sentiment.

The Magician of Rank asked himself, from time to time, which one of the four Smith brothers was the stupidest. Delldon Mallard the 2nd was the biggest; Whitney Crawford the 14th was the handsomest; Leroy Fortnight the 23rd was the fattest; and it appeared that the most cowardly of the set was Hazeltine Everett the 11th. But for stupidity, it was hard to choose among them, and the fact that they were his blood kin was a heavy burden to him.

"You hear me, now?" demanded Delldon Mallard. "I want no misunderstanding. That's our Granny and we love her, and if it just happens that she can't quite be brought to go along with what's needful without a certain amount of pressure being applied, all right; but she's just an old lady and she's frail, and I don't want—"

Lincoln Parradyne was completely out of patience. The man would ramble on for half an hour if he wasn't stopped, and all of it nonsense.

"I don't want to hear what you don't want," he said tiredly. "I have no *interest* in what you don't want! Your requirements were quite clearly specified, Delldon Mallard—you wanted Granny Gableframe in a state where she could not interfere with your plans, and I've provided you that. If she were one of the servingmaids, I could also have seen to it that her condition wasn't marred by . . . irritation. But this is a *Granny*, cousin, not a dithering girlchild."

Leroy Fortnight snorted from the foot of the bed, where he was alternately kicking the bedpost with his boot and punching it with his fist.

"What's the matter?" he asked, snickering. "Isn't your magic good enough to keep her down? One little old scrawny woman?"

"I don't believe I'd talk to Lincoln Parradyne like that," hazarded one of the others. "Not unless you fancy him laying you out the same way as the Granny. You think you'd like that, Leroy Fortnight?"

Delldon Mallard cleared his throat. "That," he said firmly, "would . . . uh . . . be illegal. *Il*legal."

"Do you suppose," marveled the Magician of Rank, staring at the big man with true astonishment, "that what I've done to Granny Gableframe *isn't* illegal?"

"Well . . ."

"Well? *Well?*"

"I don't really think so," said Delldon Mallard. He was the oldest, and Master of this Castle; he felt a sense of responsibility and wanted his position made unambiguous. "I don't really think that legality enters in here, you know. I . . . uh . . . gave the matter a good deal of thought before I asked the Magician of Rank to do this. And I'm satisfied in my own mind that what this represents is a kind of . . . uh . . . contest. That is, if the Magician of Rank was to perform a Transformation like this and paralyze just *any* old lady, say, just any old lady at all, why, that would . . . uh . . . be a different kind of thing. *That* would be illegal, I'd be obliged to agree. But not with the Granny here . . . She, uh, has her own magic, and as I said—"

"Sit down!" said the Magician of Rank. "Delldon Mallard Smith the Second—shut *up* and sit *down*."

"Now I don't see that there's any call for you to speak to me like that," began Delldon Mallard. And then he saw Lincoln Parradyne set one hand on the bedstead and stretch out the other toward him, and he sat down instantly and closed his mouth.

"I believe," said Lincoln Parradyne through clenched teeth, "that I had better explain this to you gentlemen just one more time before we leave for Castle Brightwater. You do not appear to me to have it straight in your minds. Not at all."

"Now, Linc—"

"Be still!" thundered the Magician of Rank. "You listen to what I say, you listen with both ears for once! Do I have your attention?"

The silence indicated that he did, and he went on.

"It is true that the Granny has magic of her own, surely; you'd be in sorry shape if she didn't. Your girls would be born and given names at hazard, the way it was done on Old Earth, if the Granny weren't at hand to choose a Proper Name. Your crops would fail and your goats would go dry. There would be rot and mildew and dirt and vermin inside the Castle, and there'd be blight and ignorance and dirt and vermin outside it. There'd be nobody to heal your sick—I give you my word neither the Magicians *nor* the Magicians of Rank have time these days to see to your sniffles and your bellyaches. But as for there being a contest between us, between myself and Granny Gableframe . . . think of a contest between twelve grown men and one four-year-old boy, and you'll have something to compare! The odds are about the same."

"Well," said Delldon Mallard, tugging at his bottom lip, "I think we'd need an interpretation on that. I wouldn't want anybody saying as how I wasn't fair. It might could be that you know a few tricks the Grannys don't, Lincoln, I'm willing to grant you that. But I do believe your ego has a tendency to run away with you." He chuckled softly, all tolerance and indulgence, and his brothers echoed him; and the Granny lying helpless under the counterpane closed her eyes as if she could bear no more.

Lincoln Parradyne stared at the man, oldest of the Smith boys, Master of Castle Smith, and wondered whether he could control himself. I keep your Mules flying, he thought. Without my help a Mule could no more fly than it could knit. I see to your weather, so that no rain falls except where it's needed, and I control the snow and the wind and all things that have to do with the heat and the cold, with wet and with dry . . . Because of the Magicians of Rank you have never known a blizzard or a drought or an earthquake. Or a disease that lasts more than a week, and even those we could shorten to minutes if we didn't feel that the week was good for your coddled little characters. We see to—

He stopped, suddenly, in the middle of his silent recital, feeling foolish. There was some question as to just who it was he was trying to convince, since nobody could hear him. And if anyone could have, he'd of been guilty of spreading knowledge allowed only to the other Magicians of Rank and that accursed girl at Brightwater.

"No point in arguing with him," said the handsome brother. "No point atall. Delldon sets his mind to a thing, there's no changing it. And his mind is for sure set on this."

"You're quite right," said Lincoln Parradyne grimly. "If Delldon Mallard has his mind set to do something he knows is wrong, there's no hope of swaying him from whatever excuse he comes up with to justify that wrongdoing."

"You think we're doing something wrong?" Leroy Fortnight turned on his oldest brother. "Think he's right? If he's right, I'm here to tell you, I'm not going to go through with this, Delldon Mallard."

Lincoln Parradyne walked out of the room and left them listening attentively to their brother's endless explanation of why what might be wrong at some other time, if somebody else were doing it, in some other situation, was *perfectly* justified at this time, in this situation, with the brothers Smith doing it. He had no doubt that Delldon Mallard would be able to convince them; their consciences were no more tender than their manners, and they were accustomed to giving in to Delldon's arguments. They had spent their *lives* giving in to Delldon's arguments. He himself had no stomach for listening to it again, however, and he felt a certain twinge of his own conscience at the thought that the Granny had no choice but to endure it in silence.

If she had known what a mire of ignorance and ineptitude she would spend her time dealing with, would she have chosen this Castle as her residence, he wondered? Though someone had to, and Gableframe was a good deal tougher and better fit to manage it than most. For himself, if it were not that to leave would have meant abandoning his own kin . . .

Outside the door, he nearly fell over a cluster of the Smith women, all hovering there wringing their hands—always excepting Dorothy, who was convinced that her father's plan was a brilliant stroke. She smiled at Lincoln Parradyne, and then curtsied slowly, a deep court curtsy ending in a wobble that turned her face a dusky red.

"Better practice that some more," he said. As if he didn't know how many hours she had spent practicing it, standing in front of the tall mirror in her bedroom. The flush on her cheeks deepened, and he thought for a moment that she would cry. She cried easily, fat tears always right at the surface and trembling in her eyes. It was a curious characteristic in a female like Dorothy, who was just plain *mean,* right down to the core; no doubt she'd outgrow it.

"How is Granny Gableframe?" asked one of the women, her voice tight as a banjo string in dry weather. "How does she feel?"

"She feels thoroughly miserable right now," said the Magician of Rank, "as would you, if you were in a similar condition."

"But she's all right."

Lincoln Parradyne sighed. They were so determined, these Smiths, to have all their cake, frosted and frilled on the shelf, while they savored it to the last bite.

"She is not 'all right,'" he said crossly. "Of course not. There are perhaps a dozen different ways to cause a person to suffer from motor paralysis, some of them more unpleasant than others, but none of them could be said to be precisely desirable. However, she's in no danger, if that's what you mean."

"It must be terrible—not being able to move anything but her eyes . . ."

"No," he said, making his way through them and answering her over his shoulder as he headed down the corridor. "On the contrary, it's very restful. Good for the Granny to have a little holiday from tearing round the Castle tongue-lashing and nagging and fretting, in my opinion. Her major problem is that she refuses to relax and enjoy it."

Her major problem, if he'd been able to explain it to them, was of course that she knew what he'd done and why, and was in a flaming rage because her own magic skills weren't adequate to reverse such a simple process.

He could feel them staring after him, and he kept his back to them till he reached a corner he could turn. The Smith women, all but Dorothy, disapproved of what was going on, which showed considerable good sense on their part. Too bad they hadn't exerted that good sense in marrying elsewhere, and left the four brothers to bachelor splendor and an end of the marred line.

They would be easier to manage once the whole group had left the Castle and was headed for the Jubilee—they'd take no chances of embarrassing their men in front of other people, whatever their personal opinions might be. He'd even considered letting the Granny go along, and manipulating her through the remaining days of the Jubilee; there were Formalisms & Transformations that would have made it possible for him to do that, and her absence was sure to create suspicion. But although her behavior would of passed well enough with the ordinary citizen, he was by no means sure that his control would not have been spotted by the other Grannys—or by Responsible of Brightwater. He had decided, finally, not to risk it, and to accept the consequences of the alternatives open to him.

In the corridor a Senior Attendant stopped him, to report that everything was ready for the Smith delegation's journey to the Jubilee.

"You're sure of that, now?" he asked the Attendant sharply. "If anything has been forgotten, it won't be amusing—for us *or* for you."

"Twenty-seven trunks they loaded on the ship," said the Attendant, stolid as always. You didn't get to be a Senior Attendant in this Castle unless you learned to hide your emotions. "Checked the count myself to make certain sure of it. And I was most particular that the one you marked with the *x*, it got put on board early this morning, and well at the back. The lizzies are out front to take you all down to the dock, and in perfect order—I had the airjets seen to not ten minutes ago, and the batteries as well, in case the cloud cover doesn't lift. Nary a thing on your list, sir, that I *haven't* seen to."

"Good man," said Lincoln Parradyne. "I appreciate good service, and I remember it."

"That's known," said the man. "And the drape of your cloak needs attention, if you don't mind my saying so."

The Magician of Rank glanced at his shoulder and murmured agreement: what was supposed to be seven neat folds in an orderly cascade was more like the casual pleating of a little girl's skirt, and that would tell him something about allowing himself to be provoked by his cousins into flailing his arms around and shaking his fists at the ceiling. He adjusted the cape's arrangement with swift fingers, and refastened the silver bar that drew the falls together and held them back out of the way of his right arm.

"There," he said, "will that do it?"

"That's proper, sir," said the Attendant.

"Then will you go along and pass the message to the rest of our group? Tell them to meet me by the front gate and look sharp about it—it'll be late in the Second Day before we reach the Jubilee, even if we have fair winds all the way." Which he'd see that they did; it was going to be crucial for them to arrive at *exactly* the right moment in the proceedings.

"I'll do that," said the man. "But I do think it's a shame Granny Gableframe went on ahead of the rest of you. It would of pleasured her a good deal to ride in the lizzy and give youall whatfor the whole way to Brightwater on the ship. Granny Gableframe's partial to water and to company, that's also known."

"The Granny would of been uncomfortable on this trip," said Lincoln Parradyne casually. "At her age and with her rheumatism?" He clucked his tongue. "It was much better for her to have me fly her in on the Mule, and avoid all that commotion."

The Attendant had known the Granny a long time. He gave him a look that couldn't exactly be described as disrespectful, but let Lincoln Parradyne know what the man's opinion was of his estimate of the old lady's constitution; and the Magician of Rank snapped at him to get a move on, before things could become more complicated than they were already. It was a fine kettle when the staff of a Castle had more brains than the Family they were hired to serve, and he sincerely hoped the situation wasn't widespread. When he got back he'd review the whole bunch, and any that showed signs—like this man—of being sharper than they needed to be to carry out their duties would have to be replaced.

And then he sighed, and went quickly to his rooms to fill in the final character of a Transformation he'd had ready and waiting for completion these last three days. He wasn't eager to do it, but it was necessary. The Granny was going to have his hide in small scraps for the work that had deprived her of movement and of speech, that could be counted on already. What she would do about this last task of his, the one that would provide the Castle temporarily with a new cat—of origin unknown, but much too beautiful not to be spoiled and watched over—he didn't even care to contemplate. If things went as he hoped, she might forgive him; on her deathbed, maybe, she might forgive him. If the Smith brothers, or one of their nervous women, made some mistake that put a kink in the plan—which was likely—she would never forgive him.

And *then* Delldon Mallard Smith the 2nd would have a chance to see his "contest"! Years of it. Years of the Granny doing her Charms and Spells, setting them against him with her little mouth puckered tight as her heart must be in her chest;

and years of him, Lincoln Parradyne Smith the 39th, canceling out each and every one of them. The chance of the Granny getting one past him was too small to be worth considering, but the amount of *time* he was going to have to spend in the feud would pile up into a respectable amount of misery over the years. Grannys lived to a formidable old age, and he'd never known one to mellow.

It would have made things so much simpler if they could of brought her around to see things their way and cooperate with them—if not to help them, at least not to interfere. But she had told them flat out what she thought of Delldon Mallard's great plan.

"Flumdiddle!" she'd said. "Goatwallow! Cowflop!" And a half-hour string of more of the same, with a persistent refrain on how they'd all taken leave of what pitiful supply of sense they'd been born with, and the litany of ancient oaths for coda and elaboration.

Lincoln Parradyne didn't agree with the Granny. Every means of foreseeing he had at his disposal had been clear: the road would be a tad bumpy for what they had in mind, and its duration would depend on the skill of those carrying it out—but they *would* bring it off. That was enough for him; the potential once it was done was everything he had ever wanted and had thought hopelessly out of his reach. Well worth the risk, and the problems could be faced as they came along. He was only anxious to begin.

CHAPTER 4

OPENING DAY DRAGGED on, and Responsible dragged on through it, up in the balcony. The breeze through the windows of the Independence Room was heavy with the smell of early summer flowers, and the soft hum of the red Ozark bees on whose ministrations those flowers depended, and the combination was an effective sedative. Nothing that was going on inside did anything to lessen its effectiveness, either. She supposed she must have heard worse speeches and more boring ones, somewhere, sometime, but she could not during that interminable day think of an example. If the overdose of tedium didn't take any of the starch out of the Traveller delegation, it could only be due to their bizarre practice of spending all of every Sundy listening to a single extended sermon, *with* elaborate developments and codas and commentaries and extrapolations, and emendations on the extrapolations, and scattering slightly truncated versions of the same throughout the rest of the week. They were callused to this kind of thing, both ears and rears, and could of endured a lot more of it, she supposed.

Everyone else, however, including their allies the Farsons and the Guthries, was exhausted long before the Closing Prayer. The way some of the delegates had slumped down in their seats by midafternoon had all twenty-seven Grannys still present—and for sure still straight as spikes in *their* seats—clicking their tongues fit to drown out their knitting needles.

Responsible was satisfied with the effect. She much doubted that the population had stayed glued to the comsets to watch the proceedings of *this* day, and she figured to of lost the majority of them well before noon. She doubted even more that they'd tune in their sets to more of the same tomorrow, and that suited her purposes. If there was going to be a battle on the floor of the Independence Room, the fewer Ozarkers that knew about it and had time to get excited about it, the better. And she had seen to it that there were plenty of other ways to spend your time than sit at the comsets, or even in the balcony, while the days of the Grand Jubilee went passing by.

There were four different plays—one religious, one historical, one comedy, one adventure—going on in Capital City at all times, and enough different ones in their repertoires to be sure there'd be no repetition. Three dance troupes were on duty, two indoors and the other moving around the city, and ordered to make themselves available anywhere they were asked. Four sports exhibitions, including one laid on especially for the tadlings. Checkers tournaments everywhere she had a leftover corner. Two speech competitions, tours through the caves for the romantic of mind and tours through the farms for the practical. Mule races for the daring, and all-day nonstop sermons for the conservative. Down at the Landing there was an inexhaustible picnic, where you could sit and eat in comfort, passing your time in gossip and watching the ships come and go in the harbor. Outside the city borders the largest fair ever put on anywhere would be going on all five days, with every kind of game and exhibit and performance, every variety of food and drink, rides all the way from the sedatest of merry-go-rounds to a thing called Circle-Of-Screams that was guaranteed to make you get off and sit down for half an hour to review your sins. She had something for everybody, something for every time, and comcrews everywhere to beam out the doings to those that couldn't come to Brightwater. The doldrums on the channel given over to the Confederation Hall assembly were not going to be able to compete for attention.

There'd been plenty of opposition to the scope of the celebration, even from her grandfather, Jonathan Cardwell Brightwater the 12th, who didn't as a rule care what *anybody* spent, so long as they extended him the same privilege.

"Are you *sure* all that's needful, Responsible?"

She'd heard that till the time came when she suggested they get a sign made and save their throats. And she'd ignored it. Yes, it was needful, and furthermore it was the one and the only Jubilee she expected ever to be involved in; she'd not have it said that Brightwater stinted, or offered its guests anything less than the very best there was to offer.

"Pride, missy!" the Granny had said, shaking her finger. "Just *pure* pride! And where do you reckon it'll lead you, one of these days?"

She took a deep breath, remembering, and then, finally, the Reverend said "Amen!" and it was over, and the delegations began to file out of the Hall. The band in the bandstand at the corner of the lawn struck up a rousing march at the sight of the first man stiff and blinking at the light and the air, and that did get them moving a bit more briskly. The Grannys and Responsible brought up the rear, everybody else having left the balcony hours before, and she made certain that the Grannys surrounded her on all sides. Invisibility was her goal, and she achieved it clear to the gates of Castle Brightwater and across the courtyard to the open front doors, where the Grannys scattered and forced her to hurry for cover. A narrow cramped corridor that ran the length of the Castle and was meant to give the staff a speedy way in or out of any of the rooms had served both her and her sister Troublesome well when they were children; it served her admirably now.

Nevertheless, when she finally reached her room on the third floor, she found that all her painstaking precautions had been a waste. She could of come straight up the front way and saved herself fifteen minutes of walking time, and had a herald before her crying, "Make way for Responsible of Brightwater!"—it wouldn't of made any difference.

Lewis Motley Wommack the 33rd was waiting for her, sitting on the floor with his knees drawn up and his arms clasped around them, leaning back comfortably with his head against the wall beside her bedroom door.

"Oh, law," she said, "wherever did you come from?"

"Afternoon, Responsible of Brightwater. Same place you

did—that repository of hot wind and tiny minds we choose to call Confederation Hall."

She ignored that, and said, "Good afternoon, Lewis Motley Wommack, and you'll miss your supper if you don't hurry. The delegates are intended for the first serving in the Great Hall . . . you want to end up eating with the children?"

He cocked his head and raised his eyebrows at her, and looked her up and down, and she took one step backward before she caught herself.

"You ran away from me once," he said solemnly.

"So I did."

"You plan to repeat that?"

"If I do, you'll no doubt notice," she snapped.

He smiled and leaned his head back again and closed his eyes; it was clear he'd no intention of moving from her door. She could, of course, have had him removed—or removed him herself, if the commotion either would cause had seemed justified. It would of been an interesting problem of manners if it had not concerned her quite so personally.

It is called a Time Corner, Granny Hazelbide had said, holding her tight between knees so bony they hurt her even then, in front of all the other five year olds, *and we cannot see around it*. Could she run away from a Time Corner twice?

And then there was the question of what, precisely, *he* knew. He had glanced at her when she sat exhausted on a bench in his Castle hall, and for sure, just as the Prophecy had said, he had known her and she had known him, in some way that she could not account for. But had some Tutor told him, years ago, that the day would come when there'd be hard times for the entire population of Ozark on account of his behavior with Responsible of Brightwater, and hers with him? No matter what she did, said the Prophecy, there'd be hard times—but nowhere did it say there was a way of escaping. It might could be that he sat there now, insolent by her door as if he'd been near kin, because he too had been told that what lay before them was not to be avoided, and he wanted to get it over with and put it behind him. And it might could be he knew nothing at all, that no gossip from those little girls had found its way to Castle Wommack over those eight years, and that he sat there for reasons he understood not at all.

"Lewis Motley Wommack," she said, watching him closely, "why are you here on my doorsill?"

"To see Responsible of Brightwater," he answered, perfectly easy. "I've come for audience."

"Audiences," she said carefully, "are held with queens and kings. We've no such nonsense here, young Wommack."

He opened his eye then and looked at her, and Responsible turned her own eyes swiftly away and stared at the floorboards of the corridor, that were polished and gleaming for the Jubilee till she could see a dim reflection of herself staring back at her. She was in no hurry to look at him directly; one look into those eyes of his and the world had swung away from beneath her, once before. In the seconds it had lasted she had fallen endlessly, before she had managed to break free and run.

"You are a kind of royalty," he said, and she could feel his smile like sunlight on her flesh. "I don't know what kind, nor does anybody else—but I mean to find out."

"You talk rubbish," she said.

"And you tell lies—and we're even. Look at me, Responsible of Brightwater, her that travels round the Castles on Solemn Quest, with boots of scarlet leather and whip and spurs of silver . . . her that can command a Magician of Rank as easily as I command an Attendant—oh, yes, my fine young lady, we *do* hear these things, and the servingmaids *will* talk, for all you caution them . . . *Look* at me!"

Because she had the feeling that escape, if escape there might be, or perhaps the mercy of delay, lay specifically in *not* looking, she shook her head like a stubborn child ordered to recite, and stared unrelenting at the floor. And that was her undoing. You can't keep a wary eye on a serpent unless you watch him, and his hands were gripping her shoulders before she knew he'd moved.

"I tell you," he said in a voice that held the promise of endless patience, "look at me! Am I so ugly as all that? So terrible I'll turn your face to stone?"

She struggled in his hands and turned her head away, and with no trouble at all he used one of those hands to hold her fast and the other to tilt her face up. She could feel the warmth radiating from him where he stood, not half an inch between her body and his, and she put all her strength into pulling away from him, with her eyes tight shut.

"Responsible of Brightwater," he scoffed, "I expect you were not Properly Named. Poor little girlbaby, your Granny clabbered the thing. Timorous of Brightwater, that's more like it. Cowardice of Brightwater, might could be. My little sister has more courage than you."

That bothered her not at all. She'd been hearing nonsense intended to provoke her to foolishness all her life, and except for that single mistake with Granny Leeward, none of it had succeeded in a very long time. What she'd heard from all around her lately made his taunting no more than prattle. But his physical strength was a different matter. There was no legal way she could break loose from his grip, short of screaming for help like a terrified child—and nothing would of brought her to such a shameful pass.

There was no help for it. And once her mind was settled to that, she wasted no more time. She opened her eyes and looked at him.

No one would have called him handsome, but he was wondrously beautiful. His head was thick with curls of coppery Wommack hair, copper with lights and fire in it, and she knew from the look of his wrists and throat that naked he would gleam in the light with that copper everywhere. He had the beauty gnarled trees and rough cliff faces have, with no elegance to him anywhere—except for his eyes. They were blue, like any Wommack eyes, but a blue so dark that it put her in mind of the violets that grew deep in Brightwater's forests in the last days of March and were so useful for simple Spells. The eyes had *great* elegance, and an utter authority, and they were as dangerous as she had remembered; she looked full into them, mustering her courage, and once again the floor dropped from beneath her feet and she was helpless.

"Come into my room," she said to him, in a voice she had no mastery of and hardly recognized, suspended in endless blue. It was, she decided, like being trapped in glass—blue stained glass. She had a sudden image of herself in a pointed church window, marked off all around with a leading of black, and perhaps a Mule beside her and a squawker above her head, and cleared her throat quickly. Laughter would not be appropriate, however much it might tempt her.

"You're not afraid for your reputation?"

"I have no reputation," she told him. And that was so. Everything had been said of her, and much of it was true. "Are you afraid for yours? Or have you forgotten how doors work?"

He rubbed at his nose with the hand that wasn't occupied in holding her, but he made no move to touch her door.

"It's warded," he said.

Responsible gathered together enough of her attention to sniff the air, and to set aside the smell of him that flooded her senses, and was amazed that she'd not noticed the garlic sooner. Granny Hazelbide had been by here, and would no doubt have hung garlic wreaths round Responsible's neck if she'd dared.

"My doors," she told him, "are always warded, one way or another, and always will be. Make up your mind, Lewis Motley Wommack—you have waited all this time here at my door, and played a foolish child's game of Look Into My Eyes with me, and now I am going *through* that door. Do you follow me or not?" And she added, "Mind, I'm not running from you. You're free to keep me company."

Once they were inside he sat in the rocker by her window that Granny Hazelbide had chosen the night before, and she took another and pulled it over facing him.

"Well," she asked, "you suffer any ill effects from the wards?"

He looked himself over, and he took his time about it, and then he allowed that there seemed to be no change.

"I haven't been turned into any kind of varmint, there's that," he said. "Nor struck dead, nor my wits scrambled. There's that."

"Did you expect such stuff?" she marveled. "Wards are to keep evil *out*, not create it! What kind of Tutor did you have, there at Castle Wommack, that he didn't teach you even that?"

"You are highly valued, daughter of Brightwater," he answered, "though it's not considered polite to mention it. Very highly valued indeed. I've heard that song"—he sang the chorus in a pleasant enough voice that would one day be deep—

> "What did you learn as you flew out so fine,
> splendid on Muleback, dressed like a queen?
> What did you learn, daughter of Brightwater?
> Tell us the wonderful things that you've seen!"

"All the way to Kintucky," she said, wondering, "all that way, you've heard Caroline-Ann of Airy's song?"

He ducked his head, mock-humble. "Even in the Kintucky

outback," he said, "we have comsets. I know all the verses—shall I prove that?"

"Mercy, don't! I'd feel a fool for sure, sitting in my own room and hearing you sing a song about me."

"Well, then," he said, "because you are so highly valued, I'd thought it might be harder to find myself alone with you. I was prepared for... oh, at least a Granny in a fury, to bar my way."

"And so she would, if she knew you were here," said Responsible.

"And what will she do when she finds me here?"

Responsible shook her head in amazement. "Young Wommack," she said, "you are downright ignorant, not to mention insulting. Even here, 'in the Brightwater outback,' we know to knock on doors. Even Grannys don't enter rooms without leave—why should she find you here? I don't intend to give her leave."

He stood up at that, drew closed the curtains at all three of her windows and went and stretched himself full length on her bed. She liked the look of him against her white counterpane, and she told him so.

He didn't pause to acknowledge the compliment.

"You learned many things, touring the Castles, having adventures," he said. "Now come learn something useful."

She was still thinking she would do no such thing when she lay down beside him. Her counterpane was turned down, and her clothes and his lay in a jumble on her rug, and the thought still lingered. Only when she noted that she had been right, that the copper hair covered him in all but two or three specific places, did she abandon that idea and concede that she was indeed about to learn something.

"I am *not* ready for this," she announced.

And there are times when the land is not ready for the rain, but it falls all the same.

He ran his fingertips over her thighs, and set his lips to her nipples, and he was not overly careful how much of his weight she had to bear.

"I dislike that," she said clearly.

"This, too?"

"I dislike that even more."

"You lie," he said.

She surely did. Everything his body had promised, shirted

and trousered and cloaked, it delivered in abundance. Her loins arched toward his touch and she knew most clearly the meaning of longing. She was all out of patience, the aching of her body for him was unbearable, and if she had known any manner of hurrying him she would not have scrupled to use it. Unfortunately, she was operating this time from a position of total ignorance, and she could only grit her teeth till she shuddered, and wait.

"You're an anxious creature," he said finally, and he lifted her onto the gold of his belly and set her gently where she might ease her own need. It was not what she had expected at all, and certainly not what her experience in the stables and goatbarns had led her to expect, and she moaned in desperate frustration.

"It's impossible," she said. "It can't be *done* this way!"

"Lady, lady," he answered her, "I promised to teach you something useful. For sure it *can* be done this way, if you will only—there!"

Nothing she had heard or read or imagined had prepared her for what it was like to have the full thrust of his maleness within her, and she forgot everything in her determination to draw from him every last measure of the ecstasy offered.

"You see?" he said roughly.

She did, most certainly she did, and when he would have held her away from him she cried out fiercely and slapped at him, frantic in her determination to achieve something—her body knew what it was, though her mind did not—and he laughed and let her have her way for a while.

Until she hovered just on the edge of that achievement. And then, ignoring her teeth and her hands, he held her still in torment against him.

"Oh, dear heaven, dear heaven," she moaned, "let me *loose!*"

"Shhhhh . . . hush . . ."

"No! I can't bear it, I can't bear it another second . . ."

She fell against him, broken in despair, sobbing and past all pride, and he made a soft noise of satisfaction, gripped her in those sure hands, and held her while the shudders racked her, more and more swift, and her breath tore at her throat, and then he said:

"Now, Responsible of Brightwater. Now I shall show you the most useful thing of all."

And he grasped her hips and moved her, and suddenly she

knew that she would die of joy, and he muffled her screams against his shoulders and let her take of him everything that she wanted. It took a very long time, and not once did he make a sound.

She had heard women speak, married women and women of experience, of what happened *after* the act of love. Some men, it seemed, would talk to you. Others would fall asleep. Some would demand food; among the Traveller males, she had heard it said, there were those that would drop to their knees and give thanks for the blessings just received.

This man, however, was doing none of those things. He had raised himself on one elbow and was staring at her as if he had never seen anything like her before anywhere. Responsible had no illusions about her beauty, she had Thorn of Guthrie to compare herself with every day of her life; it could not be that which put such an expression on his face. And she was reasonably sure that the look he bore was not the usual afterlove expression.

"What," he demanded harshly, "was *that?* What the Twelve Bleeding Gates *happened?*"

Responsible reminded him that she had been the virgin here, not him, which made that a foolish question. "There are a number of words to choose from" she added, "always depending on your degree of delicacy. Pick the one you like the best."

"That's not what I meant." And then, "You didn't notice anything unusual?"

Responsible made an exasperated noise and climbed over him abruptly, heading for her bath. The bed was a sea-marsh, and she was not much better.

"Young man," she said over her shoulder, "I have never lain with a man before you. If there was something unusual, I wouldn't know it. What do I have to compare with you?"

He followed her into the bathroom and joined her in the hot water, still frowning, and the frown lasted until they both were clean and once again clothed, and sitting in the two rockers as sedately as if nothing but conversation had ever passed between them.

"I must have imagined it," he stated.

"No. I am convinced that it truly did happen. I was there, Lewis Motley."

"Responsible of Brightwater, do you remember what you said to me, just at the last?"

It hardly seemed proper, but then nothing they'd done in the past hour had been proper. She thought for a moment, and then answered him to the best of her recollection.

"I said... 'My lovely one, it is so wonderful to be inside you.'"

He cleared his throat, and directed her to think about that.

"Doesn't it seem to you," he asked, "that the anatomy is just a tad scrambled?"

She thought about it, and saw what he meant.

"Isn't it always like that?" she asked. "After all, it's mighty close contact."

"Not that close," he said. "No. It is not always like that. In fact, it is not ever like that."

She set her lips, and found that she was no longer afraid of his eyes.

"It *was* like that," she declared. "I was there, and so were you, and for certain sure it was precisely like that. And if you didn't want it to be like that, you should have provided a lecture as you went along."

He was going to be a very stubborn man, she thought, immovable as a mountain; a natural force like a tide or a storm, against which you could break into a thousand pieces, and he would never notice. And she thought, somewhat more than a little belatedly, of the Time Corner Prophecy. There was a lot in there about what would happen if she "stood before him." She doubted that what she'd done could be so described.

"Law," she whispered, more to herself than to him, "I wonder what will happen now?"

He swore, and stood up to stand with his back to her, staring out of her window, holding back one curtain with his hand.

In honest bewilderment she asked him, "Why are you angry?"

"I'm not angry," he said, but he didn't turn around, and she knew that now *he* lied.

"Lewis Motley Wommack," she said, "go eat with the children. They'll be serving them now."

He left her without another word, and she sat there rocking until the last light was gone from her room and she rocked in full darkness. She wasn't sorry for what she had done; nothing that pleasant could be a thing to regret. And her fear of him was gone for good and all. But the consequences of what she had done, now there was something to ponder on. For one thing, she was vulnerable to a number of unpleasant things that her virginity had protected her from until now. The Magicians of Rank would not need to be half so constrained in their constant wearing away at her, now that she lacked her maidenhead, and the first to take a look at her tomorrow would know that. As would the Grannys, one and all. But the Prophecy had been most specific: whatever it was that she would loose upon this world, she and Jewel of Wommack's brother, the harm would not come from knowledge shared by their bodies. That was laid out unmistakably.

She knew his body well now, and intended to know it a great deal better; and with his skill he no doubt knew everything there was to know about hers. But if it was not that, not that knowledge that held the danger, what *was* it then? They had not talked as much as you did over the ordinary cup of coffee.

"Botheration," said Responsible, and decided she didn't want any supper.

She would take off her sheets, for they reeked of salt, and sleep that night on her counterpane. Let Granny Leeward lie on the other side of the wall and wonder why the daughter of this Castle had not appeared for supper; the daughter of this Castle would be sound asleep and not caring.

Tomorrow would be burden enough, when she had to face them all and see in their eyes—even Leeward's—that they knew of the change in her. Tomorrow there'd be no eternal agenda of ceremonies and prayers to hold back the plans of the delegations set to bring down the Confederation, the fools! Tomorrow she would sit in the balcony and watch, alert for the slightest move, the least word, the beginning of crisis, the turn that would mean it was time to call on the loyal delegations and find a way to put the necessary words in their mouths.

Tonight, she would sleep.

CHAPTER 5

RESPONSIBLE WAS SITTING over the last cup of the pot of tea the servingmaid had brought her when the knock came at her door. She set the cup down, made sure her nightgown was decently arranged, and called, "Who's there?"

"Granny Leeward here, Responsible of Brightwater. Granny Leeward of Castle Traveller. May I come in?"

"You sound nothing *what*soever like a Granny," said Responsible deliberately. "I do believe you're a fraud and a sham, whoever you may be."

There was a silence, time enough for her to have another sip of her tea. It was her favorite cup, emerald-green china with a rim of silver, and sturdy enough to drink from half awake without worrying that she'd crush it, the last unbroken one of a set used for company meals when she was still in Granny School. She despised the cups her mother and grandmother chose to start their days with, delicate white porcelain with the Brightwater Crest on the side, big enough to hold maybe three good swallows, and so frail they felt like eggshells in your hand. She could face those later in the day if need be, but not before breakfast, and at no time did she admire them.

"Responsible of Brightwater, you bar your door to me, you'll rue it! A fine day it'll be when a wench of fourteen keeps me standing in a hall saying howdydo to the bare boards, and I'll thank you to keep that in mind, missy!"

"Ah," said Responsible, "now I hear you use formspeech, I recognize you for a Granny after all! Please to come in, Granny Leeward."

The old woman was dressed and ready for the day, all in her customary black, and her pale-blue eyes so cold in her bony face that they put Responsible in mind of two small dead fishes, side by side.

"Have a rocker," she told her, "and make yourself comfortable. Have you had your tea this morning or shall I send for you some?"

"I've been through with my tea this past hour," said Granny Leeward, chill and snappish, "and waiting till I heard the sound of your cup on your saucer so I'd not wake you. You keep mighty highclass hours, to my way of thinking."

"Proceedings don't begin at Confederation Hall till nine," said Responsible, "and it's a while yet till it strikes seven. Ample time for what I have before me today."

"You've mighty little before you, this day and some days to come." The Granny sat down in a rocker, carefully settling her heavy skirts around her, and folded her hands in her lap. "That's what I've come to tell you about—and mind, I'll have no sass from you."

Responsible had some more tea and waited the move, and after the silence had stretched a ways Granny Leeward continued.

"You'll recall, I expect, that I was present—and quite a number of the other members of our delegation with me—when you put on your disgraceful performance at Castle Traveller a while back."

"I do recollect that, yes."

"And you do agree that it was—disgraceful."

"I messed up your fan a tad," said Responsible coldly, "but I did you no harm. And I believe Castle Traveller's budget will run to a fan or two."

"Sin," said Granny Leeward, like a stone falling. "It was *sin,* what you did."

"No," said Responsible. "It was illegal. The two things are not the same."

"Only a Magician of Rank has the authority to do what you did that day," said the Granny, chopping off every word, "and *that's* the illegal part. The sinful part is a woman even knowing what you obviously know, and having no more decency than to use that knowledge, and in full daylight before a dozen respectable people on top of *that*. And it was an ugly trick, missy, a purely *ugly* trick!"

"If there was sin—which I don't admit to—it was in losing my temper and falling into the trap you and your kin set for me. I'd say that was more stupidity than wickedness."

Granny Leeward gave her a narrow look, and as Responsible had expected, there came a sudden look of understanding in her eyes. She'd be seeing that look a lot oftener than she cared to today.

"I see you've added a *new* wickedness to your inventory," said the old woman. "You're a *bold* hussy, I'll grant you that."

Responsible sighed, and set her tray on the night table by her bed.

"Granny Leeward," she said, "you've come to chastise me for my foolishness at Castle Traveller—call it sin if you please, I'll not waste my breath arguing theology with you before breakfast. Well and good; I'm not proud of it. There you sat, leading me on and fanning yourself with that black fan; and all I had to do was heat up its handle a tad to advise you I intended to be treated with respect. There was no call for me to turn that fan into a handful of mushrooms—"

"Black and *rotting* mushrooms, with the smell of death on 'em!" interrupted Leeward, and Responsible nodded.

"Quite right," she said. "The black was appropriate, seeing as how you Travellers find it the only fit color for human use, but there was *no* call to make them rot in your hand. You caught me with a child's trick, and I'm well and thoroughly ashamed that I took that bait. But it seems to me you made me pay for that already, Granny Leeward. How greedy for revenge *are* you?"

The old woman snorted, and her face was stiff with contempt.

"I wouldn't want any misunderstanding between you and me," she said, leaning back in the rocker and steepling her fingers. "Not any misunderstanding whatsoever. Might could be I should clarify this for you."

"I'd be grateful," said Responsible.

Granny Leeward counted the points off one at a time. "What you did to *me,*" she said, "practicing an illegal act of magic, and a foul one, on my person—that goes unpunished still. You lay for a day with deathdance fever, that the Magicians call Anderson's Disease, as payment for carrying out your ugliness before the Family—that's paid. Your offense to me still stands, and I'll call that in when I choose; I don't choose just yet, Responsible of Brightwater, not just yet. And that's not why I'm here."

"You're not clarifying *much,* Granny Leeward, but your narrowness of spirit. Perhaps you could try a little harder?"

"There are six delegates from Castle Traveller as will sit in the Independence Room this day, and as saw what you did," hissed Granny Leeward, "and they're ready and willing to denounce you before the entire convention of delegates, the audience in the balcony, and those watching on their comsets. That make it clearer?"

"Mighty gallant, your men," said Responsible. "It must make you proud."

"A female such as you, missy, ought not to have the gall to ask for gallantry. Well on the way to being a witch, and clear the other side of being a fornicator, and you talk about gallantry? That's for decent women, not for your kind."

"You're plain-spoken," said Responsible. "That's useful in a Granny."

"Didn't I say I'd take no sass from you? Your memory gone with your maidenhead?"

"A compliment is not sass," said Responsible, with as much sass as she was able to muster. "I judge Grannys as I judge Mules, and you rank high. Now speak your piece."

Those pale-blue eyes . . . she had not been surprised to see them like dead fish, but spitting blue fire was surprising. It would have been pleasant to think that the old woman might be tricked in return, brought to a sufficient pitch of fury to lead her into some indiscretion of her own, leaving the two of them in a more balanced position; but it wouldn't happen. To begin with, they were alone, and if the Granny was being humiliated there was no one to see or know it but herself. And to go on with, Responsible was certain the woman knew nothing beyond Granny Magic, all of which was legal for her to use.

Granny Leeward leaned forward, stabbing the air with her pointing finger, and she laid it out for Responsible so there could be no confusion in any least particular.

"Either you stay clear away from Confederation Hall," the Granny said, "where you cannot interfere in what's none of your business and never has been, or my son will stand before the entire assembly this morning and denounce you—leaving out *no* details, keep that in mind!—and the rest of those as saw you will back him up. Now I reckon that is clear as springwater, but if it's not I'll be glad to embroider it for you some."

Responsible sank back against her pillows and whistled long and low and silent. Now she'd heard it, it was obvious, but she hadn't expected it. Which was an interesting measure of her strategic skills.

"Botheration," she said aloud, and thought a word that she'd never heard spoken, though it was claimed to exist.

"Keep your botherations to yourself," said the Granny, "and the Travellers won't add to them. We've other doings to concern us, and telling that sorry tale about you would only use up another day on top of the one you wasted for us yesterday. But if you insist on coming to the Hall, spite of what I've said to you, we *will* waste that time, I promise you, and I'll not scruple to stand in the balcony and add my voice to the testimonies."

"I believe you have me," said Responsible, taking another drink of tea. "All things considered."

"That we do," said Granny Leeward. "That we surely do, and if ever a female deserved it, you qualify."

"Blackmail doesn't burden your conscience, Granny?" Responsible asked.

Granny Leeward sat straight and pale. "We walk a narrow line at Castle Traveller," she said. "We keep the old ways, and there's none of the rest of you as does. We know, the Gates be praised, the difference between a sin and its name. That's a difference not to be despised, nor yet forgotten."

"Explain me that, Granny Leeward—and its application in this matter of you and me. I don't see it."

"I'll explain you nothing! You need moral instruction, you've a Granny here, and a Reverend as well, though he's a poor thing. This universe has one primary law—as ye sow, so shall ye reap—and *we* abide by that. I come here as no instrument of blackmail, Responsible of Brightwater; I come as an instrument of justice!"

"I wonder," mused Responsible, and the Granny drew herself up in the rocker, bridling all over with outrage. Responsible had heard about people bridling, and read the phrase, but this was the first time she'd ever seen it.

"On Old Earth," she said casually, "there were those so convinced of their purity, so sure they were instruments of justice, that they put others to the rack and the fire out of concern for their immortal souls. Now I suggest to you that you might want to keep that in mind your*self*, Granny Leeward. There's ugly, and then there's ugly."

Granny Leeward stood up like she'd sat on a straight pin, shaking all over with a rage she wouldn't stoop to express, and Responsible made a mental note—this was one who did not handle well any criticism that struck at her morality. It might be useful to know that one day. And while she had it going, she drove it home.

"And it doesn't burden your conscience that you Grannys are charged to *help* me, not hinder me?" she demanded. "I find *that* curious."

The Granny's face closed, shut, and if the rage was still there she mastered it. She gave no sign that she'd heard Responsible's last question.

"I'll leave it to you to furnish your excuses for your absence," she said, looking right through the girl. "You lie easy enough, it should cause you no special trouble. Just you stay away from the Hall. And I'll have your word on it."

"You have it," said Responsible wearily. They were tiresome, these Travellers, with their never-ending insistence on guarantees. "And now you *do* have it, I'll thank you to leave. I have work to do, and I'd best get at it."

Granny Leeward headed for the door, but she stopped there long enough to shake her finger some more and say a few sentences on the subject of pride going before a fall, and peace coming to them as deserved it and misery to those as didn't, and just deserts. Responsible rode this out in silence—she had no intention of easing any wounds she might have inflicted on this one—and the time finally came when the woman had either exhausted her supply of moral justifications or tired her own tongue, and she went out the door, leaving a vast silence behind her.

Responsible lay there and whistled her way through three choruses of "Once Again, Amazing Grace," as a calming measure, and gave her situation some careful thought.

Under her bottom pillow, for example, there was a cylinder no bigger than a needle, and in it a list written on pliofilm and headed "Things To Do When I Get Home." Weeks it had been there, shoved out of sight till she could find time to tackle it, and there'd been nights when she'd had the feeling it burned her head right through the feathers and heavy pillowslips. Might could be she'd make her way through some of the items on that list after all, while she was staying away from the Hall.

And then, might could be she'd take advantage of the opportunity to just *lie* here? She was that tired.

She reached under her pillow, knowing the foolishness of the lying-about idea, and took out the cylinder, unscrewed the top, and pulled from it the sheet of pliofilm. It had been so long curled it wouldn't lie flat, of course, and she hadn't any inclination to take it over to her desk where she could spread it on the leather surface to cling properly; she made do with gripping its edges and ignoring the way it wound itself round her fingers.

Eight items she had written there, she noted with disgust. Eight tasks. And when she'd set out on the Quest in February there'd been only the first. Somehow, riding back into Brightwater in April, there'd been the idea in her head that she could get them all out of the way before the Jubilee. Like many another fool idea she'd had lately.

First of all, there was the task she'd set out with: to go over the Castle's secret account books, those that couldn't be trusted to the Economist and required her personal attention.

Next came the matter of determining whether there really had been a Skerry seen at Castle Motley; and if there had been—which she doubted even more strongly now than she had when the servingmaid had blurted out the tale to her—declaring a day of celebration separate and special for the event as custom demanded. It'd be a tad late, but better a tardy observance than none at all. Provided she found any evidence that the servingmaid's story had had a scrap of truth to it.

Third was the promise she had made in the night to the Gentle, highborn T'an K'ib. She had given her word: the Gentles would be involved in *none* of the Ozarkers' doings, as already specified by the treaties signed centuries ago. Furthermore, Responsible intended to see that every inch of the Gentles' territory taken from them by the careless mining operations of the Arkansaw Families was restored, and restored in either its original condition or with improvements to the ancient race's own specifications. T'an K'ib had not insisted on that, treating it as a minor matter, but Responsible saw it differently. The Arkansawyers knew quite well where the boundaries of their lands joined those of the Gentles, and the temptations of a few tons of ore or a vein of choice gemstones were no excuse for violating those boundaries.

Fourth, she had to see to the matter of the growing prejudice against the Purdys. Prejudice was one of the things that had driven the Twelve Families from Old Earth in the first place. They'd all been white, sure enough, but they'd heard more than they cared to tolerate about "ignorant hillbillies" and "white trash" and they'd seen the black and brown and yellow peoples of Earth suffer at the hands of ignorant and vicious people their own color. And now, somehow without anybody's remarking on it as it grew, the Purdys had become the "white trash" of this planet. When anybody did a stupid thing, the first remark you heard was "A body'd think you were a Purdy born and raised!" Nasty, that's what it was, and she would *not* have it; it shamed her that she had not noticed it sooner.

You didn't put an end to prejudice by proclamations, though; it grew slow, and it died slower. What was required was for the next few groups of Purdy girlchildren to spend their Granny School time spread all round this planet, clear away from the constant expectation of the grown-up Purdys that they would *always* fail in whatever they did. A few dozen confident, self-assured Purdy females to go home and do missionary duty—that's what was called for.

And then, for number five on her list, she had written down "Wommack superstition clear out of hand." As it was, and no doubt about it. A Wommack cut his finger, it was because of the Wommack Curse. A Wommack spoiled a roast because she had her mind elsewhere, the Curse again. Every mistake, every natural mishap that the universe laid on a Wommack—be it ever so like the mishaps and mistakes that were laid on every other soul on Ozark—lay it to the Wommack Curse. That had to be seen to, and, quickly; there had to be a sufficient run of good luck for the Wommacks to put some chinks in their curse consciousness. And thinking of Lewis Motley Wommack, she smiled to herself; she might find it possible to get in a few licks on *that* job with no strain to herself at all.

Sixth was the trivial task of making certain that nobody but pitiful Una of Clark, lost in her worship of her husband beyond all limits of decency, had been back of the mischief that had plagued Brightwater early in the year. Milk that came spoiled from the goats, mirrors that shattered, Mules that flew like squawkers drunk on fallen fruit fermented in the sun—and the one kidnapped baby, with no harm done to him. Responsible had no doubt this one was trivial, for Una of Clark had been too broken with terror the night she'd confronted her with her crimes not to have cried out the names of anyone that'd helped her—always excepting the husband. Una of Clark would have died unhesitatingly, plunged off the seacliff and into the waters boiling below her, before she spoke any word that might mean the smallest peril for Gabriel Laddercane Traveller the 34th.

Responsible tried, briefly, imagining herself obsessed in that way with Lewis Motley Wommack, convinced the sun rose when he came in the door and set when he went back out it, trembling at his least frown and melting away when he smiled on her. She ran it round her head for a minute or two, checking, but it made no sense to her any way she viewed it. Praise be for small favors.

Next to last on the pliofilm was the Bestowing of two acres of land on Flag of Airy and her husband, in recognition of their service to Castle Brightwater; and seeing that, the guilt did bite at her. Most of the things on the list she could truly say there'd been no time for; they required careful planning and ample time. But not this, this was an hour's easy work. She had plain and simply forgotten about it.

And finally . . . "See to the feuds on Arkansaw," she'd written with the stylus.

See to them!

Responsible rolled over onto her stomach and struck the pile of pillows with her fist. See to them, indeed. How was she to "see to" the incredible antics of three Families, bent on feuding, set on feuding, bound and *determined* on feuding? Guthries, Farsons, and Purdys, bad cess to them all, and the poor Gentles right in the middle of it! Just what she'd been thinking when she'd scribed there so casually "See to the feuds" she could *not* imagine. Must have been after she crashed into the side of that dockshed and addled her head.

It was a long list, and she figured that to carry it through she needed maybe a staff of fifty Magicians, and fifty more miscellaneous, and for all she knew an army wouldn't be a bad idea, whatever an army might be like. She could begin with the Castle accounts, and throw in the Bestowing in a hurry, but the rest of it?

She knew an assortment of words she was forbidden to use, and she ran through them as she'd run through the list, all the while she was rolling up the pliofilm and stuffing it back in its case to bury once more underneath the pillows. And she'd only gotten to the tenth of her prohibited pronouncements when there came the thundering at her door that she'd been expecting with half an ear for some time now.

"Come on in, Granny Hazelbide, before you destroy my door for good and all," she hollered, resigned to what could not be avoided and wouldn't improve by being put off. "Come on in here and tell me all about my sins!"

The Granny fairly flew through the door, and banged it to behind her. She had on a crackling crisp dress of shiny dark blue, caught at the neck with a brooch handed down in her family all the way from First Landing, if she was to be believed. Her feet were shod in high-heeled pointy-toed black pumps with a shine that hurt your eyes, and so narrow Responsible knew they hurt *her*. Granny Hazelbide prided herself on the neatness of her foot. And on her head was a black straw hat to match the pumps, and a black veil ready to be pulled down over her face in the latest style, with a cluster of dark-blue violets with velvet petals and velvet leaves and velvet stems wound round wire to top off the headgear. She was a regular fashion plate, was Granny Hazelbide, and she was in a fury.

"Whatever are you doing lying there in that bed like the Queen of the Shebas?" she demanded, advancing on Responsible like a skinny tornado. "You make me late for the Opening Ceremonies, girl, and I'll take a switch to your bare tailbone, for all you're near fifteen and fancy yourself full grown! I'll give you two minutes—two minutes, do you hear?—to make yourself fit to be seen and go out this door with me! Laws and Dozens, Responsible, we're late this minute!"

"Granny, Granny," soothed Responsible, "you'll have a heart attack if you go on like that, and I'll have to call in a Magician to set you right, and for sure I want no Magician hanging round my bed on a beautiful morning like this! I suggest you *calm* yourself a tad."

The old lady's lips drew tight, and her brows met over her nose, and she leaned over Responsible's bed like she was ready to whack her with her pocketbook.

"Calm myself!" she said. "When you lie there and face me down, cool as you please, and it half past eight in the morning? Have you taken sick, missy, or leave of your senses—which one?"

"Neither one, Granny Hazelbide," said Responsible. "Neither one. I've just run into a sort of a snag."

Granny Hazelbide leaned over further, and tipped the girl's chin up to look into her face, turning it this way and that till it made her neck ache. And then she let her fall back, suddenly, and Responsible was grateful it was pillows she'd had to fall on. Even so, the resulting thump shook her some.

"You call that a snag, do you," said the old woman disgustedly. "A snag! What'd you go and catch yourself on it for, if you saw it as such a hindrance, eh, Responsible?"

"Granny, darlin'—"

"'Granny, darlin'!' You mark my words, Responsible of Brightwater, there'll be a few words from your Granny darlin' about this, once she's leisure enough to speak them. But losing your maidenhead, though it's a disgrace to us all and a piece of foolishness the likes of which doesn't come by *often,* it's no excuse for you to lie in bed and miss the Second Day at Confederation Hall. Now get yourself out of there and into your clothes, and let's us *go,* Responsible! Snag, huh! *Who,* pray tell, was it got past my wards on this room?"

"I'm not about to tell you, Granny," said Responsible. "Not *about* to, so you needn't push it. Nor, I'm sorry to say, is that the snag I had in mind."

"What you have in mind doesn't bear repeating before decent folk such as myself, I'll wager!"

"How you *do go* on!" said Responsible admiringly. "You'll out-granny all the other Grannys yet, and think how proud I'll be then! Seeing as how I had the raising of you.

"However," she added quickly, before the Granny could catch her breath and start on her again, "if you plan to hear

the Opening Prayer you'd best go on, and I'll explain later. It's not a short explanation."

Granny Hazelbide stared at her, and set her arms akimbo. "Responsible," she said, "is there really an explanation? Worth my being late for?"

"You'd have to tell me that after you heard it," said Responsible. "Depends on how much you fancy the Opening Ceremonies, I'd say."

Granny Hazelbide pulled up a chair and sat down in it without a word, as Responsible had known she would; and she listened—her mouth puckering tighter and tighter with every passing minute—while she heard a carefully edited version of the mistake made at Castle Traveller and this morning's visit from Granny Leeward. And then she spoke her mind, and Responsible was glad she'd only made it a tale of giving all the staff at Castle Traveller toothaches. She'd been afraid that might be somewhat too mild to convince, since many an Ozark woman not a Granny and with no hope of ever being one picked up a scrap or two of Granny Magic, though few would dare use what they knew. Granny Hazelbide didn't find the transgression a light one; that became clear in a hurry.

"Stupid!" she said fiercely. "That's the only word for you, missy. Just purely *stupid!* How could you let yourself be wrenched round to such a state—and the Travellers, of *all* Families to find yourself beholden to! So Granny Leeward called you a whore—does calling make it so? Prior to this morning, that is! I reckon she used the word again when she was in here, and this time with good reason!"

"No," said Responsible, "as a matter of fact the word she used this time was 'fornicator.'"

"And how'd you respond to *that?* You put warts on all the Mules in the stables? Rashes on all the servingmaids and Attendants? Sink all the boats at the Landing? What kind of conniption fit did you throw over 'fornicator'?"

"Well," said Responsible, "I don't mind 'fornicator' especially. It lacks the little extra bit; it makes no claim that I *sell* my favors, you'll note. I was able to restrain myself."

"And now there you are, barred from the Hall."

"So I am."

"Shame on you, girl!"

"Want me to call her bluff and go, Granny?"

"Great Gates, no! There's no bluff to that woman. If she

said she'd make a scandal of you before the whole world and its brother-in-law that's exactly and precisely what she would do. You stay away, just as she bid you, and be glad she's not made it worse."

"Well, then, Granny, what I need from you is not more tongue-lashing. What I need is for you to go on along and be my eyes and my ears. I can watch on the comset, for sure, but it'll give me only such scraps of what's going on as the comcrews find interesting. Whoever's speaking, and a shot of the balcony now and again, and no more. I won't be seeing who passes notes to who else, or who walks out in a huff, or who falls asleep that you might of expected to pay close attention, or who gets together in huddles in the rows. I need you to watch for me, and listen close, and send word if you see *anything* that appears to you to be out of line."

"And what'll you do if I do see mischief: I'll see plenty afore this week's over, you know. What do you plan to do about any of it, missy?"

"That depends on what it is," said Responsible patiently. "Might could be there'll be nothing I can do; might could be I can be useful. But unless I have you to report to me, we'll never know which."

"And what will you be doing in between my reports, besides lolling in your bed and sniffing the posies?"

Responsible thought of her hateful list of "to do" tasks.

"I'll find a way to pass my time," she said with assurance.

"Rolling in his arms, no doubt!"

"Granny Hazelbide," said Responsible, mock-serious, "you have an evil mind."

The Granny clicked her tongue against her teeth till Responsible wondered the tip didn't bleed.

"Shiftless *and* shameless!" she ranted, shaking her finger at the girl smiling up from her pillows. "What would your *mother* say?"

"That she couldn't believe any man would of wanted me," said Responsible promptly. "You know that. Especially when there's such competition as Silverweb of McDaniels around, all unspoken for and never been kissed. Now do please go on to the Hall, dear heart? Please? It'll be time soon for the Travellers to begin their move, and I'd be pleasured to know how they open the game. You can come back tonight and lecture me on my morals till you drop in your tracks if that appeals to you; so far as I know, nobody ever talked a maidenhead back into its place, but I'll listen respectfully if you fancy trying. But not now, Granny Hazlebide, not *now!*"

The Granny went out of the door, proclaiming woe and thunderations all the way down the hall, and Responsible locked her hands behind her head and stared up at the ceiling until she could hear her nattering no longer. And then she stared a good half hour longer, thinking. She might have put her list away, but she could still see it plain as plain in her mind's eye.

"This very day," she told the ceiling at last, "this very *morning*—what's left of it—I'll see to the Bestowing of Flag of Airy's two acres."

And then what? the ceiling gave her back.

"And then," she said, carrying it on, "I believe I'm going to need some help. I do believe that I'd better send for my sister."

That silenced the ceiling. What it would bring on in the way of response from other sources, once it was known that Troublesome of Brightwater might be coming down from her mountaintop and into the city, would not be silence. Responsible chuckled, thinking about it.

And realized that, come to think of it, she *missed* her sister. Mean as she was, outrageous as she was, impossible as she was sure to be, she missed her. And she'd had no idea.

CHAPTER 6

THE BESTOWING WAS drawn up in black ink on snow-white paper, marked with the Brightwater Crest and sealed with the Brightwater Seal, before noon of that day. Responsible had looked over the Kingdom's maps, displayed for her on the comset screen, with great care; and she had chosen two acres plus a bit of riverbank left over, a nice piece of land only eleven miles out from Capital City, tucked into an arm of the river between two big farms and overlooked this long time because it was so small.

"Too small to be any use," said her grandmother Ruth of Motley when Responsible carried it downstairs to the small sittingroom.

"Too *large,* to my mind!" her mother had objected. "We've almost no land left to give, Responsible; if somebody actually did a deed worthy of gratitude, Castle Brightwater would be hard put to it to find any acres to Bestow. I don't approve, myself; I don't approve at all."

"Responsible didn't expect you to," said Ruth of Motley

comfortably. "It'd spoil your image. *I* approve, and I'll speak for both my husband and my sons: none of them would grudge the young woman her two piddling little acres."

"I don't see," said Responsible's mother stubbornly, "what Flag of Airy has done to merit a Bestowing. The last one we gave—and it's been eleven years ago, mind, before Responsible ever saw daylight!—was twelve acres to the young man that tried to save the lives of Jewel of Wommack's family. You remember that, Ruth?"

"I'm not senile," answered Ruth of Motley, giving Thorn of Guthrie a look as she bit through a strand of embroidery floss that spoke of a preference for setting her teeth elsewhere.

"Grandmother, you'll ruin your teeth," said Responsible automatically. She'd been saying that ever since she could remember, and she'd learned it from hearing everyone else say it. But Ruth of Motley never paid it any mind, and her teeth gleamed bright as they ever had. Then she realized what Thorn of Guthrie had said, and she looked at her mother and tried for a casual face.

"I didn't know that happened here," she said. "Thought it was on Kintucky."

"*No*-sir," said Thorn of Guthrie. "The Wommacks were here at Brightwater on a visit, the old man and that young wife of his—she was no more than a child, and he had no business marrying her, if you ask me, not that anybody ever has—and Jacob Donahue Wommack's wife, and the two children. Praise the Gates, they left the tadlings home... But the others went down in the river, there where that root tangle is just past the bend, right out there beyond the Castle grounds. And they all died, trapped in the roots and sunken logs, with the boat turned over on top of them. And," she wound it up, "it was the young man as near drowned him*self* trying to save them that had the last Bestowing of land from this Kingdom. They were perfect fools, you know—going out on the river, and it in flood, and not knowing what kind of mess there was trapped in that tangle, but they wouldn't hear no; nothing would do but they should have a day on the river—and they paid in full."

"That was a sorry day," Ruth of Motley added. "Everybody carrying on about the Wommack Curse, like it wouldn't of happened if anybody else had been in that fool boat. I remember it well."

"And *that* young man did something worth notice, Responsible. He must of gone down a dozen times trying to free the Wommacks, and at the last they had to hold him back to keep him from having another go at it when he was so exhausted he'd never in the world have come up again himself."

"Mother," said Responsible reasonably, "do think. If, as you put it, somebody did something that *really* called for a gift from Brightwater, those two little acres wouldn't serve anyway. But they'll please Flag of Airy and her husband, both of them fine young people. There's room enough for him to raise a house, and her to put in a garden that'll feed the two of them and a few tadlings as the years go by. Don't be selfish, Mother— it's not becoming."

"Wait till the men are home," said Thorn of Guthrie, "and we'll see what they say. Not to mention Patience of Clark."

"I'm not likely to make any Bestowing without the whole Family's approving," protested Responsible. "What do you take me for?"

"Responsible," said Ruth of Motley mildly, "don't tempt your mother."

"Yes, ma'am."

"The document's well drawn, and you were wise to do it and have it out of the way. Put it in the desk over there, and then after supper tonight we'll call a short Meeting and send the vote around. But there'll be no trouble."

"I *still* say—" Thorn of Guthrie began, but her mother-in-law cut her off. Enough was enough.

"Thorn of Guthrie," she said, "for two long *months* Flag of Airy saw her own babe suckled at the breasts of Vine of Motley, so her milk would not dry up before we Brightwaters got Vine's own child back to her arms. And in that two months she bore a heavy load. Responsible is quite right."

"Fiddle!" said Thorn of Guthrie. "I've suckled two daughters myself, one of them there before you, and I'd have welcomed anyone that cared to take the task from me. I don't see it."

Ruth of Motley rolled her eyes toward the ceiling, and then bent over her embroidery in silence. She was doing a panel of ferns and flowers that required a good deal of attention, and she intended to waste no more effort on her sharp-tongued companion.

There they sat, the two of them: Ruth of Motley with her needlework, one piece after another till the Castle was smothered in the stuff, and Thorn of Guthrie with yet another of the endless series of diaries she'd been scribbling away at for thirty years. They were almost alone in the Castle. It wasn't large, as Castles went; but today, with nearly everyone gone to the fair or the Hall or some one of the other entertainments, it seemed a vast echoing cavern.

The question Responsible had been dreading came just as she thought she was going to make it out the door without either of them thinking of it.

"Responsible!"

"Mother, I'm just on my way to put this Bestowing document back in my desk for safekeeping."

"Your grandmother said to leave it here, and you heard her; and besides, I want to ask you something."

Thorn of Guthrie sounded determined; Responsible turned back with a sigh, went to put the Bestowing document in the sittingroom desk, and then stood waiting.

"How come you aren't down at Confederation Hall your*self* this morning, along with the Grannys?" her mother asked her, and Ruth of Motley looked up from her work for the answer.

"Don't plan on going," said Responsible, short and sharp.

"You don't plan on going?"

"Echo in here," said Ruth of Motley, as was her habit.

"Whatever do you mean, you don't plan on going? All the fuss you've made, all the dust you've raised over this week of nonsense—and you stand there and tell me you don't plan to go?"

Responsible stuck to her guns.

"That's right, Thorn of Guthrie."

"Well, that beats all!"

Her rescue came from an unexpected source. Ruth of Motley had turned back to her work, but she spoke attentively enough.

"I think that's wise of you, Responsible," she said. "I think that's *very* wise. Not a thing you can do to change what's going to happen in that Hall, and for you to sit there and watch it going on and torturing yourself over it would be pure foolishness. You're better off keeping busy here till it's all over and we know how far they've gone. Not to mention the fact that there's plenty of neglected work right here for you to turn your hand to while everybody else is off gawking at the delegations and going to carnivals."

That satisfied her mother, and Responsible blessed Ruth of Motley for her solid common sense. Here she'd been fully prepared to face them all down and just plain refuse to *say* why she was staying away from the proceedings, same way she'd refused ever to say who she'd learned had kidnapped the McDaniels baby, and to bear the fuss that went with the refusing. Just because no amount of thinking had brought a plausible reason to her mind. And now Ruth of Motley had taken the load right off her back, all unexpected and unasked. And while Thorn of Guthrie was still occupied in counting off all the things she wanted Responsible to see to while she was staying home and not tormenting herself, she slipped away, much relieved. It was time she turned on the comset in her room and had a look at what was happening; by now they'd have finished with the Opening Prayer, and whatever leftover trivia there'd been from the day before—and unless she was far wrong in her thinking, Jeremiah Thomas Traveller would of been recognized by the Chair and would be holding forth.

She wasn't wrong, either. She sat in her favorite rocker, the blue one with a back high enough to rest her head against, and paid the figure on the wall the compliment of *her* attention. Like many another thing in Castle Brightwater, the comset could have done with some repair. That had been sacrificed to the budget for the Jubilee, and every so often the projections ceased to be threedys and became flat as paper cutouts. But the sound was reliable, and that was the main thing; she knew well enough what they looked like.

Jeremiah Thomas had just begun, and the speech promised to take some time, for he was not only Master of his Castle, he was a Reverend, ordained before he passed his sixteenth birthday, and he knew how to spin out the sentences.

She had tuned him in just as he was finishing off his thanks to the Brightwaters for the "splendid program" of Opening Day—the hypocrite!—and allowing as how it had been a historic occasion fitly and abundantly observed. But now it was time for them to turn from ritual observance to the serious business of this meeting—and he proceeded to explain just what that meant to him.

"Mister Chairman"—he rolled it out—"Senior and Junior Delegates and Aides, gentle ladies that honor us by gracing the balcony of this grand and glorious Hall . . . and all the citizens of the six continents who join us this day through the miracle of technology . . . I stand before you now with a heavy heart. A *heavy* heart!"

Responsible hoped it was heavy. She hoped it was a stone of Tinaseeh marble in his sly vicious breast, and well supplied with sharp little points.

"Why, you ask, is my heart heavy?"

I don't ask any such thing.

"Because, my dear friends, my dear colleagues, I have no choice open to me today but to speak the truth. Oh, not that I am not reluctant to be the first to do so—for many among you know what that truth is, and did I wait long enough you might well speak it for me! Not that the truth does not stick in my *throat* . . . no! I *am* reluctant! I *do* find it hard to force the words to come forth, as come forth they surely must! But I tell you all, my conscience will not let me rest until I have said what *must be said.*" He let his voice fall to a hush. "All night last night I knelt on the bare boards of my chamber floor—"

There wasn't a guestchamber in Castle Brightwater with bare boards to its floor, nor a servant's room either, but Responsible could see that it wouldn't of sounded nearly so dramatic for him to talk of kneeling for hours on soft rugs.

"—and I *wrestled* with my conscience! *Must* I, I asked myself . . . *must* I, I asked the Holy One Almighty . . . must I, Jeremiah Thomas Traveller the Twenty-sixth, be the one to speak this truth?"

He paused to let that settle over the heads of his listeners, and then he answered his own question.

"And the answer came back to me—it came back YES! And it came back YES! again!"

Just like him, thought Responsible, pleased to see him go flat and black on her wall, barely a flicker, to drag the Holy One into this and spread the blame.

"Oh, my friends," he said, "oh, my colleagues—"

Careful! You'll be saying dearly beloved next!

"—I shuddered then. I shuddered . . . for the truth I must pronounce, the truth my conscience *compels* me to pronounce—that truth is not a joyous truth! That truth is not a merry truth! That truth is not a truth cast in a spirit of gaiety . . . unless, unless . . . but let me come back to that! For now, let me only tell you that the truth is sometimes a sad and solemn burden, and that this is such a time—but I *will* speak it, nonetheless; and I do not fear to do so."

He went on then, to remind them one and all of the reasons that had brought the Twelve Families from Old Earth to Ozark one thousand years ago. He talked of the air of Earth, that could not be breathed; of the water of Earth, that no one dared drink till it had been made so foul by chemicals that it burned the throat and offended the nose; of the soil of Earth, so poisoned that the food it grew was unfit for human beings to eat, that had taken in pollution till it could give back nothing else. He talked of the pollution of human*kind* as well, every hand set against every other; of the dank misery of the slums where the world's poor had scrabbled from dole to dole. He spoke of the shame of the so-called holy men who threw out in their daily garbage the finest foodstuffs chemistry could produce, while billions lay swollen-bellied in the dust, dying of starvation. He talked of the politicians, that lived like great ticks upon the bodies of the citizens they had sworn to serve, bleeding them of their substance and fattening upon it till the bureaucracies were swollen to monstrous size. He spent a number of superb sentences upon the doctors, become so callous and so arrogant and so divorced from the people that they could heal nothing but their bank balances; and a few more upon the lawyers, who had lusted after the suffering of others and profited by it; and still more for those that had dared to call themselves teachers, while they spent their useless lives spreading ignorance and demanding ever more money for the pitiful job they did . . .

On and on and on . . .

Would he *never* stop? Responsible tried to imagine any gathering of women where such a monologue would of been tolerated past the five minutes it took to see where it was heading, and failed. No female would of sat still for the wasted time. Not a word that he said, looming there in his antiquated black suit, flickering with the straining of the comset—which was certainly poorly—standing there with a *tie* round his scrawny neck as a symbol of his bondage to the ancient nonsense he spoke against—not a word they hadn't all heard a hundred dozen times. Not a turn of phrase they didn't hear every three Sundys or so at Solemn Service . . . and he had no skill of control. He had the preacher's skill. He could put one word after another without ever a stumble or a pause; but they sat for his mellifluous bombast out of politeness, not because they enjoyed it—and because they were men, and had no better sense.

Granny Hazelbide had said it as well as ever she'd heard anybody say it, long ago at Granny School. "Men," she said, "are of but two kinds. Splendid—and pitiful. The splendid ones are rare, and if you chance on one, you'll know it. What I tell you now has to do with the *rest* of 'em—as my Granny told me, and her Granny told her before that, and so back as far as time will take you." They'd all leaned forward, because her voice told them something important was coming, and she'd gone on. "If," she said, "a man does something properly, that's an accident. That's the first thing. As for the sorry messes they make in the ordinary way of things, that's to be expected, and not to be held against them—they can't help it. That's the second thing. And the third thing—and this is to be *well remembered*—is that no man must ever know the first two things."

Granny struck her cane on the floor, three times hard, to underline that. "When a man spills something, it's your place to catch it before it touches, snatch it before it falls, and be sure certain he thinks he caught it himself. Men—all but those rare splendid ones—they're frail creatures; they can't bear much."

"And a woman?" one of the little girls had asked timidly. "How about a woman?"

The Granny had gripped her cane till her knuckles gleamed like pearls. "There is *nothing,"* she said in a terrible voice like ice grinding together, "more despicable than a woman who cannot *Cope!"*

Thump!

"You remember that now!" she told them. "You keep that *firmly* in mind!"

"It's not fair!" It had run all around the circle, where they were sitting on the floor with their legs tucked neatly under them. "It's not fair atall!" And she'd turned on them, brandishing the cane over their heads—Responsible remembered how that cane had seemed ready to crash down upon her head, and how she'd trembled—and she'd said, *"Fair!* This is the real world, and it is as it is. Let me never hear any more from you about *fair!*"

She jumped, then, no longer a five year old at Granny School, once again a woman near grown watching a foolish man and listening to his useless words. The word that had made her jump, thundering out of the wall, had been "Jubilee!" She had missed, in her reverie, the part where he'd compared all those tribulations of Old Earth with the tribulations he now claimed to see building on Ozark, and had laid them at the feet of the Confederation of Continents.

It didn't matter, she'd heard it from him before, along with the part about the money wasted by the Confederation that should be staying in the treasuries of the individual Kingdoms where it belonged, where it had been honestly earned and should be honestly disbursed. She knew where he was in the speech—it was time now to make the motion to dissolve the Confederation—and what was he yelling Jubilee about? She leaned toward the wall, not wanting to miss this.

"A Jubilee!" he was saying, voice like butter melting, voice like syrup on cakes, voice like rosy velvet against the cheek, "A Jubilee is a time of rejoicing and coming together in celebration. And I wouldn't have you think I begrudge you your Jubilee—you have *earned* your Jubilee. I do not propose to take it from you. What I propose . . . what I propose is that we make this a new Jubilee, a true Jubilee, a Jubilee in honor of the celebration that will then go on for all the days that remain of this week! A celebration not of serfdom, not of slavery, but of independence! A celebration of our decision to stand upon our own feet at long, long last, sovereign states governing themselves as befits *men* . . . no more cowering under the skirts of Brightwater! Let us, my dear friends, oh my dear friends, let us celebrate not the Jubilee of the Confederation—but the *Jubilee of Independence!*"

The whooping and the cheering and the shouts of "I so move!" and "Second the motion!" came through loud and clear, and Responsible had to admit, much as she despised to do it, that that had been a clever touch. Grim old Jeremiah Thomas, he'd managed to get rid of the role of ghost at the feast, managed to paint himself benevolent and warm of heart and in *favor* of people enjoying themselves—and at the same time, the motion to dissolve the Confederation permanently had been passed and set up for debate, just as he'd wanted it to be.

She reached up and switched off the comset, no longer interested. It would be the standard procedure now, and it would take all of the following day at least. Every Senior Delegate would be allowed to speak to the question, first of all. Then every Junior Delegate, should any of them want to add something—and most were sure to, they had so few opportunities to be heard. And after that, there'd be the round of rebuttals, when anybody that wished to raise objections to the speeches could put that in. And the final summing up by the Chair . . . all of that, before the motion could be put to a vote. It would be tedious.

She could count on some of them. The McDaniels, the Clarks, and the Airys, for sure; she could count on them to point out and underline what it was going to be like for the frontier continents with no comsets and no supply freighters, hacking out their existences with a few thousand people that hadn't been here to vote for any such condition. She could count on the Travellers to scoff at that and allow as how people weren't such puny creatures as some thought they were, and how a hard life here meant a fair life Hereafter, and how misery was what built *men*—she could be sure of that. There'd be the Purdys, saying nothing . . . and the Smiths helping them . . . but doing it at great length, trying to play both sides against the middle they could only just barely glimpse. The Lewises and the Motleys, they'd help specify as far as they dared what sovereign statehood was going to be *like*, once the rhetoric was done with and the hardscrabble was before you . . . And the others? No way to know, and nothing much to do but wait. It seemed to her the chances were good, in *spite* of the rhetoric, and she was sick to death of watching the delegates caper about, and weary to death of hearing them talk, and she turned them off as she would have pinched a bug between her fingers.

And because of that, she missed the entrance of the Smith Delegation, filing sixteen strong into the back rows of the room, just in time to add their "Ayes!" to the vote for the Traveller motion. And she didn't hear, until after Granny Hazelbide came to her room just before supper, of the stir it had caused when people had seen that Granny Gableframe wasn't with them.

CHAPTER 7

JEWEL OF WOMMACK was out of her bed at the first sound from Lewis Motley's guestchamber and into her nightrobe; by the time he closed his door—so softly—behind him and turned around, she was standing outside her own door with her arms folded over her chest and her foot tapping on the cool stone floor.

"Hush!" he said at the top of his lungs; and then he roared at her: "You mean to wake up the whole Castle? Don't you have any consideration at *all* for other people? You think you're the only person in this Castle that—"

Jewel backed hastily into her room, dragging her laughing brother after her by a death grip on his left earlobe. Scandalized, she pushed the door to with her free hand, praying that nobody had heard his carrying on.

"Lewis Motley Wommack!" she said, stamping her foot at him—a wasted effort on the thick rug with its pattern of intertwined roses and ivy, but the only gesture short of biting him that she could think of in her fury. "You are a worthless, wicked man, and a disgrace to our Family, and you will drive me clean to *distraction* if you do not cease your dreadful ways! Haven't you got any shame at *all?*"

"No," he said, "I don't suppose I have."

She glared at him, back to the door and determined he'd not go through it without going through her as well, determined she'd not cry no matter what he said or did, and silently cursing the mother who'd left her with this burdensome animal to torment her all her life long. He'd never marry, not him, she knew it; he could not bear the idea that there was anybody that had a claim on him, anybody he had to answer to for any smallest thing. She'd be a creaking old woman of ninety-nine and she'd *still* be accountable for his behavior.

"I wish I was dead," she announced bitterly. And then she changed her mind. "No, I wish *you* were, and then I'd have some peace!"

Lewis Motley Wommack the 33rd, all in black like a Traveller male, and a hood to cover the copper hair that might catch the glint of a stray light and give him away, lifted his little sister into the air and shook her gently at arm's length, well beyond the reach of her nimble fingers.

"Nasty, nasty child," he said, "wishing your one and only brother laid out in his cold narrow grave, and him only nineteen! Whatever would people say if they could hear you now?"

"That you'd driven me *mad,* that's what they'd say! And they'd be right!"

"*What* do you care about Responsible of Brightwater?" asked Lewis Motley in his most reasonable voice. "What has she ever done for you that you should have such tender scruples about her?"

"My scruples," hissed Jewel of Wommack, "my scruples are for any living creature that strikes your fancy! *Any* creature—always excepting your Mule, of course. You take right good care of your Mule."

He swung her down into his arms, gave her a hug that took all her breath away, set her back on the bed she'd come tearing out of, and allowed that he did see to the comfort of his Mule.

"A Mule," he said, "is worth a man's respect. Won't do fool things no matter who tries to make it; keeps itself to itself and has no patience for human nonsense; works hard for its keep and asks no quarter of anybody or any thing; and'd take your hand off as soon as look at you if you don't play fair. Mules, my dear, are *entitled*."

"And women? They don't do for you and make over you and plain lie down and beg for the privilege of dying for you, Lewis Motley Wommack? They're not worth the consideration you give a Mule, just because they won't bite your hand off?"

"The day I find a woman that's as admirable as a Mule," he declared, "I promise to treat her well. *You,* for example; you show signs of developing into something as valuable as a Mule. Provided you get over spying on every move I make."

"Lewis Motley," she said, shivering all over with simple fury, "how many women now have you notched off to your count? How many girls are there in Kintucky that get up from their beds in the morning crying and go back to them at night with the tears not dry on their faces, because of you? How many now have you taken on, molded to your liking—law, you turn every *one* of them into the same pitiful slavish creature, over and over again—and then dropped the way you'd drop a playpretty? How *many,* dear brother?"

"You've been keeping my count for me," he chuckled. "I don't bother."

And he added, "Responsible of Brightwater's a different matter. I think you can leave her off your list."

"I should think *so!* I should just purely and completely think so . . . And the idea that you are off to bedevil her again . . . Lewis Motley, you break my heart, you truly do."

"Think I *can* bedevil her, do you? I appreciate the compliment."

The tears flooded Jewel's eyes, in spite of her resolve, and she hated her voice for the way it betrayed her, quavering and quaking like a little girl's.

"Why do you spy on her?" she managed to choke past the lump in her throat.

"Why do you spy on *me?*" he countered. "The Grannys ordered you to, I suppose."

Jewel bit her lip and glared at him, though he'd gone all blurry through her tears. As if she'd answer that!

"Little sister," he said then, "you might just as well resign yourself and sleep the sweet sleep that's due you, because there is no way in this world you can change a single thing that's bothering you. Hear me, Jewel? No way atall. No way you can change me into a staunch and upright stick of a Lewis—or another version of my righteous brother Jacob. I have only four more days and nights in Brightwater, and if I'm to discover Miss Responsible's secrets I have no time to waste. The days are useless, since I have to spend them in that Hall listening to the idiot pontification of the pack of fools we've chosen to call Continental Delegates... And if you interfere with my use of the nights... Jewel, love, I can't let you do that."

"Whatever secrets Responsible of Brightwater has," said the girl wearily, knowing it was no use and never would be, "they're none of your business."

"I intend to *make* them my business," he told her. "I intend to find out why it is that a skimpy little female, not yet fifteen and homely to boot, is bowed to and scraped to like she is. I intend to find out what there is about her that is so special it sets her apart even for the Grannys—and I intend to find out why the Magicians of Rank speak of her the way they do."

"Which is what way?"

"Like a pestilence," said her brother. "Like a plague. Like an evil that goes far and beyond all other evils. That scrawny little piece! I intend to know why."

"*Why* must you know that?" she shouted at him, no longer caring who heard; might could be if somebody heard they'd come along and object and he'd be ashamed to go prowling the halls in the middle of the night. "Even supposing it's true—and I don't see it, Lewis Motley, I don't see it at all, I think it's all your imagination and Responsible has just had the sorry luck to be born to a do-nothing mother and a scandalous sister and a pack of worthless men that leave everything to her to do, and have since she was old enough to talk—and the only difference between her and a couple dozen other girls I know is that the family as makes a slave of her happens to own the oldest Castle on Ozark instead of a poorscratch farm! But just suppose you're right—why must you find out about it? What business is it of yours, that makes it your place to go prowling the Castle where we're guests when decent people are in their beds; poking and prying—what gives you the right, Lewis Motley?"

"Ah, Jewel," he laughed, "you can't expect me to let a mystery like this go by me! I may never get another chance at it—I may well never get off Kintucky again, and Kintucky's got not a single mystery to call its own. A *secret*, Jewel of

Wommack, exists for but one reason—to be found out. And I'm off now to worry at this one."

The heavy door closed behind him, but she wasn't fooled; she knew him far too well. She let the minutes pass, let him stick his head back in and bid her a mocking goodnight with his apologies for forgetting, before she really let herself weep. He hadn't caught her that way for over two years now, and she was proud of the record.

She looked up at the ceiling and found no answers written there, and announced to the Holy One that she had by the Twelve Gates and the Twelve Corners done her best, for all that she'd failed as usual, and then she lay down and cried herself to an exhausted sleep.

Lewis Motley was grateful to his sister in the long run; though he wouldn't ever have admitted it to her, he found her a good deal superior to any Mule—or any female—he'd ever encountered, and he enjoyed her company even when she was at her most frantic. Jewel of Wommack was never dull, and there was no putting her down by any fair means; give her another year or two and she'd be a match for anybody, himself included. She had a way of finding the strands of an argument, laying out each one casual as if it were nothing at all—with all its subpropositions attached—and then tying the whole thing off, while everybody else was still muddling around in search of their opening remark. He admired that, if it did sometimes cause him inconvenience; and this time, with her futile protest, she had saved him a half hour's boring wait at least. As it was, he'd no more than reached the narrow corridor running the length of the Castle, the one Responsible thought she used so discreetly, and found himself a narrow niche to hide in, when she came along. The timing couldn't of been better.

She was wearing a long traveling cloak for which there could be no excuse in the warm May night if she'd nothing to hide, and she fairly flew along the corridor and out the door at the back of the Castle, with him right behind her. They crossed the Castle yard and took the path down to the stables, a parade of two; and he saw in the last fading light of Ozark's three moons that she had a gathering basket over her arm. At one o'clock in the morning, whatever did she need with a gathering basket? He could feel himself warming to his task.

Not a Mule brayed as they came up to the stables, and that

wasn't natural. The Mules should of been raising the devil of a fuss. If not about her—he was willing to admit that it was just possible the Brightwater Mules had seen to it that all the others stabled there these nights knew who she was and that she had every right to be there, seeing as the fact they wouldn't mindspeak a human didn't mean they wouldn't mindspeak one another—then about him. Any Mule worth the price its tail would fetch for a loomwarp would be braying to warn her he was behind her in the night, and the Mules in these stables were the very finest of their breeds. Something was all wrong, delightfully and fascinatingly wrong, in the Kingdom of Brightwater.

He waited by the stable corner, back pressed to the wall and only that smallest part of his face absolutely necessary to see her come out not hidden; and in three minutes flat there she was, without the awkward basket, mounted on a Mule with two sets of saddlebags over his back. He had barely time to throw himself bareback on one of the Mules that Brightwater had made available for its guests before hers had taken to the air and gone over the Castle wall into the darkness.

He followed her at a safe distance down a street where the flowering trees arched thick and met over the roadway, making it a tunnel of heavy scent—how the citizens of Brightwater stood it he couldn't imagine, it was so sweet it turned his stomach. She was a tiny figure ahead of him, the street curving away down a hill and out of his sight, but her Mule had a white blaze to each ear, and he marked her by that. He'd have no trouble keeping up with her, and no chance of losing her, especially with the mysterious silence that had somehow been imposed on every living thing that could ordinarily have been expected to sound an alarm.

And then she was gone.

One moment she was there, the two little white spots in the darkness clear as two candles ahead of him, and the next there was no sign of her anywhere. Only the darkness and the absolute silence and the perfumed night air, and him alone like a fool and with no idea how to get back to the Castle. He'd been far too interested in where she was going to pay any attention to the route they'd followed.

But he'd learned something that would be worth the wandering around hunting he'd have to do to retrace his path. He went a bit farther, and he got down from the Mule and walked a few nooks and crannies to make certain sure, but he hadn't really had any doubts. A Mule, a highclass and expensive and well-trained Mule, had a top speed of sixty miles an hour. But there was a way the Magicians of Rank had, called SNAPPING, that took those Mules from point to point as near instantly as made no difference. *Only* the Magicians of Rank could do that. The Grannys couldn't. The plain Magicians couldn't. Just the nine Magicians of Rank, and no other living creature.

Except Responsible of Brightwater. That she had SNAPPED somewhere, and would get herself back the same way, he had not the least doubt. Lying in her bed, feeling not just their bodies mingling but somehow their minds as well, so that he was her and felt her deep within him, and she was no longer a maiden on her way to being a woman but was *him*, taking her own maidenhead, he had known there was more to her than just the knot of political intrigue he'd suspected. And for the sake of knowing what it was he'd fought back the gorge that rose in him at the sensation of being female, at having the privacy of *his* body invaded—let alone the privacy of his mind! He felt cold sweat on his forehead, remembering; it had been like having something you would never put your hand to, something you'd carry out of an old barn wiggling at the end of a rake and at arm's length, with your head turned aside, and having it moving in your head, somewhere back of your eyes...Lewis Motley shuddered, for all the warmth of the night air.

Oh, he was not surprised that she could SNAP a Mule. He would not of been that surprised if he'd seen her SNAP without the Mule beneath her; and the word "witch" came to him all unbidden. It would be a good question to ask the Grannys: what happens to a man that takes the virginity of a witch?

He turned his own Mule and took it back through Capital City, watching for the towers above the trees till he found the Castle, flew over the high stone wall and down to the stable door, and put the Mule away in its stall with a ration of grain for its trouble. Then he found himself a place to sit against the stable wall, hidden behind a rack of hanging bridles and gear, and settled in to wait for Responsible's return. And still, not a Mule brayed.

It was almost three when she came back, and he had fallen asleep in spite of himself. Bad enough trying to stay awake all day while the men in the Hall droned on and on with their everlasting nonsense; to make a nightwatch of it as well, two nights in a row now, was beginning to tell on him. Jewel would of been pleased to know that, no doubt. What woke him was the sound Responsible made transferring something—a number of somethings, and it frustrated him mightily that he couldn't see what they were—from the Mule's saddlebags into the gathering basket.

The Mule was lathered, and she set the basket aside, hung the saddlebags on a hook in a corner of the stall, and began to rub it down... He could hear the rough hiss of the stable blanket against its hair. He sat bolt upright against the wall, doing his best not to breathe, and was pondering what to do next when she spoke up.

"Lewis Motley," she said briskly, right along with the rubdown, "you'd be a good deal more comfortable in your bed than you are against that wall. We pride ourselves here at Brightwater on making our guests comfortable... but then we've never had to allow for them sneaking up and down the halls and through the stableyards and roaming all around the town half the night. Might could be our arrangements'll need to be changed. Tea, maybe, served for the guest with a sudden urge to go riding after midnight. And a sofa in the stable instead of that hard floor."

The idea that she'd known he was here all along, let him follow her down the garden path, and expected him to be waiting—the humiliation of it left him without a word to say.

"Well?" she said. "No answer, Lewis Motley? You Wommacks have curious manners, if I do say so myself, and I surely do. Only person I've ever known with more gall than you is my sister Troublesome, and she has her reasons. You have your reasons, young man?"

He cleared his throat, took a deep breath, and launched into an ordinarily reliable account of the manner in which he ached for her fair white body and was willing to spend any number of waking nights on hard floors for an opportunity to clasp it to him once again. It wasn't his very best version, but it was the one that came quickest to his otherwise vacant mind, and she listened to it all the way through politely enough.

"Do tell," she said, at the end of it, and he wasn't all that surprised. It had had its uses with any number of young females, the ones Jewel expected him to worry about their crying and puling through their days and their nights. But it was not all that likely to prove effective with the daughter of Brightwater—he'd heard the welcoming speech she gave the delegations, and noted the easy way she lulled them.

"Shall I try a different one?" he asked her. "I have an assortment."

"Never mind," she said. "Considering you spent most of last night sitting out in my hall and got nothing for your trouble, and then most of this one in the company of our Mules, I'll settle for the piece you just recited. Now I suggest we go to bed, or you'll be late back to your room and the whole Castle will be scandalized."

He followed her warily, feeling no more lust for her than he'd felt for the borrowed Mule. It had been far too easy, and he'd gotten off much too lightly; he might have been led round the barn, but he wasn't so addled he didn't realize *that*. Not to mention that she must know he'd seen her disappearing act, seeing as how she knew everything else he'd done this past forty-eight hours or so. And he tread the halls softly, knowing they had barely an hour before the Castle staff roused to start this day. To say nothing of the Grannys, that felt anybody abed after five in the morning wasn't worth spitting over, and tended to set even that hour back once they passed the century mark. Might could be that with the press of time and the number of curious circumstances he'd not be called upon to muster up even a pretense of that absent lust; which would be just as well.

But he needn't have worried. Responsible of Brightwater had him naked in her arms with a speed that made him wonder if she was still using witchcraft, and in ten frantic minutes it was all over, tangle of bodies, tangle of minds, and all. He lay there drenched with sweat beside her, trying to get his breath, and complimented her on her efficiency.

"I'd of preferred a more leisurely course to things," she said, "*if* I'd had my druthers, but there are times when every second must be made to count. This was one of those times."

"Well, I thank you for your hospitality," he said lamely; he hoped he had strength enough to get back down the corridors and up the stairs to his room. Maybe he could claim he'd broken a leg and buy himself a few hours' sleep—for a few hours' sleep, at that moment, he would of been more than willing to break a leg.

"Tired, Lewis Motley Wommack?" she asked him.

"Oh, no," he said. "I can hardly wait to get to the Independence Room and sit through today's round of speeches on the cursed *Confed*-eration."

"Law, how you lie!"

"Right enough. And I wish you'd tell me, before I rush off to my important affairs of the day, how you *do* that."

"Do what? Lie? It's you as does the lying."

"Tell me how you run around inside my head like you do, Responsible of Brightwater... Tell me that, and stop your throwing dust in my eyes."

Responsible raised herself on one elbow and stared at him, and he thought what a shame it was she wasn't beautiful, plain witches not really fitting his concept of the thing, and she said with an absolute seriousness that inclined him to believe she spoke the truth: "If I could keep from it I wouldn't do it, since I'm well aware you dislike it."

"You can't keep from it? That's a dubious claim."

"I don't go where I'm not wanted," she declared. "Not deliberately. Might could be that as I get more practice at this, I'll learn to control my head somewhat better. I get... carried away, you see. It's a distracting sort of activity."

She did indeed get carried away, and he prudently made no comment on that. She was a lusty woman, and he pitied any man handed the task of keeping her satisfied for the next fifty years.

Just the thought of it and the sweat turned icy on his body, making her go "Tsk!" beside him.

"I'd warm you up, my friend," she said gently, "but there's not time. Nor time for you to shower, I'm sorry to say. Unless you want every Granny in this Castle to see you sashaying down the halls, you'd best get yourself under way and save the tidyup for your own rooms."

"Tell me one thing," he said.

"If you don't ask," she cautioned, "I won't be obliged to refuse you."

"Where did you go?" he continued, determined to gain as much as he could. "Near on three hours you were gone, Responsible of Brightwater—where were you?"

She was silent, except for the laughing; and he sighed and dragged himself out of her bed before he could fall asleep in it. He wasn't going to find out by asking, she'd made that clear; and the idea of turning her into the sort of maudlin mess he was accustomed to producing, where she'd do or say anything just to keep him from leaving her side—that was ridiculous. He was young, but he wasn't stupid.

"I intend to find out, you know," he told her, pulling his clothes on any old how. "I do intend to find out."

"Intend all you please," she mocked him—mocked him, damn her! "I'll not spoil your fun by telling you."

"And how do you know I won't get up today in front of the Grannys and the whole world assembled, and tell them that you disappear in the night on a Mule, and have the power to lay silence on the creatures, and make something indescribable of the act of love?"

She was calm as a pond. "I know that," she answered, "because first of all that would put an end to your fun, for sure and for certain—you'd never find anything out that way. And secondly, because for all the wickedness you so pride *your*self on, young Wommack, you have a code of honor of your own—and it doesn't include tattling. You'd never stoop to that."

"Might could be I'd see it as my duty as a citizen to speak up," he said, struggling with his hood. "If there's anything I can't abide, you know, it's failing in my duty as a citizen."

"Like Jeremiah Thomas Traveller?" she teased. "Burdened with the truth and heavy of heart, but oh, law, you asked the Holy One Almighty if you should tattle and the answer came back YES! and it came back again YES!"

He closed her door behind him as loudly as he dared, leaving her still chuckling on her drenched narrow bed among the pillows, and limped desperately toward his rooms and a scalding shower. He was by no means confident he'd live through this day, nor certain he cared to; and the Gates help anybody that crossed him till he'd had a chance at some sleep.

When Jewel of Wommack stuck her head out her door at him as he passed it he said only, "Don't chance it!" and she popped it right back in again without another word.

CHAPTER 8

RESPONSIBLE SAT AT her desk, the private account books before her, and worked, doggedly. It was work that had needed doing before she had left the Castle in February; it was work that needed doing now; and it would make an excellent device for forcing the hours of this day to go by.

At nine o'clock sharp she'd tuned her comset for automatic printout, and she would not miss one word spoken. The speeches and their rebuttals, the Chair's summary and the results of the voting—assuming they got to the voting today, which was not all that likely—would be transcribed silently onto pliofilm and deposited in the comset slot where her copy of the day's news still lay unread. She had waked up that morning, an hour after Lewis Motley Wommack left her bed, to the sound of a late spring rain drumming on the roof and against the north windows, and usually that would of been her idea of an ideal setting to curl up in her bed with the news-sheet and her pot of tea. But she'd had no stomach for the "news" this morning. None of what had happened at Confederation Hall would be news to her—except the things that mattered most but would not be printed on the pliofilm. And anything new that had happened beyond the narrow focus of her present interest, anything that was of importance and might deserve her attention, she did not want to know about right now. She had no attention left to give such things, and would do a slapdash cattywampus job of tending to them—far better to have them wait till this meeting was over and she knew where matters stood.

She was tired, from tension and from lack of sleep; the shower she'd had before her tea had not driven away the gritty feeling under her eyelids nor the ache in her muscles. Nevertheless, she sat at her desk and she studied the columns of figures, forcing them not to blur by squinting fiercely until she added a headache to her other problems and was tempted—just *slightly* tempted—to squander a Spell or two on her self.

"Pay attention, Responsible," she told herself sternly, "and don't be such a frail little flower." A good hard pinch would wake her up fairly effectively, and save the energy she might well need for real magic before this week was over. She applied the pinch, swore softly, and looked again at the columns of numbers.

There was, for example, the one hundred thirteen dollers entered under the ambiguous heading "Herbs Needed." Herbs needed by whom? For what? And how could anybody spend one hundred thirteen dollers on herbs at one time? The Grannys gathered their own herbs, as did she and the Magicians; only the Magicians of Rank were considered so busy that their herbs must be provided for them by others.

She laid down her stylus, cross at the ambiguous entry, cross that she hadn't demanded details when it had come through on the private budget line in the first place, and went to the comset. She punched in the computer locations for the budget category, seven numbers in sequence, and the infowindow lit up for readout on such matters as the cost of goatfeed and Mule blankets in the month of April 3012, which was not yet quite what she wanted. The restricted access code numbers switched the computer's search to the areas that interested her.

She typed in the date of the entry, the words, and then, AMPLIFY.

GAILHERB EIGHTY DOLLERS EVEN

BENISONWEED	THIRTY-THREE DOLLERS EVEN
SOURCE	MARKTWAIN WILDERNESS NORTHEAST EDGE, 2119.4 BY 941.0 APPROX
GOAL	CASTLE AIRY
BENEFICIARY	CHARITY OF GUTHRIE

The readout winked off, flashed once more as a concession to her human frailties, and winked off, leaving the word WAITING behind.

Responsible thought about it.

IS REPEAT DESIRED? The computer was short on patience.

She ignored it, and thought some more. Then she typed in: DISPLAY ALL OTHER DETAILS RE ENTRY.

ALL DETAILS DISPLAYED. WAITING.

"Wait, then," said Responsible, and turned it off. She was satisified. Charity of Guthrie, widowed Mistress of Castle Airy, took in every damaged creature that Ozark produced. Any citizen involved in some shabby Family altercation that would not bear the light of day or of the courts; any girl suffering the nine-month effects of careless love; any young person unable to face the long haul up through the world from servingmaid or apprentice or hired man to heading an independent household; any weak or shamed or injured or frightened person, anyone simply in need of refuge, could be sure of a warm welcome at Castle Airy. And three Grannys lived under that roof, to help Charity live up to her name. If she'd felt she needed one hundred and thirteen dollers worth of gailherb and benisonweed, so be it.

Responsible checked the item off and went on to the next one. And then her stylus slowed as she wondered . . . had any of the Twelve Kingdoms planned ahead, against the possibility that the Confederation would fall and they would no longer be able to depend on Brightwater for such things as herbs? It was very simple for them now; whatever their Castles required, they punched in their order on their comsets and it arrived by supply freighter. And in an emergency, there'd be Veritas Truebreed Motley the 4th, Brightwater's own Magician of Rank, SNAPPING in on his Mule with the supplies in his saddlebags almost before the person asking had stopped entering the order. The Castles had been taking that for granted for hundreds of years now, like the weather; might some of them have thought about preparing for a new kind of winter?

Sure enough. The computers told her, as they'd have told her sooner if she'd had sense enough to ask. In the last six months there'd been a steady series of orders in from Castle Traveller. Herbs, they'd ordered, both healing and magic. Magic supplies in abundance. Bags of the holy sands from Marktwain's desert, and flagons of the sacred water from its desert spring. Lengths of fine cloth needed for the ceremonies of the Magicians and the Magicians of Rank. Gold cloth for the sails permitted only to the small silver ships of the Magicians of Rank. Unguents and potions; musical instruments and bolts of velvet; silver horseshoes and silver daggers. And coarse salt, in huge amounts.

The list was too long to represent genuine need, and she ought to of seen it; but they'd been clever about it. A little here, a little there, and all of it scrambled to look like the ordinary orders of a busy Castle . . . Only when the computers had it neatly sorted and totaled could you see what they were up to. They'd been stockpiling, had the Travellers, hoarding all those items they might find themselves hard put to locate for a while if they didn't have Brightwater to call upon.

The hypocrisy of it made Responsible's mouth twitch. Independence! Oh, yes. Stand on your own feet, be boones, be true *men;* no more hiding behind the skirts of Brightwater. But first, be very sure you've bled Brightwater of all the necessities for that independence.

Castles Guthrie and Farson, on the other hand, that ought to have been doing the same thing, had put in nothing more than a few routine orders. They were so obsessed with the details of the fool wrangling going on on Arkansaw that they'd had no time to spare for the obvious. Responsible had no illusions that they would of refrained from hoarding on any kind of moral grounds.

She typed in rapid instructions; there would be no more deliveries of supplies to Tinaseeh, nothing else to Castle Traveller, that did not have her personal approval. She'd not have a legitimate need neglected, but neither would she allow Castle Traveller to strengthen their hands any further at Brightwater's expense.

Noon passed, and still she worked, and the soft hiss as each filled sheet of pliofilm landed in the OUT slot on the comset never stopped; they were working right on through dinner, then, at the Hall. She kept grimly to her figures and her bits of data, refusing the temptation to take a look now and then at the words that might be on those sheets. There were only a few alternatives, and as her magic had truly told her, every one of them carried trouble with it. Should the Confederation stand, there would be trouble: the anti-Confederationists' resentment would be greatly increased by their defeat, and by their public humiliation at the Jubilee. The plotting, the niggling attempts to undermine the assembly, the constant dragging of feet when action was needed, would go right on as they had all these years, disrupting the equilibrium of Ozark. Should the Confederation fall, there would be trouble: twelve sovereign states to establish themselves, to construct alliances and formal relationships one with another—a way of life entirely new and untried. And then there was the possibility about which she could make no reliable prediction: the most militant of the anti-Confederationists—say, the Travellers, the Farsons, and the Guthries—they might simply *secede*. That was also possible, if things did not go their way, and if the problem of saving face seemed to them heavier than the consequences of secession.

At which point she realized that her method of concentrating on her work and refusing to think about these things was to run them round and round her mind, thinking all the time, "I absolutely refuse to think about what will happen if . . ."

"Dozens!" she said out loud, and then, "Bloody oozing Dozens!" If there was a worse oath than that one, she didn't know it; if there was any justice, she'd be struck dead here where she sat, and then she wouldn't have to worry about any of it any longer. "As I sow, so shall I *reap?"* she demanded of the universe in general. "How about You doing a little reaping, now I've done so benastied much sowing?"

The small message bell on her comset rang then, a poor substitute for the bolt of lightning she was lusting after; there was a message for her. No doubt the Farsons wanted their rooms changed; they always did, whenever they came to visit, as a matter of principle.

She laid down her work, doing it little harm, since she'd been paying no real attention to what she was doing for the past half hour at least, and pushed the MESSAGE stud.

"Twelve Corners and Twelve Gates!" the thing squawked at her; she didn't even recognize the voice. But the voice was prepared for that, which meant it had to be somebody accustomed to the vagaries of Brightwater's low-budget communications equipment. "It's Granny Hazelbide," it went on. "You turn your comset on, missy, this minute—the Smiths have just demanded to be heard out of turn because, by their lights, they've already missed *several* turns—as if that was anybody's fault but their own, but your uncle's fallen for it—and from what I see before me, unless you look quick you're going to miss something like you never imagined in all your borned days! And so am I if I tarry *here* any longer!"

TERMINATE, said the computer.

Responsible frowned; she had no desire to miss out on anything that had brought the Granny to that pitch of excitement, but the suggestion that anything the Smiths might say or do would be worth her time was one of the more dubious ideas she'd heard lately. A Granny tumbled over the balcony edge from leaning too close, a Junior Delegate gone berserk and racing up and down the center aisle—something like that might be interesting, but the Smiths? The Smiths were dullness raised to its utmost potential.

Nevertheless, if Granny Hazelbide thought there was something happening, it was likely there was, and Responsible hit the proper switches. And there stood Delldon Mallard Smith the 2nd, risen to give *his* speech on the subject of the motion to permanently dissolve the Confederation of Continents. And his brothers, all three of them, and all four eldest sons, standing in the row alongside him—to give him moral support, no doubt.

She scowled at his image—the man'd never said a word worth hearing in all the years of his life, if what people said of him was to be credited, and her own limited experience with him led her to believe that it was—and listened for a clue to what had had the Granny all in an uproar.

"—that I . . . uh . . . understand from the very depths of my *man*hood, the utmost recesses . . . uh . . . of my soul, the plea that my distinguished colleague from Tinaseeh has made to all of us and its . . . uh . . . its significance. It strikes a chord that resonates in *this* breast!" And he pounded on the breast in question to demonstrate the awesome sincerity of his feelings;

Responsible snickered. "But we Smiths," he went on, "we Smiths were not taken by surprise at Castle Traveller's move, nor do we . . . uh . . . take it lightly . . . uh . . . lightly. Knowing, knowing I say, that it was sure to come at this Jubilee—my friends, it was long *overdue!*—we turned our finest minds to what it must mean . . . for all of us. Not only for Castle Smith, but for every Castle on this planet. And what came to us, like a . . . uh . . . *revelation!* . . . was that since First Landing our people have been ignoring something of great importance. *Great* importance!" He paused dramatically, a great bulk in a swath of cloaks that must have been torment in the heat, and clasped his hands before him, leaning toward his audience.

"Think!" he said. "What *was* it that First Granny herself said, as she waded out of the waters of the Outward Deeps and set foot on this gentle land, one . . . uh . . . one thousand years ago? Every schoolchild knows the answer to that question! She said—she *said:* 'Glory be! The Kingdom's come at last!' The *Kingdom!* I tell you, my friends, my colleagues, gentle ladies, citizens all over this beautiful and bounteous . . . uh . . . planet—we have missed the significance of what First Granny said for *one thousand long years!* For that, that was a *Naming!*"

Responsible was glued to the set now, not because what he said was so fascinating but because for the life of her she could not see where it was going to lead. What *could* he be trying to get at?

"Now," he said, clearly warming to his subject, "what *is* a Kingdom? Is it a piece of land? Is it a building? Is it a set of . . . uh . . . coordinates? That may well sound like a simple-minded question to . . . uh . . . some of you—but I ask you, I ask you to give it some serious thought. When one of our Grannys names a girlbaby Rose, we ask ourselves—what does that *mean?* We add up the values of those letters, and we look carefully and with respect at their . . . uh . . . total, and we ask ourselves—what is their *significance?* And we don't call that simpleminded, for we know that Naming is serious . . . that the very . . . uh, the fabric of our lives depends upon Proper Naming! And when First Granny called this a Kingdom, what, we must ask ourselves—one thousand sorry years late!—what did she *mean?"*

As any fool knew, Responsible thought, tapping her fingernail impatiently against her front teeth, she meant that we'd finally reached a homeplace and that she was fervently grateful to be off The Ship and out of the water and once more have her feet on solid ground. So?

"I'm not going to *tell* you what she meant," Delldon Mallard said, his voice heavy with layers and layers of dramatic emphasis—he must have practiced, thought Responsible—"I'm going to *show* you!"

For a moment she lost sight of him, as the comcrews swung their cameras round the room and up toward the balcony to give their viewers a glimpse of what was happening. On the floor of the Hall, where Delldon Mallard stood with his three brothers in their places and the four eldest sons each at their father's elbow, an Attendant rose at every one of them's right hand, and waited at rigid attention. And up in the balcony, the Smith women were standing, each with a servingmaid at *her* right hand! Marygold of Purdy, wife of Delldon Mallard and Missus of their Castle; the wives of each of the three brothers, lined up beside Marygold in the back row; and Dorothy of Smith, eldest daughter of the Castle. All over the Hall, the Smiths and their staff were standing—to do what?

The cameras swung dizzyingly back again—the comcrews must have been flustered by the turn of events—and focused on the Master of Castle Smith. His face was the very picture of a man with grave thoughts on his mind, though Responsible doubted he'd ever had a truly grave thought, and he jerked his chin imperiously toward the Attendant that flanked him.

Responsible watched it; but she didn't believe it. Even seeing it with her own eyes, she thought that last night's labors, last night's revels, and this day's tedium had driven the last of her senses to distraction. It could not be that she was really seeing the Attendant lift away—with a flourish—the heavy cloak that covered his Master, to reveal beneath it yet another cloak; this one of purple velvet, sweeping from the high ruff at his throat all the way to the floor and trimmed all the way round its edges and its sleeves with a foot-wide border of snowy fur. Nor could she really be seeing the magnificent velvet outfit, all tucks and smocking and studding, beneath that purple cloak, or the—yes, dear heaven, it was a scepter—suddenly in his hand!

"You are seeing it," she told herself sternly. "*Be*hold . . ."

From a carven box the Attendant took something else, and he placed it with laborious pomp upon his Master's brow. A crown, beyond all question a crown. It shone under the lights the room required in the gloom of the rainy day, a heavy golden crown with a puffed insert of velvet and fur to match the cloak . . .

She began to believe it, and she sank right down on the floor to watch the spectacle as it was repeated all over the room at the Hall, flickering there on the screen. His brothers weren't quite so splendid as Delldon Mallard, their heads were decked with coronets and they held no scepters; the sons, miniatures of the brothers except for an extra gewgaw or two on the costume of Delldon's boy, looked miserable with both the heat and the attention. And up in the balcony, while every Granny clutched her knitting to her breast in shock, the servingmaids removed the outer cloaks of the Smith women and completed the final touches to *their* gaudy array.

"I give you," bellowed Delldon Mallard Smith, "my brothers—the Dukes of Smith!" He swung his arm wide in a gesture of presentation, and the Attendant next to him ducked hastily, but not quite hastily enough. "I give you my son, the Crown Prince Jedroth Langford Smith the Ninth! My nephews, who will be Dukes one day, and now bear proudly the title of Baronet! I give you my wife and my consort, Queen Marygold of Purdy, Queen of my Kingdom!" And on and on down the list, ending with the Crown Princess, Her Gentle Highness Dorothy of Smith.

Dorothy, that had always been a pincher. Marygold of Purdy, that had never sent in an order totaled correctly in her life, even when it was for just one item. The Royal Family.

Delldon Mallard Smith wasn't through, of course; that would of been too much to expect. "That," he went on, giving the back of the seat ahead of him three solid thumps with his scepter and making everybody sitting there jump, "*that* is what a Kingdom is! It has a King! A Queen! All those things that properly . . . uh . . . belong to a Kingdom, it has those things! And when every Family of Ozark has fulfilled its responsibility to First Granny, when every Kingdom has its King and its Queen, *then* at long last we shall see an end to the tribulations that we have suffered these last ten centuries . . . For it was not the Confederation of Continents that bought our troubles upon us—begging your pardon, Delegate Traveller, but that is . . . uh . . . a misinterpretation. It was the failure, the failure to establish twelve *proper* Kingdoms as First Granny intended us to do!"

An Ozarker hesitated to shoot at a sitting duck; but there

was one careful question, put by a delegate with his eyes fixed on the ceiling above him and not on the man he addressed. He wondered, just wondered, why First Granny had never seen fit to *mention* this dreadful mistake.

It didn't bother the King of Castle Smith. The whole thing having come to him in a dream, it all being a *revelation*, as he reminded them he had already stated, he knew the answer to that.

"Just plain stubborn," he said flatly. "She wouldn't stoop, not First Granny! If we were such plain fools we couldn't see it, why, we could . . . uh . . . just suffer the consequences. And we *have*—and we've deserved them every last one. It tears at the heart to think of it, First Granny sitting through all those long years waiting, waiting for . . . uh . . . somebody to see the light, and going to her grave with her wishes still denied her . . . It makes a man . . . it brings a man close to tears." And he wiped ostentatiously at the corner of one eye with a bit of his white fur cuff.

Responsible would have given half her repertoire of Formalisms & Transformations at that moment for a chance to see the faces of the Grannys up in the balcony, listening to a pitiful fool make out the first of their number to have had less sense than *he* had.

There was more, but she was past hearing it. She had thought, she truly had thought that she had considered every possible alternative. But she had been sorely mistaken, for this had never crossed her mind. Not only had it not come in a dream, like a revelation, it had not even drifted through a nightmare! Why, even on Old Earth, even before the Twelve Families left it in disgust, there had been no more Kings and Queens that she knew of. Maybe somewhere in the backwaters of that dying world there'd been a relic monarchy or two, but for the true nations of Earth the days of royalty had been the days of fantasy and fairy tale—and that was one thousand years ago.

What would they do now, she wondered, not sure she really cared anymore; she couldn't decide which word was more fitting—"tragic" or "hilarious"—and her head felt entirely scrambled. This explained a number of things, all in a swoop. Why Granny Gableframe wasn't here; no Granny would have countenanced such a charade. Why the Smiths had come late—to call even more attention to their foolish selves and their ridiculous plan, and to avoid the consequences of coming so unhandily late in the alphabet. Why the Smiths had so rudely shut their Castle doors to Responsible when it had been their turn to show her hospitality on her Quest—they'd been afraid that she would see something that would give their scheme away and lose them the advantage of surprise.

Surprise they had, and no question about it. The loudest silence Responsible had ever heard lay over the Independence Room; she fancied she could hear that silence spreading out all the way to the Castle. And Delldon Mallard Smith, fool that he was, was not such a fool as to lose that advantage. While he faced no more than a pack of stunned and dumbfounded males, with the females above him helpless to interfere, he called out, "Mr. Chairman, I move we put the motion to a vote *now!* With no further delay!" "Second!" bellowed the Dukes of Smith in chorus. And the Chair, her own uncle, in his own state of shock, quavered, "All in favor say aye," and the ayes came out of mouths that no more knew what they were saying then if they'd been babes in the cradle—and the act was done.

And in the Smith row, where she'd not seen him before, Responsible saw the beaming face of Lincoln Parradyne Smith the 39th, Magician of Rank of Castle Smith. He was pleased, ah, he was *delighted;* he'd be dancing in the aisle any minute now. What had he done to Granny Gableframe, she thought, to keep her away, and keep her from warning Responsible that this monstrous thing was in the planning? If he'd harmed the old woman, Responsible would see that he paid . . . but he no doubt knew that. It there'd been any hazard he'd not of been grinning the way he was.

It was over. Over!

Not done properly, of course. Few of the delegates had had their opportunity to speak, and no rebuttals had been offered. Any one of the neglected men could of cried "Point of order!" and demanded that the procedures be observed, that had been their right; but they had not. The Travellers had no doubt been holding their breaths for fear someone *would* come to his senses enough to halt what Delldon Mallard had set in motion. And the Brightwaters, like everyone else, had been vacant-minded with amazement, and miserable with embarrassment, and had let the opportunity pass by and the ayes fall from their mouths as if they didn't matter . . .

"Men!" shouted Responsible then, outraged to the point of

physical sickness, and she kicked the ailing comset with all her strength. "Bad cess to every last *one* of them!"

She was not alone in her opinion.

Down the center aisle of the Independence Room strode a figure that ought to show Delldon Mallard Smith and his Dukes and Princes what majesty was. She stood almost six feet tall; she was slender as a blade of grass, but there was no hint of frailty to her; a black braid was wound round her head in a coronet that was natural in its magnificence and needed no gold to set it off. And her beauty! In the long periods of time that passed between her rare opportunities to see her sister, Responsible tended to forget the almost awesome beauty that Troublesome of Brightwater carried so casually. She wore a riding costume of plain brown leather, faded and worn, and the heels of her riding boots rang against the polished marble floor, and there was no ornament on her anywhere. She needed none, and Responsible hoped the Smith women were aware of the contrast, them in their gleaming crowns, and their necks and hands hung with baubles like something up for sale on the cheap!

Troublesome needed nothing to carry her voice, either. She gave the Chair—Donald Patrick Brightwater the 133rd, him of the popular name—one glance of contempt that should have withered him into fragments right then and there, and turned to face the remnants of Ozark's government. And while she shouted at them, her voice echoing back from the walls, Responsible wept and clapped and cheered, and so did the Grannys, one and all.

"Now you've done it, you cursed fools!" shouted Troublesome of Brightwater. "Now you've gone and done it! I've seen foolishness in my day, I thought I'd seen all the kinds of foolishness there were, but you have topped it all! The year three thousand and twelve, this is; a time when we could if we so chose travel from star to star across our skies; a time when the marvels of magic have taken from the backs of our people the burdens that other ages thought the natural lot of humankind forevermore. A time of wonder—if we chose that it should be . . . But you, you Smiths! You *Smiths!* You choose to throw us back into the darkest of Dark Ages; shall we have the pox, too, to make our Kingdoms more authentic? Eh, *Your Majesty?*"

She waited, and when nobody challenged her, she went on. "And I'm a fool, too," she said, "to stand here wasting my voice on youall. My fellow fools, I should be saying. My dear, fellow fools . . . You've done it, you're a Confederation no longer; you've thrown away five hundred years of striving toward a respectable system of government, thrown it away for a mass of confusion and a pile of chaos, thrown it away for a cheap parlor trick that left you all gawking at the funny man and his funny hat and his funny scepter . . . I speak for Brightwater—no, dear Uncle, you stood and let this pass without a word, don't you interfere with me now, and don't you *presume* to speak for us!—I, Troublesome of Brightwater, *I* speak for this Castle and this Kingdom, and I tell you to get out of this room and out of this Hall and out of my sight! You sicken me, you disgrace this ancient building . . . Goats have more sense than you, I'll let them in here; Brightwater will stable its Mules in here, they have an intelligence that merits it. But you! Fools! In the name of the Twelve Bleeding Suffering Gates, begone from here before I take a whip to your pitiful *backs* . . . and don't you think, don't you think for one breath, that I wouldn't! You deserve whatever happens to you now . . . and Brightwater will weep no tears for you!"

Her voice ran them from the room as surely as if it had been a whip, and in the magnificence of her rage she was as sure a scourge as an earthquake or a flood would have been, and even the Magicians of Rank went scurrying out of the Hall with all the speed they could manage.

As for the Royal Family . . . they were a tad encumbered in their heavy velvets, and no doubt suffering greatly from the heat in them. And Responsible cackled like a squawker in its coop to see two of the Baronets—Baronets! they could at least have gotten the titles right!—chasing down the aisles after the little golden circlets that had fallen from their unaccustomed heads.

CHAPTER 9

GRANNY HAZELBIDE CAME straight to Responsible's room to tell her about what she'd missed.

"Law, you'd of been proud of your sister!" she said, rocking fast. "You saw her order that pack of cowards and ninnies out of the Hall; you should of seen 'em scurry, like something was yapping at their tailfeathers, and all the 'royal' Smiths tripping over their purple trains!" The Granny smacked her knee and chortled deep in her throat. "And then your sister went all around that Hall, child, and she locked every window in every room, all three stories of them, and she locked the back door and the side doors, and then she threw the bolts and slammed the front door as well. Left the place tight as a cast iron egg, she did. And then she marched out to get her Mule—know where she'd hitched it?"

"To the statue on the lawn, I expect," said Responsible.

"Quite right, *quite* right, and tied up to First Granny's left ankle! She untied that Mule and rode it right down the street and out of town with never so much as a look back at anybody, but there was no trouble atall reading what she was thinking purely from the look of her back! Not to mention the Mule's, but we'll leave that lie. I never thought to see such a sight as I saw today, never in all my life—and I'm sorry you weren't there. Your delegates were damned fools, which comes as no surprise; but your feisty sister! Law, Responsible, she was a privilege to behold and an honor to observe!"

"I didn't even get to say hello to her," said Responsible slowly. "And I wanted to, Granny—I realized, the other day, I've been missing her."

Granny Hazelbide stretched out her hand and tucked in a strand of the girl's hair that had come loose from the ribbon binding it back. "She came when you sent for her, child," she said gently. "There's nobody else alive she'd do that for."

"I suppose I'll have to make do with that."

"I reckon you will—and appreciate it."

"Granny?"

"Yes, child?"

"Tell me how that happened."

"Tell you where one end of a wedding ring starts and the other ends, you mean? It's that kind of question."

Responsible ignored her, and kept worrying at it.

"How," she demanded, "after all the planning, and all the discussing, and all the saying what we'd do if this happened and how we'd do if that happened, and all the rest of it . . . *how could such a fool thing happen?"*

"You've put your finger on it," said Granny Hazelbide. "We had all our preparations made, like you said, for many a different come-along; but we never thought to prepare against a *fool* thing! And that is how they got us. You can use all the logic you like, seeing what this cause will do for this consequence . . . but nobody's so wise they can plan for fools. There's no logic *to* a fool, Responsible, just no logic atall—remember that."

Responsible swallowed hard, and nodded, not that it would do her much good to remember it.

"What's happening now, Granny Hazelbide?" she said. "I don't have the heart to go see for myself."

"Just about what you'd expect to be happening," said the Granny. "As fast as they can pack up, the Families are riding out of here, flying out of here, sailing out of here. They can't look each other in the eye, and for *sure* they can't look at the

Brightwaters! They're stuffing their faces in the diningrooms, making their hastiest excuses to your mother, and then heading for their homes like the sorry shamed creatures they rightly ought to consider theirselves."

She fanned herself briskly; she'd come as close to a run on her way here as a woman of ninety could get, and she was feeling the warmth.

"It'd of been a mighty different thing if it'd been done *right,*" she went on. "Say the Confederation *had* fallen, in spite of the speeches and the rebuttals, there'd still have been the other three days of the Jubilee. Jeremiah Thomas Traveller would of organized it all so each of the Twelve Kingdoms could of met in smaller rooms of the Hall, and he'd of had trade treaties going, and plans drawn up for Parliaments or some such all around, and brand-new Ambassadors flying back and forth from room to room, feeling important... It wouldn't of been what we wanted—but it would still of been a Jubilee, and done with dignity! This was a Mule of a different breed, Responsible. None of 'em quite realizes yet what's been done, none of 'em wants to admit they behaved like tadlings deciding who's to be It—they just want to be gone, with their tails between their legs. Purple velvet tails, in the case of the Smiths."

"Well," said Responsible bitterly, "the Economist should be happy. This will save Castle Brightwater three days' rations for near on two hundred people, and a respectable number of Mules."

"It's a sorry mess, child, and a scandalous waste."

"Not just for us, Granny—think of the Lewises. They've got no money to spend on frills like trips to Brightwater, but they sent twenty-four, and every last one of them in Sundy best... I know how long they had to save to do that."

"There was no way we could have known," Granny Hazelbide insisted.

"There should of been!"

"And there should be only bliss and glory, but there isn't. How many nights did you spend casting Spells, trying to see your way through this, Responsible? Not even the Magicians of Rank could say how it would come out. All any of you got for your efforts was 'There'll be trouble'! *I* remember."

She stood up then, and brushed her skirts down, looking grim. "And I'm sorry to have to tell you that there's a piece of trouble left over," she muttered.

"Ah, Granny! A piece of trouble—we haven't even seen the beginning of the troubles yet!"

"This is something . . . more ordinary."

"What? What's happened?"

"Well, now, it seems as there's a Bridgewraith."

"Oh, Granny Hazelbide!" Responsible knew she must look despair doubled and pleated, but it was too much. "Not now!"

"Now," sighed the Granny. "You recollect that little bit of a bridge on Pewter Street, the one they call Humpback, though it has about as much of a hump as I do—that's where she is."

"You know who it is?"

"For sure I do. It's Mynna of McDaniels. But there being strangers in town, and young people as weren't here when Mynna died—she's been taken home twice already. They say her mother's in a sorry state, Responsible; Mynna's been dead it must be twenty years this October. Two of the Airy Grannys are down in the diningroom this minute telling those as are left eating not to pay Mynna any mind no matter how she cries and begs; but it won't be easy. Mynna was a pretty little thing, and she's standing on the bridge crying fit to kill, wearing the blue dress she had on the day she tripped and fell off that bridge into the water. Hit her head on a rock, Mynna did, and drowned in water not even six foot deep, and her a good strong swimmer for a girl of ten. I remember it like it was yesterday."

"I'd better—"

Granny Hazelbide stopped her, pushing her back into her chair with one firm hand.

"You'd 'better' nothing—you stay right here," she said. "I'll be going along to Humpback Bridge myself, soon as it's dark, and I'll take Mynna of McDaniels' hand and lead her back to the graveyard where she belongs. That's Granny business, and not suitable for you to concern yourself with it."

"She won't *stay* in the graveyard, Granny—they never do."

"Then I'll go down and lead her back every night for so long as it takes to convince her, and two or three times a night if it's needful. And some of the other Grannys'll spell me. A month or two, she'll settle back down."

Responsible rubbed at her eyes with both hands; the sandy feeling was a torment, and tonight, somehow, she'd have to get some sleep. But she said, "I don't mind going down there, Granny."

"Nor do I," said the old woman, "nor do I. And I'm not

worn out with all this the way you are. At ninety a body doesn't need much sleep."

"I thank you—and I do mean it."

"I know you do, child. And I'll have a little something sent up to you to *see* that you sleep this night. Mind you drink it all down, you're falling over in your tracks."

Responsible nodded, and leaned her head back in the chair, weary to her bones and beyond.

At the door, the Granny stopped suddenly and stood with one hand on the knob.

"One more thing, Responsible," she said, "and I reckon you'd best hear it from me. I'd be averse to your hearing it from Granny Leeward, for example, and if I know that one she'll be at you with it before supper—or your mother will, one. It'll be no surprise to you."

"What is it, Granny?" Responsible wondered if there ever would be an end to this day.

"They're saying that the Bridgewraith's come out because Troublesome was here in the town."

Responsible closed her eyes and smiled.

"They would say that," she said. "What else have they got to blame things on? Couldn't be their own fault, after all."

"Like I said," the Granny answered. "I didn't think you'd be surprised. And now I'll be going."

The door closed behind Granny Hazelbide, and Responsible sat and rocked and thought and rocked and thought some more. She sent a tentative thought out, feeling for Lewis Motley Wommack, and found him already on board a ship pulling away from the Brightwater Landing, and skittish under her mindtouch as a wild Mule colt. Taking note of that, she let it drop; he had a right to his privacy.

It wasn't as if he hadn't made it amply clear to her how he felt about mindspeech and mindtouch—exactly the same way the Mules felt about it, so far as she could tell, though he'd not done to her yet what the Mules did when a Magician was fool enough to try to take advantage of their telepathic abilities. The headache she had was from having the world fall in on her; she couldn't lay it on the shoulders of Lewis Motley.

PART TWO

CHAPTER 10

AT CASTLE SMITH, Lincoln Parradyne Smith the 39th was not at all surprised to find something sitting on the Castle's front steps waiting for him. It was a beautiful cat, grant him that, but he didn't care much for the look of it at that moment. Its back was arched like a snare, the claws on all six paws were out and at the ready, its long silver hair stood out all over it like the quills of the fabled Porkypine; and it hissed and spat at him in a remarkably eloquent manner.

The Magician of Rank had been expecting his reception; in the trunk marked with an *x* there'd been packed not only the thirteen crowns, the king's scepter, and the rest of the royal paraphernalia, but also a sack of heavy leather with a drawstring round the top. He whipped that out of a deep pocket inside his cloak, dropped it over the cat—that had been too occupied cussing him out in her limited vocabulary to be wary—and pulled the string tight. Then he tucked the bag under his arm, much like carrying a bag full of snakes but perfectly safe, and headed up to his rooms at the fastest pace consistent with the dignity of his position.

Inside his rooms he lost no time; he went straight to the heavy magic-chest, hewn of the precious cedar that only Lewises could coax to grow, and pulled out what was needful, laying the squalling sack inside it where he could slam down the lid if the animal thought of anything he hadn't anticipated. He drew a pentacle of adequate size on his floor, pouring out the coarse salt that made its borders well over an inch wide for safety; and at each of its five corners he laid two silver daggers set down in a cross. He stepped back and looked at it, and decided that though it wasn't elegant it would serve, and then in one swift motion he loosed the pucker-string to the sack, threw the thing into the middle of the pentacle and leaped back well out of harm's way.

"You *are* angry, you dear old thing," he murmured at the cat, that's fur had now taken to giving off sparks all on its own, "and I can't say I blame you. Hold on a minute, and I'll give you a chance to tell me what a vast number of unspeakable things I am."

He had a sudden temptation, almost overpowering, to run the Granny through a set of changes on the way to her proper shape—say a mourning dove, first; and then maybe a ponderous turtle; and then maybe a nanny goat; and so on. But he fought it off. She was going to be trouble enough as it was.

He set up his Structural Index and his Structural Change with great care—it wouldn't do to alter so much as the sprigged flowers she'd had in the pattern of her dress goods—and he raised his hands to trace the double-barred arrow in the air. It was a simple Substitution Transformation, and it didn't take long; one quiet crackle from the golden arrow, and there stood Granny Gableframe good as new and twice as fractious.

The pentacle had been more than sufficient to hold the cat, furious as it had been; the Granny was something else. She hitched up her skirts to avoid the salt, kicked aside a set of the crossed silver daggers with one pointy-toed shoe, stepped contemptuously right out of the magic shape and right up to *him*, and jabbed her finger into his chest. He felt the blood come, even through his tunic, and sighed; it was one of his favorite tunics.

"Now, Granny—" he began, but she cut him off in midsyllable.

"You," she said, "are so far beneath contempt that you're not worth wasting spit on. If you were sitting on the edge of a piece of paper, you'd be able to swing your legs, you're that *small!* You are a worthless, sorry, vile excuse for a Magician of Rank, and if I'd the power I'd strip you of that rank, for you don't deserve it any more than your *bed* does. Oh, I can't do it, I know that well, but I can wish, and I'm a powerful wisher, Lincoln Parradyne, just a *powerful* wisher! And it might could be the just One as runs this universe'll see fit to do what I can't—I can pray for that, *without* ceasing! And when you've laid me in my grave at last and think you're shut of me, Lincoln Parradyne Smith the Traitor, you watch, you watch close—you'll see my face in every mirror and it'll be telling you what filth, what slime, what blasphemy you are . . . You'll see my face in every cup you lift to your lips, you'll hear my voice at your ear all the day long and all the night long and it'll be cursing your immortal soul, *without* ceasing! Vile serpent, vermine out from under a swamplog, you and your false lying tongue, you'll find me in your pocket when you reach in for a shammybag, you'll find me in your shoe when you stick your stinking foot into it; you'll find me in your buttonholes when you . . ."

It went on and on, earning his considerable admiration before it was over, and he didn't doubt a single word of it; and all the time that fingernail in his chest, poke, poke, poke, and he took it in silence. He had every bit of it coming to him.

"Never before," she said finally, her voice gone to a gravelly rasp but not one bit weary, "never before in the one thousand years we've watched this world turn under the three moons, *never* has a Magician of Rank raised a hand—by magic or in ordinary human mischief—against a Granny! You are the very first to have that sorry distinction, Lincoln Parradyne Smith, and whatsoever it may have gained you now it will bring you more evil in payment than you ever knew existed! The universe, false Magician, *is not mocked!"*

"Granny Gableframe," he hazarded then, since she appeared to have at least paused for a breath, "do please notice that I've done you no harm—none. I know the staff of this Castle, they'll have fed you on breast of fowl and thick cream all the time we've been gone, and the servingmaids'll waste days hunting for their lost pretty pet. You have my word you missed nothing at the Jubilee, if *that* is worrying you; it was a boring mess from beginning to end. Look at yourself, Granny Gableframe, you're just as you were—not a hair on your head is out of place."

She raised her index finger straight as a spike beside her temple, and she fixed him with a furious eye.

"You have tampered with my *person!*" she hissed. "You have tampered with my freedom! You have made a lower animal of a woman that was doing magic, and doing it with skill, before ever you were born! Don't you tell me you've done me no harm, you sorry piece of work—and you'd of done more if you dared. A Magician of Rank, using his Formalisms & Transformations against an old woman—phaugh, it'd make a worm puke for shame. Now stand aside!"

And she marched out of the room, with him following her at a discreet distance and feeling that it wasn't going well, and down to the parlor where the Family had gathered for coffee and ginger cake. They sat up nervously when she sailed into the room, he noticed, and Dorothy—now Princess Dorothy—began to bawl.

Delldom Mallard spoke up first, his voice warm and sticky with his confidence in his own righteousness, and bid the Granny good afternoon.

"Sit down and have some coffee and some of this good cake with us, Granny Gableframe," he said. "We have a lot to tell you, now we're home."

"I wouldn't sit with you," said the Granny, "if both my legs'd been removed. *Which* you might very direct your toy Magician of Rank over there to do next, I reckon!"

"Now, Granny," said Delldon Mallard, "when you hear what we have to tell you, you'll forget all about your mad. You'll be sorry you didn't go along to be part of it all, and you'll be proud of this Family. Sit down, Granny, and let us tell you about it."

"Don't you put yourself out to tell me anything," she spat at him. "I know all about what happened—and you know who told me? A *Mule* told me, in your own stables, that's who! A Mule won't stoop to mindspeech with a human being, but it's perfectly willing, I discovered, to share minds with a cat—and I know all about it. Ever hear a Mule laugh, Delldon Mallard? They haven't left off laughing since you made your speech!"

"Granny Gable—"

"You hush!" she declared. "Don't you talk to me, you pitiful excuse for I declare I do not know what! And as for you females, you'd best really settle in to your weeping and your wailing, for you've got a lot of it to do down the road, and a long and lonesome road it is, mark my words. I'll not stay under this roof another night, just for starters; not one night. I'm a decent woman, raised decent, lived decent, and plan to go on the same way; I'll not cast my lot with such trash as you—cover your worthlessness with royal velvet, will you? Might as well go crown the goats! You pitiful females, you hear me now—there's no velvet heavy enough to cover you, ever again!"

"Granny," Lincoln Parradyne objected, "you're frightening the women."

"Am I? Am I? I should surely *hope* I am! They know their duties in this world, and well they know what they've done—oh, Dorothy of Smith, don't you shake your head at me, your crown'll fall off; and I raised you my own self, don't you *dare* tell me you don't know what you've done. Shame on you!"

"Granny, please listen for—"

"Silence!" she thundered, and struck the floor with her cane so hard she dented the planking; and they made not another sound.

"You think you're a sovereign Kingdom now, do you, with a royal court, and a King and a Queen, and a Crown Prince and a Royal Princess and a passel of Royal Whatnots and Flumdiddles . . . and all of it blamed on First Granny, bless her soul as is whirling somewhere, I can tell you! And here you sit, on the southwest corner of Oklahomah, sharing this continent with Castle Clark and Castle Airy, neither one of which'd give you a crossclover leaf to play at casting Spells with. It's many a long and weary mile to Kintucky and Tinaseeh, clear across the Ocean of Storms—and there'll be no help for you from either Traveller or Wommack, they'll have their hands full and running over with their own troubles."

"Granny Gableframe," put in Marygold of Purdy—and then waited a minute, till she was sure the Granny planned on letting her speak—"that makes no special difference. It's no more than a step over to Arkansaw, no more than half a day's flight by Mule from here to Castle Guthrie. We've near neighbors, and near friends."

Granny Gableframe sniffed. "Marygold, you pay as much

attention to what goes on in this world as the squawkers do, you know that? You needn't expect help from Castle Guthrie, not yet the Farsons... Might could be the Purdys would be willing to help, seeing as you're their close kin, but they won't dare. Guthrie and Farson are feuding, and Purdy's caught in the middle playing looby-loo and trying to keep their skirts out of both puddles. They'll have nothing to spare for you for a very long time. I think you're about to find yourselves mighty lonely, you Smiths—thank the Gates, Lincoln Parradyne, I am a Brightwater by birth and not one of this line. Envy me that, don't you?"

"Granny Gableframe," said Delldon Mallard, brushing ginger crumbs off his smocked velvet trousers, "I know you feel obligated to granny at us, and I... uh... must admit you're doing a right fine job of it. But there are things you don't know—things we *men* know. There's nothing that the other Kingdoms ever did for us we can't do for ourselves, and I'm not all that willing to humor you any longer in your tirade at these innocent women. It's not... uh... called for."

His brothers the Dukes allowed as how they agreed, and the women looked at the floor, and the Granny just looked amazed.

"Part of that, the part about humoring me, I'll ignore," she said disgustedly. "It's not worth my time. But I suggest you think again about your claims to being so sufficient. *True*—you'd be hard put to it to remember calling on most of the other Families for anything. You've never had to. Never been any need, so long as youall had Castle Brightwater for a sugartit to do everything for every last soul on Ozark—all the rest of you, you've just hung there, hundreds of years now. You've forgotten all about what Brightwater's been doing for you, same way you don't think on what the sun does for you, nor the air... Well, Brightwater'll do for you *no* more, pretty ladies, fine gentlemen. *No* more!"

Lincoln Parradyne could see by their faces that not a one of them knew what the old woman was talking about. Possibly Dorothy might of had a glimmer, since as eldest daughter she had more to do with the Castle accounts than any of the others, but she was so wrapped up in her own hysterics he doubted she'd even heard the Granny's words, much less understood them.

"Granny Gableframe," he said at last, leaning against the

wall and crossing his arms, "you're wasting your breath on this group. They don't follow you, my dear lady."

"I am not your dear lady, nor never was, nor never will be," she informed him, and he begged her pardon.

"Nevertheless," he said calmly, "*I* am here. And what this Castle can't obtain by trade agreements from the other Kingdoms, I can produce for them myself."

The Granny stared at him, flabbergasted, and shook her head slowly from side to side.

"The *depths* of your ignorance!" she breathed. "It's a bottomless well, a pit with no end to it! You see yourself, do you, using Insertion Transformations to feed and clothe and heal and otherwise provide for the needs of every man jack of this Kingdom? Is that what you mean, Lincoln Parradyne Smith? You that it takes half an hour's preparation and an hour's restup to come up with one little old peachapple for a demonstration, when the Tutors call you in to show the little boys what a Magician of Rank can do? You see yourself materializing tons of grain, and bales of herbs, and . . ."

Her voice trailed off into silence, and then what was clearly a snicker, and Lincoln Parradyne felt a small tinge of uneasiness. It was true, he'd be busy, but he'd had no doubts of his ability to handle whatever the ordinary economic processes wouldn't be adequate for, no doubts of his ability to bring the Kingdom through this brief period of adjustment. And he had no doubts now, really. It was just the way the Granny was looking at him, as if she knew something he didn't and had no mind to tell him what it was. He turned his back on her and stared at a painting of some ancient Smith, hanging on the wall; he'd had all he chose to take from the old crone. Let her rail and rant at the rest of them; he was through listening.

She had one question left for him, however, and she didn't mind directing it to his backside.

"Think on *this*, Lincoln Parradyne!" she said. "You plan on taking a great deal out; what do you plan on putting back *in?"*

Dorothy stopped her blubbering for a moment, and spoke to her father.

"Daddy," she started out, and then when he cleared his throat and frowned at her, she began again with, "*Sire,* I mean to say—"

The Granny clapped her hands. "Sire, is it?" she cackled.

"Sire? Such as the goats have, and the Mules? And you plan on addressing your mother as 'Dam,' you do?"

Dorothy could be stubborn, too; she ignored Granny Gableframe and put her question. "Sire," she said doggedly, "you heard what Granny Gableframe just said to Lincoln Parradyne. I would like to know what it *meant*."

The Granny snorted.

"While he tells you, Your . . . uh . . . Highness," she said, "while he tells you all the marvelous things the *men* know that are going to be such a comfort to you, I'll be getting my Mule saddled and bridled—I've earned that much for my services here—and I'll be on my way. I don't want anything else from this Family, thank you very much—give it away, or burn it, or better still, keep it. When you run out of everything you can divide it up among you."

Marygold's voice was not much more than a whisper, but it was honest. "Granny," she said, "please don't you leave us. If I'd of known it would end this way, you leaving us, I never would of gone along with it all."

"And if you'd suspected the sun came up in the morning, no doubt you'd of pulled your windowblinds, Marygold of Purdy," answered the Granny. "What precisely did you *expect* I would do after this shameful carryon?"

"Well, the men were sure you'd see it their way after it was all over; even Lincoln Parradyne there, with his back to us all like he'd had nothing to do with it, he was positive you'd be pleased when you saw us be a true Kingdom, the way First Granny wanted it done . . ."

And Delldon Mallard ran it past her one more time, all about what First Granny had said, and how it had been a Proper Naming, and how now that the Kingdom was taking that road it couldn't help but prosper. "And so you see, dear Granny Gableframe," he wound it up finally, "there's no call for you to be going anywhere, and no call for you to be breaking Marygold's heart the cruel way you're doing. Your place is here, with your Liege Lord."

Lincoln Parradyne turned around at that; if the Granny burst, which seemed to him likely, he didn't want to miss it. And he bit his lip to keep his face straight; it wouldn't do to undermine the Liege Lord's confidence by laughing at it. It was going to be useful, having a King with no more sense than Delldon Mallard, but it was going to have its embarrassing moments.

"My place," said the Granny in a voice of silver needles and icicles, "is at Brightwater. And that's where I'm going, this minute."

The King leaped to his feet and struck the table with his scepter, making all the dishes rattle and dance and splattering coffee far and wide.

"You'll do no such thing!" he roared. "It's treason! I *forbid* it!"

The Granny looked him up and she looked him down, as if she couldn't believe her eyes or her ears, and Lincoln Parradyne rather expected she couldn't, when it came right down to it. He wondered when anybody had last forbidden Granny Gableframe, that was Bethany of Brightwater by birth, and a McDaniels by marriage, any least thing she chose to do. Eighty years or more, he supposed; he much doubted her husband had dared cross her, even before she was a Granny.

She didn't bother replying to the King's forbidding; she turned her back and walked right out the door into the hall, down the corridor and out the side doors that led to the stables, and they all heard the braying of the Mules not five minutes later. It seemed to Lincoln Parradyne that it would not be far off to say that the Mules were laughing.

After she was gone, he found himself facing a solid wall of glares; and a man that had been only one of the Smith brothers yesterday morning but was a Duke Hazletine Everett of Castle Smith this afternoon stated it for all of them.

"You told us," said the Duke, "that the Granny would get over it. You allowed as how she'd be *mad*—and that's reasonable—but you never told us she'd leave."

The Magician of Rank bowed elegantly. "My apologies, Your Grace. The Granny was proved me mistaken—and given her temper, I'd say we're well rid of her."

"Would you, now?" The Duke did not seem soothed. He nodded toward his wife's swollen stomach, and asked: "What do you propose for us to do, Lincoln Parradyne, if my Duchess has a girlbaby? Who's to name her, now the Granny's gone? I never heard that anybody but the Grannys knew the ways of safe and Proper Naming, and Granny Gableframe was the one and the only Granny in this Kingdom!"

"I can't see either Castle Airy or Castle Clark," said his wife, her hands folded protectively over the shape of the possible girlbaby, "seeing fit to loan us a Granny when my time comes."

"Well, I can," said Lincoln Parradyne. "Charity of Airy would send aid to the Devil himself if she thought he needed it. Put it out of your mind, and should it prove necessary we'll send to her for help."

"I don't much like being beholden to Airy," said the King. "They're Confederationists to the last . . . uh . . . servingmaid, over there."

"You like the idea of an Improper Naming any better?" demanded his brother Hazeltine. "You like the idea of a curse such as hangs over Castle Wommack, and I don't know how many generations since the babe there was Improperly Named?"

"Allow me to point out," said the Magician of Rank, "now that you've brought it up, that that particular error was made by a Granny. Are you quite sure, all of you, that the rule which says only Grannys can name female children is anything more than a superstition?"

Too far, too fast. Their shocked gasps and the thud of his Liege Lord's scepter falling right out of his hand onto the floor told him that.

"That Granny," said Dorothy of Smith, "*that* Granny, she was at her very first Naming, and it's known she was poorly at the time besides, with a woman in the Castle using illegal Spells against her and not caught until nearly two weeks after it all happened? Everybody knows that!"

"All the same," he shot back at her, "the Wommack Curse has lasted over four hundred years. The Granny's circumstances at the time do not seem to have been taken into consideration by the Powers—which makes very little sense. If even you can see that the Granny ought to have had allowances made for her, it does seem that the Holy One could have mustered up the same amount of wisdom!"

"Oh, Lincoln Parradyne," said the Duchess Linden of Lewis, wife of Duke Whitney Crawford Smith and undoubtedly the most capable of the women there—which was saying very little—"you walk a narrow and perilous line!"

Which he most assuredly did. He was aware of that, and the beads of sweat stood clammy on his forehead. But he'd risked far too much to see it all go sour now for lack of courage to stay on that same dangerous line she referred to; it was the path he'd chosen, and the point of no return had gone by some time ago—he had no intentions of looking back. The biggest problem in this Castle for the next few months, he was willing to wager, would be morale; as the Granny had said, the Smiths were going to be mightly lonely in their pomp. And it was by no means certain that the people of this Kingdom, that for quite a while would find their new rulers as ridiculous as Granny Gableframe had, could be easily controlled. It would not take many crowds of laughing townspeople and farmers to drive the Royal Family to a shaky condition.

He wanted that, of course; it was his intention that *he* should rule this Kingdom, and that required a shaky King and a vaporish Queen, and all the rest to match, and the Gates knew he had promising raw material to work with. But they had to be able to at least put up some kind of front.

"I suggest," he said quickly, "that we put this out of our minds for now. We're all tired, and we've all been under a strain—and we've been cheated of three days' holiday by the dainty sentiments of the other eleven Families, with, I'm sure, a judicious amount of pressure from Brightwater and the rest of the Confederationists. This is no time to be debating policy, or philosophy, or any other subject. It's a time for changing our clothes and spending the rest of the day quietly relaxing. Tomorrow we'll have a great deal of work to do, and we'll be in no shape for it if we go on squabbling like this among ourselves."

"I'm not sure," said the King, pulling at his beard, "that I feel . . . uh . . . *safe* without a Granny in the Castle. There's always been a Granny here . . . I've never heard of a Castle that has no Granny, and I don't believe I like it. It's not . . . seemly."

"Maybe Granny Gableframe'll get over her conniption fit and come back," suggested one of the Duchesses.

"No she won't," snapped Dorothy. "No—she's made her mind up for good and all."

Firmness was necessary here, and confidence; Lincoln Parradyne provided both.

"I don't know that I can go along with your concern," he said casually, "or that I think being without a Granny is necessarily any problem. But I do see that it matters deeply to you, and I think I can set it right. I know of a Granny that has no Castle she calls home."

"There's no such Granny!"

"There is. Granny Graylady, her name is, and I know where

she is to be found. Give me a few hours to rest, and I'll saddle a Mule and head out to where she's camped and ask her to join us. No doubt she'd be glad to be settled at last, like all the other Grannys, instead of living all alone. You leave it in my hands; I'll see to it."

They believed it. He could see their faces relaxing. And though he knew perfectly well that no inducement on this planet could have brought Granny Graylady into Castle Smith or any other Castle—she preferred the cabin she lived in in the Wilderness Lands, and the role she filled there—he was equally certain he could find an old lady somewhere in one of the towns who'd be willing to play at grannying for a while if he offered her a large enough sum. All he needed was a female sufficiently old, sufficiently scrawny, and sufficiently venial; *anybody* could use the formspeech proper to a Granny, seeing as how everybody spent much of their lives listening to it.

As for himself, he had no reason to believe that a Granny was necessary to the safety of any Castle, or anything else. But he knew the power of superstition. It was power that worked in his favor, day in and day out, and he intended to accord it the proper respect.

CHAPTER 11

"FRANKLY, GRANNY HAZELBIDE, I'm surprised at you," said Thorn of Guthrie. "A body'd think there was nothing to get done around here that required any attention from that girl . . . you realize what time it is?"

"I'm not yet addled," said Granny Hazelbide. "It's near on one-thirty, by my reckoning."

"*And* mine," said Ruth of Motley. "Who ever heard of anybody not on their deathbed sleeping till one-thirty in the afternoon?"

"If you'd happened to drink the brew I sent up to Responsible last night, and had the servingmaid stand over you to be sure you drank it every drop down, you'd still be asleep, too, I guarantee you that."

"Oh, you potioned her, did you, Granny?"

"If I hadn't of done, she'd of worked all night long last night the way she has the past three. Since when do either of you, or anybody else around here, have to worry about Responsible pulling her weight? The problem's always been keeping her *from* working, not getting her to keep at it, as *I* recall."

"Nevertheless," said Thorn of Guthrie, "it's a purely disgraceful hour for her to be still in that bed! If you say she's overworked, I'll take your word for it, but she could at least get up and sit in a chair. She's fourteen, Granny, not fifty; she'd make it through the day."

"Fifteen," said the Granny, staring hard at Responsible's mother. "Fifteen years old on the eleventh of May—which it happens to be, this very day."

Ruth of Motley frowned at her daughter-in-law, and exchanged looks with Granny Hazelbide, and then she asked: "Thorn of Guthrie, did you forget that child's birthday again?"

"Third year in a row," observed the Granny.

"May have done," snapped Thorn, with a high flush on her cheeks that only made her more beautiful.

"I notice she always remembers *yours*."

"It makes no smallest nevermind to Responsible, and you know it," Thorn told them both. "Why you nag me about it when she's got no natural affections whatsoever, I cannot imagine, and I don't choose to listen to any such trivial clatter on a day like this, thank you very much all the same."

"Well," mused Granny Hazelbide, pursing her lips, "I suppose as a woman reaches your age her memory does begin to suffer a tad, Thorn. No doubt Responsible knows that—and as you say, it won't worry her a mite. *Not* a mite!"

The Missus of Castle Brightwater drew an exasperated breath, and the high flush flared higher still, but she was not about to take bait that obvious.

"*I* think," she declared, "that she should get up. And that's my last word on the subject."

"I'm pleased to hear you say so," answered the Granny, "seeing as how you've already said too many and some left over. You leave the girl alone; the staff's seeing to clearing up after that mob we had in here, and that's what we pay 'em for. No reason Responsible should be doing *any*thing. For sure she's not missing anything in the way of inspiring conversation."

"Since it's her birthday," said Ruth of Motley pleasantly, "I'll side with you, Granny."

"You might just as well—because I'm letting nobody near her till she's slept out, and that's all there is to it. The load on that child's back is going to be mighty heavy from here on out, and I'm glad she's not having to think about it for a little while."

Thorn of Guthrie tightened her lips, but she held her peace, and only the speed with which her stylus scribbled at the diary page betrayed her.

As it happened, Responsible was not asleep. She was awake, and had been since a little past one; but she was not brimming with energy. She felt like she'd been drowned in honey and then had it harden round her—that would be the ebonygrass Granny'd put in the potion. It was rare stuff, and saved in the ordinary run of things for people that'd been through some hellish kind of experience. The little Bridgewraith's mother and daddy, for example—it would of been appropriate to potion them with ebonygrass, and Responsible hoped somebody had thought to do it.

She lay there, determined to move, thinking every minute she would move, and only sinking deeper into the languor that held her fast. Her conscience would never have brought her out of it alone; what finally did it, right around four in the afternoon, was the hunger gnawing at her stomach and the leftover taste of the potion. Her mouth put her in mind of the cavecat's den she'd spent some unanticipated and unpleasant time in back a few months, and that did at last drive her in search of her toothbrush.

When she'd first waked up, just for a second, she'd thought "Fourth Day of the Jubilee!"...Just for a moment she'd forgotten the shambles things were in. It would have been wonderful; just imagine, if things had gone the other way, if the delegates had told the Travellers and the Smiths to take their "free men and sovereign states" hogwash and throw it into the Ocean of Storms. There'd of been a party at Brightwater this night to end all parties; she'd set aside a quantity of strawberry wine, that's price would of fixed every comset in the Castle, against just such an outcome. Now they'd be able to put it down in the cellar as an investment; not likely it would get any less expensive. Perhaps King Delldon Mallard of Castle Smith would buy it off of Brightwater for his state dinners.

She spat into her basin, getting rid of the taste of the ebonygrass but not the taste that the thought of the Smiths brought to her mouth. Bitter, it was. And bitterest of all was the thought that nagged at her, that if she'd stayed home till the Jubilee and passed her time at her magic—instead of taking off on that fool Quest all around the Kingdoms—she might well have discovered what the Smiths were intending. She was *supposed* to find out such things, and make provisions to deal with them, she bore the label for that. But she'd had no slightest inkling.

Which she rather expected could mean only one thing. The Smiths had been truly, genuinely, wholeheartedly convinced that what they were up to *was not wrong*. How they'd managed that was a marvel to her, but given the awesome depths of their stupidity, might could be any kind of nonsense was possible for them. They surely had not been backward about turning up in their gaudy array before all the Kingdoms assembled, not any one of them, so far as she could tell. Ignorance, like innocence, was a powerful talisman.

And then there was the memory, rankling at her day and night, of how she'd sat still for it without a murmur when she'd gotten the letter from Dorothy of Smith saying it wouldn't be convenient for Responsible to visit Castle Smith on her Quest. It was just that she'd counted on Granny Gableframe to keep things in at least rough order, and the idea of a Magician of Rank actually turning magic against a Granny had never entered her head. It was an unnatural idea, like a Mule playing a fiddle; if it *had* entered her head no doubt she'd of thrown it right back out again.

"Things," she said to her own face in the bathroom mirror, "things are entirely *out of hand* on this planet!"

And what was she to do about it? She doubted sleeping all day was a productive way of tackling the problem.

There were times when she wondered if it wouldn't have been an easier row to hoe if it'd been runaway technology she had to deal with instead of runaway magic. They'd been so careful about the technology. No robots, not even in the fields and the mines where robots could do the work far more efficiently than human beings ever could hope to. No nuclear *any*thing; she doubted there were more than a score of human beings besides herself who even know the word. No chemicals in the food or on the soil, no synthetics . . . Without Housekeeping Spells to smooth the heavy wools and linens they wore, the women of Ozark would of spent many hours with their irons. And they'd thought long and hard before they allowed electricity, according to the Teaching Stories, deciding finally that it was a natural thing with its roots in the lightning—and even so, the Travellers wouldn't use it. Not in their Castle, not in their Kingdom. They'd had to move clear to Tinaseeh to escape its taint, and they'd done it with a grim enthusiasm—and believed that it was magic that powered their comsets.

She smiled, remembering the way the Traveller delegation had behaved about the switches that turned things on in Castle Brighwater; she'd seen a mother smack her tadling's fingers for touching one, like he'd put his hand into goat droppings.

No, they were pure as pure, using the power of sun and wind and water and plain old-fashioned muscle—and magic. Which was where the trouble lay. Magic. Common Sense Level, available to everybody unless they just plain weren't interested, same as the times tables and the alphabet were. Middle Level, for the ambitious, or those as didn't care to be overdependent on the Grannys. Granny Magic, for the Grannys only; Hifalutin Magic, for the Magicians. And for the Magicians of Rank, the highest level—the Formalisms & Transformations. Power there and to spare—at least you could turn a robot *off!*

She decided she hadn't the courage to send down for tea at this hour of the day; it was twenty minutes till time for supper. She pulled on a plain blue dress, left her feet bare to irritate her mother, and padded on down the halls and stairways to the kitchen. She could ask for coffee, anyway.

"Evening, Miss Responsible," said the women when they saw her, and a servingmaid smiled and said she was pleased to see her looking rested.

"Thank you, Shandra of Clark—ladies. Do you suppose I could have a cup of your coffee?"

They settled her at the big kitchen table with a mug of coffee strong enough to make the spoon stand up straight in it, and she began to feel that she might be able to face the Family for supper after all. She'd rather far have stayed in the kitchen, or eaten in the staff's own diningroom—but that was for tadlings. And she was going on fifteen.

At which point in her musings, the Senior Servingmaid set down a long narrow basket in front of her and said, "For you, Miss Responsible, from all of us, and many happy returns," and she realized that she'd stopped going on fifteen and gotten there.

"Youall spoil me," she said, and it was true. They did. For all they had to take from her in the way of scolding about the dust on the furniture and the polish not being high enough on the floors and too much salt in the cornbread—they spoiled her all the same.

"Open it, miss," said the Castle Housekeeper, that somebody'd just brought in to see the event. "Go on, now."

The basket was new woven, with a handsome *R* worked right into the lid, and two strong handles, and she'd of been satisfied just to have that for her birthday gift; she looked up at them, surprised.

"Open it!"

She lifted off the lid and looked inside, and saw why the basket had had to be such a big one and needed a braced bottom. Inside was a little dulcimer, like the one she'd lost on her Quest, dropping it right off the Mule's back into the ocean—only much prettier. It had inlays of shell all along the soundingboards, three hearts and a rose with two leaves to it. Her old one had been just plain wood.

"The basket won't do to keep it in, Miss Responsible," said the Housekeeper apologetically. "We had to tip it to get it in there just for the giving. But I expect you'll find a use for a big basket like that all the same, and we wanted you to have both."

Responsible smiled at them, and turned red, and wished she could think of something to say. People being nice to her was too rare for her to have developed any skills in dealing with it; it always took her aback and left her foolish.

And even more, she wished that she could sing decently, but there was no use wishing that. Might as well wish for wings. She settled for taking the instrument out of the basket, laying it across her lap, and playing them three verses of the easiest song she knew.

"Ah, it has a sweet tone!" she said, then, while they clapped—spoiling her some more—and laid it to her cheek. "I thank you . . . so much."

"It pleasured us to do it," they said, and then the Housekeeper spoke up on the subject of what Thorn of Guthrie would do to them if supper was late to the table, and they scurried around the kitchen while Responsible sat and glowed at them.

"Sally of Lewis," she asked the Housekeeper, "just how did youall know I wanted another dulcimer?"

"The way you'd treasured that one the Granny had made for you when you were a little bit of a thing? And then losing it like you did? Why, miss, it didn't take all that much brains to puzzle it out that you'd be yearning after another one. It's small, but then so was your lost one. We did wonder about that. Might could be you'd rather of had a proper one, instead of a child's. But you were so fond of the other one . . ."

"You did just right," Responsible assured her. "I couldn't manage a bigger one. It's beautiful, and I love you one and all for thinking of me. It must have taken a precious long time to make it—and the basket, too."

"We all worked at it, miss," said Sally of Lewis. "It went fast that way."

"Bless your hearts," said Responsible.

"We'll need more than our hearts blessed," the Housekeeper told her, "if you don't get yourself on in to supper. They'll be waiting on you."

"Law! I'd forgotten all about it!" Responsible touched all the hands she could reach, tucked her dulcimer under one arm and the basket under the other, changed her mind and hid the dulcimer away in the basket again while Sally of Lewis fretted, and hightailed it for the diningroom.

And then as she went out the door the woman called after her suddenly, "Oh, miss!"

"Yes?"

"I didn't want to forget . . . one of the stablemen was up here not thirty minutes ago, saying as how that Mule of yours is acting up."

"Acting up, Sally of Lewis?" Responsible turned back and leaned against the doorframe. "He have any idea what was wrong with the creature?"

"No, miss—he'd had the Granny down to look at it; and he told me the Granny said you were to go see to the Mule yourself, after supper. I expect you'd best ask *her* what the trouble is."

Responsible nodded slowly, thinking, and stared at the floor.

"Is something wrong, miss? You look right peaked to me—and you're about to crush that basket."

"It's the potion Granny gave me last night," said Responsible quickly. "That and lying in bed this whole day long."

"I know what you mean—nothing makes a person feel more like leftovers than lying all day abed doing nothing. You go on in and get a good meal under your ribs, you'll feel better."

"And then she'll be turned around entirely," commented one of the servingmaids. "Sleep all day, you can't sleep that night . . . it goes on and on."

"Half a potion this night," agreed another one. "To straighten things out. You speak to the Granny, miss; and we'll see to it your tea's brought up as soon as it's light tomorrow morning."

Responsible thanked them, and they wished her a happy birthday one more time, and she thanked them for that, and then she headed with a pounding heart for the diningroom.

Granny Hazelbide, seated at Thorn of Guthrie's left hand, looked a little peaked herself, Responsible thought, as she slipped into her own place at the corner of the table where her left elbow wouldn't always be poking people as she ate.

"Nice of you to honor us with your presence," said her mother, tart as bad vinegar, and Ruth of Motley moved right in over that with "Happy Birthday, Responsible!" and the salutations ran round the table.

"Thank you kindly," she said.

"How does it feel to be fifteen?" asked her uncle Donald Patrick. "You find gray hairs on your head this morning?"

She was of the opinion that her hair would be snow-white by the *following* morning, if the message about her Mule was what she thought it had to be, but she didn't intend to tell him that.

"Just one," she said. "And I pulled it out."

Emmalyn of Clark, Jubal Brooks's wife, set down the forkful of fried squawker she'd had halfway to her mouth and shook a warning finger.

"I hope the goodness you *burned* that hair, Responsible of Brightwater!" Emmalyn declared. "No telling who might find it, you know."

The other women at the table avoided one another's eyes, and Responsible waited, wondering if her mother would be able to resist the chance to make a remark about how Responsible hadn't even been out of *bed* the whole day and couldn't therefore have found any gray hairs among the black ones. When her mother said nothing, she was pleased; perhaps, as time went by, she'd mellow.

"I took care of it, Emmalyn," she said courteously. "But I thank you for the reminder."

"You're welcome, I'm sure," said Emmalyn. "You can't

be too careful these days. Such goings-on I'm sure I *never* heard of before as we've had since this year began. It makes me nervous."

"Emmalyn of Clark," said Granny Hazelbide, "you wouldn't be nervous if you didn't dwell on everything. It's not healthy, the way you do, and it's time you gave it up and had babies instead."

It wasn't especially nice of the Granny, saying that, seeing as how it was due to her judicious alterations here and there in Emmalyn's diet that she and Jubal Brooks were still without a single babe and them married almost six years now. But Granny Hazelbide was out of sorts, and Emmalyn irritated her rather more than somewhat.

"Now, Granny Hazelbide," put in Ruth of Motley, "I'm sure Emmalyn does the best she can."

"Emmalyn has *always* been delicate, haven't you, Emmalyn?" said her sister Patience of Clark demurely.

Emmalyn gloried in being called delicate, and while she was glowing with pleasure and Jubal Brooks was patting her hand to show he too appreciated her frailties, she forgot all about Responsible's one gray hair and the hazards thereof.

"Responsible," said Thorn of Guthrie, "you going to tell us what you've got there in that basket by your feet, or not? It's big enough to hold a morning's firewood, or a couple of babies set head to toe, if they scrunched up a tad. You can't expect us not to be curious."

Responsible hadn't realized she'd been so obvious with the basket; that showed how distracted she was, and Granny Hazelbide clucked her tongue.

"A birthday present from the staff," she said, and showed them all the lid with her initial worked in, and the dulcimer tucked inside.

"Law," said Thorn of Guthrie, "here I was so grateful when you lost the old one, and now you're all equipped again. They must be out of their minds."

The uncles chuckled, and Emmalyn fell in behind them, and Responsible gave the basket a shove with her toe to get it out of sight under the table. "I had no plans of singing to you, Mother," she told Thorn of Guthrie. "I believe you can stop worrying about it."

"Won't be caterwauling under my window in the middle of the night, eh?"

There went Thorn—prick and poke, poke and prick. Responsible had been six years old, and the dulcimer Granny'd given her brandnew, the year she'd decided it would be appropriate to celebrate Thorn's birthday by serenading her from under her bedroom window. It had not been a great success.

"No, ma'am," said Responsible. "Set your mind at rest."

Jonathan Cardwell Brightwater the 12th put his oar in then. "Thorn," he said, "you are downright mean. I don't know what keeps you from pickling in your own juices, I *tell* you I don't. Pass your girl some food here before she faints away—that's the least you can do, I happen to know you forgot her birthday again—and stop your jabbing at her. Listening to you, I understand why Troublesome stays on top her mountain and won't come down; shows good sense on her part, if you ask me. You trying to drive Responsible off the same way?"

Ah, thought Responsible, the bosom of her family. However, at one hundred and nine a man had certain privileges, and Thorn of Guthrie apologized charmingly to her father-in-law, who responded that he should think she *would* be sorry.

"You get my message, young lady?" Granny Hazelbide asked, as if it had been maybe something about piece goods.

"I did," said Responsible. "And I'll see to it."

"You do that," said the Granny. "Pass the gravy, Emmalyn!"

Jubal Brooks was a swift eater; he pushed his plate away and concentrated on his coffee, and Responsible felt him looking at her from under his thick black brows.

"Something on your mind, Jubal Brooks?" she asked him. Might as well be helpful.

"Yes, as it happens," he said. "I'm wondering. You've had a day off now—don't remember you having one since that time you were taken so sick three years ago. And the Jubilee's over—for five hundred years or forever, whichever comes first. Now I'm wondering what you plan to do starting *tomorrow* morning."

"Well," said Responsible, "I plan to be busy."

"So Granny Hazelbide told us," said Ruth of Motley, "and she was right sharp about it, too."

"Details!" said Jubal Brooks. "That's what *I* want to hear."

Emmalyn smiled proudly. She fancied her husband something of a power in the Castle, especially when he was being forceful like he was now. And Responsible gave up pretending to eat.

"First thing that happens tomorrow," she told them, "is we

cut back the comset power till it transmits only to the borders of this Kingdom. For example."

Both the uncles whistled long and low, and Jonathan Cardwell swore a round oath, women or no women. "You don't plan on the grass growing under your feet, do you, missy?" he demanded. "You really think it has to be done that fast? Law, and I was calling your *mother* mean!"

"Has to be done," said Responsible, "and it won't be a whit easier next week than tomorrow. Whatever a whit is."

"But what will people do?" quavered Emmalyn. "How'll they get messages around and how'll they get the *news?* And what's going to happen to the lessons for the older kids, and—"

"Emmalyn," answered Responsible, "I don't have any idea *what*soever what 'people' will do. That's 'people's' own problem."

"Responsible," said Donald Patrick slowly, "this isn't going to be much help to business, you know. Are you sure we oughtn't to have a kind of transition period here, while some other arrangements are worked out?"

Responsible stared at him.

"As I recall," she said coldly, "when the delegations of the Twelve Kingdoms began whooping and hollering their votes to dissolve the Confederation of Continents, you made no least move to stop them—though you were chairing at the time and the whole procedure was out of order. I don't recall you even saying 'point of order,' Donald Patrick."

"The sense of the meeting was *clear!*"

"It was that. And a part of the sense of the meeting was that there was to be no more central government, am I not right? And that we were, as of the moment that fool vote went around, twelve separate and sovereign nations, each to its own self. You correct me, Donald Patrick, if I'm wrong."

When he didn't answer her, she went on.

"I can't quite see how, without taxes from the other eleven Kingdoms, we could manage here at Brightwater to continue a planetwide communications system. You ask the Economist what it costs to run the comsets if you think it can be done for the price of eggs, dear Uncle. Furthermore, it appears to me that sending out comset broadcasts from *this* separate and sovereign nation into the other separate and sovereign nations would constitute interference in their national affairs. I surely wouldn't want to be guilty of that, would you? Downright unboonely. Sticking our noses in where they're not wanted."

"Responsible," said Donald Patrick, "when those comsets go dead, all over this world, there's going to be an uproar like . . . like . . ."

"They'll have to send their uproar by ship, Mule, or lizzy," said Responsible grimly. "They'll not be sending anything else by comset."

"Oh, now," said Jubal Brooks, still staring at her, and his coffee going stone-cold in his cup, "I object! There's no need to go off into ex*tremes* like that, and you never said a word of warning before the vote."

Granny Hazelbide saved her the trouble of answering.

"You mean to tell me," she demanded, beating her fork on the edge of her plate to point out her opinions, "you mean to sit there and tell me that a whole roomful of grown men, and those men trusted these past I don't know how many years with the governing of this *en*tire planet, they needed to be told such baby stuff as that?"

"Well, Granny Hazelbide, I don't know that I care for your tone!" he protested. "We were fully cognizant of the political facts. *Fully* cognizant!"

The Granny snorted and went back to her eating, talking through the mouthfuls.

"Would of done you a sight more good to be just a tad cognizant—cognizant!—of the practical common-sense facts," she said. "I'm with Responsible; it never would of entered *my* head that you men all assumed the Kingdoms could pull out of the Confederation and put crowns on all their pointy little heads and still count on all the services to go on just like they always had. And no reason it should of entered Responsible's head, either—it was obvious to a plain fool. You men made your decision; now you can live with it."

"You can be certain," put in Responsible, "that Castle Traveller had thought of every one of the practical consequences. And were mighty careful not to point them out to any of the rest of the baagoats in the room, *who*—I might add—it is not my place to lead by the hand and pick up after. Why didn't you *think!*"

"Responsible, you can't talk to Jubal like that," said Emmalyn, and then jumped as Patience pinched her under the table.

"I beg your pardon, Emmalyn," said Responsible, "but I suggest you consider carefully what your Jubal, and the rest of the Brightwater men present at the Hall—not to mention our so-called friends and allies—allowed to happen. Then, you care to speak sharp to me on their behalf, I'll listen to you."

"Responsible—"

"If," she went on, "*if* procedure'd been held to, as Donald Patrick had full authority to insist that it should be—he was Chair, remember?—if there'd been the rest of the speeches for and against, and the rebuttals, as the law calls for, then there'd of been time for these matters to be raised. One of the Lewis delegates, someone from Castle McDaniels or Castle Motley, *some*one among you distinguished gentlemen, would no doubt have asked the necessary questions. Such as: how did the others plan to get along without the comset system, that's been broadcast from Brightwater these many hundred years? Such as: what happens to supply deliveries, that have been worked out and run by the computers at Castle Brightwater since the day they were hooked up—and the only Kingdoms with shops large enough to serve as supply transport are Brightwater and Guthrie?"

"I do believe this is going to be interesting," said Thorn of Guthrie crisply. "And Responsible is quite right, Donald Patrick. If you'd not just stood there like a gawk—pardon me, *sat* there like a gawk!—and let that vote go by you, those questions would have been raised."

"And we would, I expect, have a Confederation this minute," added Ruth of Motley. "Not a happy Confederation, I daresay—but a Confederation. Jacob Jeremiah Traveller would of found it a good deal harder to get his point across if there'd been ample time to talk about just what it might *mean* to be boones."

"Castle Traveller," said Granny Hazelbide, "doesn't especially care about the comsets. Anything they want to tell, they just walk round the one town they've got and tell it. Not to mention that from their point of view the end of broadcasts just means one less source of corruption for their tadlings. And I reckon they've been laying in supplies now for a good long time. Right, amn't I, Responsible? Yes, I thought I was!"

And she threw in something extra about lying in beds after people made them.

"The *Smiths* are to blame," Donald Patrick sputtered. "Youall make it seem to have been me—"

"Nope," said Responsible. "Not you by your own self, you can spread that blame around for a considerable distance. But you *were* Chair, mind—and you could have ordered the Smiths to sit down and shut up, as was proper, and gone on to conduct that meeting as it should of been conducted."

Donald Patrick Brightwater's face was a ghastly white, and sweat stood out on his forehead.

"I was taken completely by surprise," he said, almost whispering. "I was expecting everything to go in order, and then all of a sudden there stood Delldon Mallard in his purple velvet and his crown, and all those Attendants kneeling all round the room, and his wife up in the balcony being crowned a Queen . . . I swear I didn't know what was happening till it was over, and too late!"

It had gone far enough, and Ruth of Motley slid smoothly into the breach.

"Son," she said, "anybody would of done the same in your place. I recall you weren't feeling yourself that day anyway, and you shouldn't of *tried* to force yourself to go on with the chairing of that meeting."

"You know how Donald Patrick is, Ruth," added Patience of Clark. "There's no way a person can get him to think of himself, not if he's convinced there's a duty to be done and his name on it."

"Responsible had no intention to criticize you, Donald Patrick." That was Thorn of Guthrie, adding her careful bit to the orchestration. "She's just upset that things went like they did."

They went on, soothing the men as automatically as they braided their hair in the mornings; and Responsible let them handle it. For one thing, she had no intention of pointing out to them that her purpose in cutting off the comsets so quickly was not revenge—it was just the most effective leverage she had for forcing the other eleven Kingdoms to fall to at once and get their affairs in order. They had to be weaned, and she knew no swifter means of doing it. If this pack of her relatives couldn't see that on their own, so be it; she had other things on her mind.

For example, she had a trip to make down to the stables—to see a Mule.

CHAPTER 12

RESPONSIBLE BEGAN BY making it very clear to the Mule what she was prepared to tolerate.

"Sterling," she said, leaning over the front gate of the stall, "you give me one of those headaches you're so good at passing around, I'll give *you* one with a two-by-four. I hope that's clear?"

The Mule rolled her eyes and flattened her ears, but it was no more than a ritual response, the same way the two-by-four was a ritual challenge. Sterling was breathing as easy as stirring thin soup—an angry Mule huffed and went on till you could hear it a hundred feet off.

"I *won't* have it," Responsible warned. "I *mean* that. I'll potion your oats and do an Insertion Transformation that'll mean things you never dreamed of in your tail; you hear me?"

The ears came up, and Sterling made a gentle whuffling noise.

"All right, then," said Responsible, and unlatched the stall. She went inside and went over to the Mule, and laid her face for a second—all any Mule would tolerate of such stuff—against its neck. And then she leaned back against the stable wall, noting it needed a new coat of whitewash, and waited.

THE OUT-CABAL CALLS YOU.

"Drat you, Sterling!" Responsible clapped her hands to her head. "What did I tell you? Gently, you ornery creature, gently! Human minds are not suited for that blasting away you do—*mindspeech,* we use! *Not* mindbraying!"

The Mule whuffled again, and thrashed its tail.

MY APOLOGIES, DAUGHTER OF BRIGHTWATER.

That was better, though not yet exactly pleasant. Responsible nodded her approval, and dropped her hands.

"Go on, then," she said. "And mind you don't forget."

THE OUT-CABAL HAS ASKED ME TO PASS ALONG A MESSAGE TO YOU, AND WHILE I DON'T LIKE THEM, NEVER HAVE AND NEVER WILL, I HAVE A CERTAIN REGARD FOR *YOU,* DAUGHTER OF BRIGHTWATER. THEREFORE I WILL TELL YOU WHAT THEY SAY.

"And tell them what I say in return," Responsible reminded her.

IT WOULD BE A WASTE OF MY TIME, OTHERWISE.

"All right, then . . . What do they want *this* time?"

The first time, she had been only ten years old, and she'd been scared half out of her wits. Like the Grannys and the Magicians, she had known the Mules were telepathic, but along with that knowledge went a stomach-twisting familiarity with the stories of what had happened to various foolish humans that had tried to take advantage of that fact. The Mules out-Ozarked the Ozarkers; they kept themselves to themselves, and they intended that everybody else should do likewise. When Sterling first mindspoke her, Responsible had waited, holding her breath, for her brain to be battered at and bounced around her head like a child's play ball. It hadn't been that bad, but it hadn't been any fun, either; the only good thing about that first time had been that it hadn't taken very long.

They were the Out-Cabal, they wanted her to know; they represented a group of planets called the Garnet Ring; their resources of magic were sufficient to simply remove Ozark from the sky like blowing out a candle, if they so chose—under certain conditions established by their laws, which it happened had not yet been met, lucky Ozark—and they were merely setting up relations.

The second time, three years ago, they'd directed her to call all the Magicians of Rank together at the Castle and put them through their paces. They'd wanted an idea of what, precisely, the abilities of "the current crop" were. And Responsible had gone outraged to Granny Hazelbide, and been told in no uncertain terms how to proceed. "You get those men here," the Granny'd said, "and you lose no time. *No* time!" She'd done it; and she'd lain near dying for eleven days afterward from the effects of their hatred. The Magicians of Rank didn't take kindly to a twelve-year-old girl in pigtails being able to call them in and set them to doing Formalisms & Transformations like you'd show off a fancy Mule team at a fair—and they took even less kindly to not knowing why they were unable to refuse her, or why they were unable to speak of it afterward. Nine Magicians of Rank, all concentrating their hatred on her over the course of the long day the Out-Cabal had requested... Remembering, Responsible shivered. She wanted no repetition of that pain, beside which the pain of deathdance fever was no more than a needleprick to a careless finger.

THEY PUT YOU ON NOTICE, said Sterling, THAT THIS PLANET IS NOW UNDER THEIR FULL SURVEILLANCE.

"It has *always* been under their surveillance, so far as I know."

FROM TIME TO TIME, SINCE YOUR PEOPLE CAME TO THIS LAND, THEY HAVE CHOSEN TO WATCH YOUR BEHAVIOR AND YOUR DEVELOPMENT. NOW, IT WILL NOT BE FROM TIME TO TIME. IT WILL BE AT *ALL* TIMES.

"Why? What makes us so much more interesting all of a sudden?"

YOU ARE A PLANET RULED BY THE LAWS OF MAGIC, NOT THE LAWS OF SCIENCE; THUS, YOU FALL WITHIN THEIR INFLUENCE.

"That has always been so," said Responsible stubbornly.

BUT OTHER THINGS HAVE CHANGED. UNDER ONLY TWO CONDITIONS DO THE LAWS OF THE GARNET RING ALLOW THE OUT-CABAL TO INTERFERE IN THE AFFAIRS OF A MAGIC-BOUND PLANET: WHEN THERE IS A PLANETARY CATASTROPHE, SUCH AS FAMINE OR PLAGUE OR WAR, THAT THREATENS TO DESTROY ALL THE POPULATION—

"I know the laws!"

DO NOT INTERRUPT ME, DAUGHTER OF BRIGHT-WATER!

Stars danced before her eyes, but she knew she deserved it.

"Sorry," she said. "Beg your pardon, Sterling."

AND THE OTHER IS: WHEN THE PLANET IS IN A STATE OF ANARCHY. THAT IS TO SAY, WHEN HUMANS HAVE THE GOOD SENSE TO RUN THEIR AFFAIRS AS MULES DO. I FIND THIS SECOND CONDITION FOOLISH.

Responsible didn't doubt that for a moment.

"There are differences between humans and Mules," she said.

Sterling's silence was both eloquent and insolent, and Responsible longed to pull her braided tail.

PLEASE TELL THEM, she said instead, switching to mind-speech herself for discretion's sake, though she'd set wards before she came in, PLEASE TELL THEM THAT WE FACE NO PLANETARY CATASTROPHE. WE ARE WELL FED, WE ARE IN FULL HEALTH, AND WE ARE NOT AT WAR NOR HAVE WE EVER BEEN.

There was a moment's silence; then, I HAVE TOLD THEM, said Sterling.

AND TELL THEM, STERLING, ESTIMABLE MULE, THAT WE ARE NOT IN A STATE OF ANARCHY.

After the pause, the Mule stamped a front foot for emphasis.

THEY SAY THAT DOES NOT APPEAR TO THEM TO BE FULLY ACCURATE.

IT IS, said Responsible, A MATTER OF DEFINITION.

THEY DEFINE ANARCHY, the Mule responded, AS AN ABSENCE OF GOVERNMENT. YOUR GOVERNMENT WAS THE CONFEDERATION OF CONTINENTS, WHICH HAS NOW FALLEN. THEREFORE, THEY SAY, YOU ARE WITHOUT A GOVERNMENT.

THEY ARE IN ERROR, said Responsible. WE ARE NOT WITHOUT GOVERNMENT... UNFORTUNATELY, WE HAVE AN *EXCESS* OF GOVERNMENT.

The pause was longer than usual.

THEY WOULD LIKE AN EXPLANATION, said the Mule finally.

PLEASE TELL THEM: WE HAD ONE GOVERNMENT, THE CONFEDERATION OF CONTINENTS. THAT HAS

BEEN DISSOLVED, LEGALLY AND BY DUE PROCESS. AND NOW THAT IT NO LONGER EXISTS, WE HAVE *TWELVE* GOVERNMENTS, EACH SEPARATE AND SOVEREIGN. WE ARE TWELVE TIMES AS GOVERNED AS WE WERE BEFORE THE CONFEDERATION FELL. PLEASE TELL THEM THAT, STERLING, EXACTLY AS I HAVE STATED IT.

She waited, then. A Mule in the next stall brayed in what she would have taken for sympathy in any creature except a Mule. Mules did not sympathize.

THE OUT-CABAL SAYS THAT THAT IS ONE POSSIBLE INTERPRETATION OF THE PRESENT SITUATION.

IT IS THE *ONLY* POSSIBLE INTERPRETATION!

THEY DISAGREE, DAUGHTER OF BRIGHTWATER. I TOLD YOU . . . I WILL TELL YOU AGAIN: THEY SAY IT IS ONE POSSIBLE WAY OF LOOKING AT THE MATTER.

AND?

AND WHAT?

AND WHAT ELSE? WHAT ELSE DO THEY SAY, STERLING? ARE THEY MOVING AGAINST US IN THE MORNING, DO WE HAVE THREE DAYS TO PREPARE, ARE WE ABOUT TO BE TURNED INTO A SMALL DENSE CUBE? WHAT WILL THEY DO NOW—WHAT IS GOING TO HAPPEN?

PLEASE BE STILL. I AM LISTENING.

BEG YOUR PARDON, said Responsible again.

DAUGHTER OF BRIGHTWATER, THEY SAY THAT YOU ARE NOW UNDER THEIR CONSTANT OBSERVATION. THAT IS HOW THIS BEGAN; I AM NOT IMPRESSED.

WHAT DOES IT *MEAN?* WILL THEY TELL YOU?

IT MEANS THAT THEY ARE WILLING TO CONSIDER THE POSSIBILITY YOU SUGGEST, BUT THAT ONLY BY WATCHING ALL DAY AND ALL NIGHT, EVERY DAY AND EVERY NIGHT, CAN THEY DETERMINE WHETHER YOU ARE RIGHT OR WRONG. THEY HAVE NO RESPECT FOR PRIVACY, THAT IS OBVIOUS.

THEY WILL SEE TWELVE ORDERLY GOVERNMENTS, GOING ABOUT THEIR AFFAIRS. TELL THEM THAT. TELL THEM THEY CAN WATCH TILL THEY FALL OUT OF THE SKY, BUT THEY WILL SEE NO FAMINE, NO PLAGUE, NO WAR, AND NO ANARCHY. TELL THEM

THEY HAVE MY WORD ON THAT.

DAUGHTER OF BRIGHTWATER, I APOLOGIZE . . . THEY ONLY REPEAT THEMSELVES. THEY SAY THEY WILL BE WATCHING. AND THAT IS ALL THEY SAY. THEY HAVE NOTHING TO ADD.

Responsible braced herself; the Out-Cabal liked to end their conversations with a little exhibition of the potency of their arcane skills, and there was no predicting what form it might take.

ALTHOUGH THEY HAVE SAID THEY HAVE NOTHING TO ADD, Sterling said disgustedly, THEY HAVE ADDED SOMETHING.

YES?

THEY SAY NOT TO WAIT—NOTHING IS GOING TO HAPPEN. THEY SAY THAT THEY ARE NEITHER CRUEL NOR UNREASONABLE AND THAT YOU ALREADY HAVE TROUBLE ENOUGH ON YOUR HANDS. THEY SAY THEY FEEL NO NEED TO ADD TO THAT.

She refused to thank them; she closed her mind firmly so to indicate. But she was nevertheless grateful. Once it had been a whirling column of lightning that had chased her all around the stable; the second time it had been towers of flame ringing her in, burning up just to the distance where the heat began to be torture, burning just long enough to cause her genuine fear, and then flickering out and leaving no mark behind. Not a charred spot, not a singed stalk of grain. Only the stinging of her skin and the heat of her clothing. If they felt obliged to be more spectacular each time, she couldn't bring herself to look forward to it. Not that either of their displays so far had been anything she couldn't of done herself. It was the things she'd heard they could do, and not knowing what to expect, nor how far they'd go, that made it uncomforatble.

She marched back to the Castle, getting angrier with every step she took—she was halfway there before she remembered the wards, and had to go back and take *them* off—and went to find Granny Hazelbide.

Who had, she discovered, acquired a partner.

"Hello there, Granny Gableframe!" she said, almost surprised out of her mad. It wasn't like Grannys to go visiting; they didn't have time.

"Evening, Responsible," said the Granny.

"Granny Gableframe," explained Granny Hazelbide, "is asking for our hospitality."

"Only for a little while, mind," put in the other. "I've been Granny-in-Residence at Castle Smith now over thirty—law! over forty—years, and it's been nothing but outlandish misery the whole time. What I fancy now is a little house in a near village, if you can spare one, where I can granny for decent folk a change, instead of that pack of . . . unspeakables . . . at Castle Smith. Seems to me Granny Hazelbide needs no help here."

"You're welcome ten times over, Granny Gableframe," said Responsible. "And as for your settling, that'll be no problem. There's no such thing as too many Grannys in a Kingdom. I'll send the word around, and we'll have the Magician take you to see the towns that apply for your services, and let you choose at your leisure."

"In the meantime," said Granny Hazelbide, "I've told her we can use her here—if she can abide our plain ways, that is. We're a tad short of scepters and crowns and suchlike."

"You've a wicked tongue and a cold heart, Hazelbide," said Granny Gableframe, "and you'll live to regret it."

Granny Hazelbide chuckled, and patted her friend's knee, and then turned serious.

"They'll quiz you to a nub, come breakfast time," she warned. "Thorn of Guthrie will want every last smidgen, every last *de*tail, and those two boys of Ruth's are more curious than's healthy . . . and Jonathan Cardwell Brightwater is worse for gossip than seven old ladies not fit to granny. You want to keep to your room and put all that off awhile?"

Granny Gableframe hummphed; and then did it louder.

"*No*-sir," she said, tart enough to pucker metal. "I have no intentions whatsoever, just *no* intentions, of furnishing that lot with the tale they're after. Here I am, and that's the end of it, and if they won't have me on that basis they can throw me a pallet in the stables with my Mule. I'll not discuss it, I put you on notice here and now. And you needn't go to any effort to prepare them for it, ladies, for I'm fully capable of telling them where to take their nosy questions when the time comes. Just leave it to this old Granny, thank you kindly."

"You sure?"

"Sure as sure, Responsible," declared the old lady. "It'll be a day to remember when I can't manage a few Brightwaters with their mouths flapping."

"Fair enough," said Responsible, "and I'll enjoy the spectacle. Now has anybody seen to your rooms?"

"Sent a servingmaid to do that, it'll be half an hour ago now," said Granny Hazelbide. "There's an empty room two doors down from me, looking out over the meadow and the creek, and has its own bath and a nice little old fireplace in the corner. Just the thing. It'll be ready whenever Gableframe cares to go up there."

"All taken care of, are you?"

"That I am," said the Granny, "or do seem to be. Depends of course on how clear Hazelbide's instructions were, and whether she fancied a mudtoad or two under my pillow as a welcoming gesture."

Responsible smiled; they were going to enjoy themselves, those two, and perhaps with a little time to recover from whatever outrage Lincoln Parradyne Smith had perpetrated on her, Granny Gableframe could be cozened into staying at the Castle permanently. She'd be company for Granny Hazelbide, and the idea of two Grannys on call at all times appealed to Responsible in the strongest terms just now.

"Want to give me a bit of advice, you two?" she asked suddenly.

Granny Hazelbide jerked her chin toward the other Granny.

"Already told her about it," she said. "We've just been waiting on you to ask."

"What do they want, blast and blister them?" asked Granny Gableframe. "I do believe they are the most... Hmmmph. I wish they'd mind their own business."

"Almost said a broad word, did you, Granny?"

"Never you mind. What'd they want?"

"Well," said Responsible, "we had a little talk, by way of my Mule. It *does rankle*, you know—having to use a Mule for interpreter. Lacks a certain dignity."

"You be glad the Mule is willing," cautioned Granny Gableframe. "You thank your lucky stars and comets for that small favor in a cold world! Cause there is *no* way that the human being could pass mindspeech directly with the members of the Out-Cabal and stay sane! It's been tried, and what was left over afterwards was not pretty to look upon."

"Died in a locked room, she did," said Granny Hazelbide,

nodding her support, "and nothing any level of magic could do for her. Crawled around in her own filth and howled, day and night, and just plain luck that the next Responsible was already nine years old at the time and able to get through the muck that was left of her mind when it was needful. You *appreciate* the Mule filtering that down for you, hear? You want your brains burned right out of your head?"

"The *point,*" said Responsible, "is that it makes it look as if the Mules are more stable of mind than we are. I don't fancy that."

"Faugh!" said Hazelbide. "It's not that atall. The Mule's just closer in its perceptions to the Out-Cabal than humans are, and the sharing seems to be no strain for the creature. Might could be they're Mules themselves, in which case we've no call to be embarrassed. Now what did they want, or you plan to sit there going on about your dignity all this night?"

Responsible told them, and they put in the necessary Granny noises at all the proper places, and approved of the stand she'd taken.

"Handled it right well, I'd say," said one; and the other allowed as how that was accurate.

"Got'em on a *neat* point, didn't you, missy? I'm proud of you."

Responsible thanked Granny Hazelbide for the compliment, pulled up a rocker, and began to rock. She was still mad, and the distraction provided by Granny Gableframe's sudden arrival was beginning to wear off. The chair started to creak in protest at her speed, but she didn't care; if it fell to pieces, it might relieve her feelings some.

"Responsible," observed Granny Hazelbide, "why don't you just take an ax to that rocker? It'd be quieter and quicker."

"Why've you got your dander up, anyway?" asked Gableframe. "Seems to me you bested them; aren't you satisfied?"

"No, I am not!"

She rocked harder, which wasn't easy.

"Law, she'll take off any minute and fly chair and all out through that window!" said Granny Gableframe. "Girl, what *is* your complaint? The Mule give you a headache?"

Responsible stopped rocking so suddenly that she nearly fell out of the chair. "I just don't understand it," she announced. "And what I don't understand, I purely *despise!*"

"Well, you're not the first," said Gableframe. "Nor will you be the last. The time comes the Out-Cabal lets four five years go by and no message sent, then I'll begin to fret—we'll know then they're up to some devilment."

"We don't know, and we wouldn't know," Responsible said, flat out, and struck the rocker arm with her fist. "We just *assume!*"

Granny Hazelbide sighed, and shook her head.

"There she goes again, Gableframe," she said. "Been through this with her I don't know how many times now, and her only ten years old the first time, and her pigtails pulled back so tight they made her ears stick out—and she's not changed since. My, but she's stubborn!"

"I say," said Responsible, "and there's nobody to say me nay, either, that we have no proof the Out-Cabal can do anything they claim. No proof there's any such group of planets as the Garnet Ring. No proof that there is any such thing as the *Out*-Cabal, far as *I* can see, and I'm not exactly shortsighted!"

"Now, Responsible—"

"Never mind your 'now-Responsibles'! You give me one bit of evidence, one solid piece of anything to show me I should believe in all this stuff; I'll back down. So far, you've had nothing to say that sounded any more sensible than Emmalyn of Clark prattling about unbrellas inside the house and spitting when you see three white Mules, and I'm purely sick of it."

"You recall that other young woman, Responsible, if you want proof—she had the same problem you have, and bad cess to the Grannys advising her that they couldn't keep her from pushing it to where she did! Her mind didn't leave her on account of fairy tales, Responsible of Brightwater, and she did no more than insist that they speak directly to her and not through the Mules. She didn't defy them, nor question their existence!"

"And what about that lightning they chased you with, and the fire all round your pretty little feet last time? *Not* to mention they know *everything* as happens here on this planet, when and as it happens! You forget that?"

Responsible drew a deep breath, and began to rock again, careful to keep it slow and sensible.

"Look here," she said to them. "Let's just look at what you say, and no more of this carryon, fair enough? I don't know about that other Responsible, though I'm for sure sorry about her; that's been two hundred years ago or more, and the circumstances that went with it wrapped up in more mysteries than an onion has layers—I don't consider that evidence. Being that nobody but the Grannys and one lone woman in every generation *knows* about the Out-Cabal, it's understandable that we don't have much in the way of details on the subject . . . but for all we really know she just had too hard a row to hoe and wasn't strong enough to bear it. As for their fancy effects—I've got *Magicians* as could do everything I've seen them do, and Magicians of Rank that make their magic look like baby fooling. Knowing what goes on on Ozark'd be cursed easy if you just happened to *be* on Ozark, let me point *that* out! And if they're so all-fired omnipotent and powerful, if their magic's as far superior to ours as a spaceship's superior to a river raft, like they claim, then why haven't they shown us some of it? Why haven't they rattled things around a bit? Moved some mountains? Canceled some of our weather? Ruined some of *our* magic, at least? *Shoot!*"

The two Grannys traded glances and allowed as how that was quite a speech, fit to try the patience somewhat more than somewhat, and added a half dozen more platitudes to the broth, until Responsible got disgusted with them, too.

"I made you a speech," she said wearily, "you could at least make me an answer. Two of you—you ought to be able to work up something."

Granny Hazelbide rocked and knitted, and rocked and knitted some more, and they all waited, and then she said: "Let me ask you a question, Responsible of Brightwater."

"At your service."

"Say there's no Out-Cabal. Say there's no Garnet Ring, no group of planets all bound by a single system of magic and out to add to their numbers. Say that long-ago Responsible *did* scare her own self insane. Say all the things you propose are true. But then answer me this: if it's not them, if it's not Out-Cabal, then who or what *is* it?"

"Someone on this planet," Responsible muttered. "Somebody right here on Ozark."

"For hundreds of years? Child!"

"For just as many hundreds of years," insisted Responsible, "we've managed to keep all this secret not just from the people of Ozark but even from the Magicians and the Magicians of Rank. That's every bit as hard to believe, but we've done it."

"Well, who do you suspect, then?" Granny Hazelbide demanded. "Speak right up, there's nobody here but us!"

Responsible said nothing. She'd run it through the computers on run-and-destroys till she was blue, and it kept coming out with a whole passel of choices. Might could be it was a Magician of Rank—or two or three of them—passing it along to new ones carefully chosen as they grew old, and enjoying themselves tremendously at what they put the women through. Might could be it was the Skerrys—nobody knew anything about the Skerrys, what they could or would do, hidden away in Marktwain's small desert and not seen once in a hundred years—could *certainly* be the Skerrys. Could be the Mules themselves, and wouldn't *that* be a fine howdydo! She'd had some experience with what a Mule could do if it took a fancy to, and might could be they were not all that happy having their tails braided and their backs saddled and bridled and behaving in general like the Mules of Earth; might could be they'd been getting their own back, in their own way. It wasn't unreasonable; it was so far from unreasonable that she shivered.

"Look at the child! She's all aquiver!"

"I'm all right, Granny Hazelbide."

"All right, are you? Take a closer look at yourself, missy—you that has no trouble whatsoever facing down the whole crew of Magicians of Rank assembled, and knows more than all nine of them put together. You that knows more than all twenty-nine of us Grannys and sees the web of the universe laid out clear and clean before you like a tadling does a fish net—*you*, Responsible of Brightwater! And you've done no more this night than send six seven sentences back and forth between you and the Out-Cabal, filtered through the mind of a Mule to keep it easy for you, and I do believe you'll have to be carried up to your bed! What's that, Responsible, if not proof the Out-Cabal's real?"

"You speak mighty plain," said Responsible. "Guard your tongue!"

"There are times," answered the old woman, "only plain speaking will do the job. Think I want to see *you* with your mind destroyed? Just because I failed to speak up plain when my turn came? I'm not such a shirkall as that, nor yet such a fool. You *can't* walk, *can* you? Now *can* you?"

Many things were not clear to Responsible at that moment. It seemed to her, for example, that even the Grannys should realize that all that power and wondrous knowledge they claimed she had was being carried around in a head that had seen only fifteen summers go by, and half the time didn't know what to do with what it knew. It seemed to her they'd realize that her loneliness was a torment, an awful and awesome burden like the whole sky down upon her two shoulders, with no living soul to ask any questions of. It seemed to her they'd know so many things; and it seemed to them—that at least was clear—that she knew so much more than she did.

And she could not afford to have them think any differently. Not the Grannys. Not and akeep this planet stable, and all the Magicians of Rank in order, while she waited for what she knew to come to *mean* more to her. She had to make a show of strength for these two.

"If there's anything wrong with me," she said to them crisply, drawing on a source of energy she'd have to pay back in a painful coin later, "it's the potion I was given twenty-four hours ago. Wonder you didn't kill me with it, Granny Hazelbide!"

And she stood up and walked straight out of the room, steady as the stones of the Castle walls, and left them looking after her in comfortable silence.

CHAPTER 13

ALL THE WAY back on the ship, Gilead worried about her father. Jacob Donahue Wommack sat through the days, staring out over the water; at the ship's table he made little pretense of eating, picking absently at his food. And in the night she often heard him in the next cabin, pacing, hour after hour; when he slept, which was not often nor for long, he moaned like a creature wounded to the heart. Gilead herself grew thin from the nights she spent listening to him, catching only a few minutes of exhausted sleep toward morning, and the Grannys fussed at her incessantly. Did she think, they wanted to know, that she could help her father by wasting away to a stick and wandering around with two eyes like burnt holes in her face?

"I can't sleep, while he's like that," she told them.

"You do him no service, listening to him and brooding over him!"

"I cannot *help* it," she insisted.

"Then shame on you," Granny Copperdell rebuked her, "for if there's something serious wrong with your daddy he'll need your strength later, and precious little you'll have to offer him! You'll have young Jewel with that on her back as well as the minding of her brother—and that's unfair, Gilead of Wommack. Just *un*fair!"

Gilead turned her head away, and the tears burned in her eyes.

"It's just that I love him," she said, almost choking on the words. "Aren't I supposed to love him?"

"Fine kind of love that is," the Granny went on, grimly. "You do your duty, we'd have a sight more respect for your 'love.'"

"It's my duty to *sleep*, while my daddy suffers?"

Granny Copperdell turned her back on Gilead, a gesture as eloquent in its contempt as a slap would have been, and harder to bear; when the young woman pulled at her elbow she would not even look at her.

"What is it you're after me for now?" she said, rigid as a rail.

"Granny, I don't blame you for what you're thinking; I know I'm not much of a woman."

"That you're not. I'm ashamed to have had the raising of you."

"Say whatever you care to—but can't you potion Daddy?"

"He won't have it."

"You've tried, then—you've already tried?"

"I have tried, for sure," said Granny Copperdell. "Granny *Goodweather* has tried. We know our business, Gilead, we've been at it more years than you've been on this world. And your daddy has sent us both packing, as is his privilege. He's neither a tadling to have his nose held and the potion poured down him, nor yet an addled old one gone child again. He is a strong man in the flower of his manhood, and if he doesn't choose to be potioned he doesn't have to be."

"I can't bear it," lamented Gilead of Wommack, "I can't! Daddy like he is, and both of you Grannys ice and steel to me, and Lewis Motley behaving like a lunatic and driving Jewel distracted, and all the children upset—"

The Granny gave her a look, shook off her hand, and walked off and left her standing there, muttering about worthless females, and for the rest of the trip both Grannys made a point of avoiding her. When they reached Castle Wommack, they shunned her still.

"Don't pay them any mind," Lewis Motley told her once, seeing them pass her as if she'd gone invisible in the night. "What do you care for the opinions of a pair of creaking old women like that?"

"They're *Gran*nys," said Gilead. "You don't understand."

"No, I don't. Jewel has told me a mess of nonsense that's supposed to explain it, but I don't understand that either. You have a right to be worried about Jacob Donahue—I'm worried about him myself. I see no reason why you should be treated like they're doing you, just for that."

There is no harsher judgment in all this world, thought Gilead, than that of an Ozark woman for a female that can't cope. But she didn't say it aloud, it wasn't the kind of thing you said to a man; and Lewis Motley went off shrugging his shoulders.

On the morning of the second day of their return, Jacob Donahue was dead. The Attendant who took his coffee up came back swiftly, looking white and stunned, and had the Grannys go back up with him to be sure. He was down again, fast as he'd gone up, and off to the stables like he was in a hurry to get to them. The Grannys were upstairs a cosiderable time, doing what was necessary, and would let nobody in until they were through. Even then, it was only for long enough to see the dead man laid neatly on a fresh counterpane with his eyes closed and his hands folded and a single candle lit beside his bed, and they shooed all the others away, scolding. "Leave him in peace now, get on with you!"

The staff were satisfied, saying "All's been done proper; trust the Grannys," and they went back to their work, taking just time to tie a band of black cloth on their sleeves from a supply the Grannys kept handy. And then the Family went to the meetingroom and took their places round the table, leaving the Master's chair empty.

"He left a letter," said Granny Copperdell, without preamble. She reached into the pocket of her apron and pulled out a sheet of heavy paper folded in thirds, and slapped it down before Gilead. "With Gilead's name on its outside."

"Oh, no, Granny," breathed Gilead, "I can't—"

"Say you can't bear it one more time," Granny Copperdell cut in, "just one more time, and I'll send you from this meeting like you weren't yet weaned, you hear me? Now that's your *father's* letter, the last words he wrote, and they are addressed to you. I'll thank you—we'll *all* thank you—to read them in a dignified manner, as is suitable to his memory."

Gilead picked up the sheet and unfolded it, staring at the Grannys, and she asked, in a voice that nobody recognized: "Does this mean that Daddy killed himself? Does it?"

"You know anything else it could mean?" snapped Granny Goodweather. "Now will you leave off, and read what's written?"

My dearest family and my beloved friends,

I write these last few words to you, not because I mean to excuse what I am about to do, but because I would like to try to explain. Perhaps then you will find you can forgive me.

My life has never been a hard one; excepting the loss of my dear wife, everything has been made easy and smooth for me, now that I look back on it. My memories are good ones, and for all that you have done to make that true, I leave you my thanks.

But I've come now to a place where I find myself too much a coward to go on—and that surprises me; I never knew I was a coward. I always thought I was a brave man—but I can't face what life will be like now, nor bear the shame of my part in making it so. Of all the delegates to that doomed Jubilee, only one was of my generation in both years *and* mind. Only that fanatic, Jeremiah Thomas Traveller, who so well lives up to his name. We are told, you know, that Jeremiah was a prophet of doom, and that Thomas was a doubter—that's Jeremiah, and I have known him many a long year. For the younger men and for the foolish ones there is maybe some excuse; there is none for either Jeremiah or for me. I leave it to the Holy One to punish him for the wickedness that rots his soul; no doubt I will be punished, too, for dying a coward's death, and a death of shame. It is a bitter legacy I leave you—never think I didn't know that.

One question will come up now, and perhaps be a source of discord. I can do at least this much for you; I can settle that question. My sons will be fine men, but they are very young; my daughter Gilead is dear to me, but she is not a strong woman. I therefore direct that the title of Master of Castle Wommack be passed on not to any one of my children, but to my brother Lewis Motley Wommack the 33rd. I make this choice without any hesitation; I know my brother. He is called a wild young man—I leave the conduct of this Kingdom and its people in his hands, knowing he will lay aside that wildness as easily as he would lay aside a cloak. Let there be no dispute on this matter, as you respect my memory. Help him, as you have helped me; support him, as you have supported me; honor him, as you have honored me.

As I look back over what I have written, I see that I have failed in this as well—I have *not* explained. And I cannot, I have no more strength than I have courage. Forgive me then, my dear ones, for love of me alone.

I bid you farewell.

Jacob Donahue Wommack the 23rd

"There! I read the awful thing!" Gilead threw the sheet of paper from her, white-lipped and shuddering.

"Thank you, Gilead of Wommack," said Granny Goodweather. She reached out and set the letter in order again, and laid it down in the center of the table. And she looked round at all the children with a pitying eye. Gilead, the eldest. The two young boys, Thomas Lincoln the 9th, and the father's namesake, Jacob Donahue the 24th. Gilead's sisters, and their husbands, and the grandchildren with their eyes like saucers. Jewel of Wommack, crying openly but without a sound, the tears pouring in rivers down her face. All these people, and the 14,000 souls—give or take a dozen—who were the people, all in the hands of Lewis Motley Wommack the 33rd.

One of the sons-in-law opened his mouth, and the Granny knew what he was about to say. At twenty-four, it wouldn't be easy for him to aceept the younger man as Master of the Castle.

"There will be *no dispute!*" she said. "He lies dead, sudden, taken in the prime of his life and by his own despairing hand; you'll not dishonor him more by moving against him now, when he cannot compel you to obedience. You put any such ideas right out of your mind, for I won't countenance them, nor will Granny Copperdell, nor will the Magicians of this Kingdom."

"That's well put," added Granny Copperdell. "Anybody as

cares to question it, they'll rue it. Mark my words."

The son-in-law closed his mouth and settled back with a look of resignation, if not acceptance, and the silence went on and on.

"Why?" Gilead ventured finally. "I don't understand why."

"He told you," snapped Granny Copperdell.

"No! It was riddles!"

Her sister Sophia agreed, and the concord ran round the table along with the questions."

"What's any of this got to do with the Travellers?"

"What'd he mean, he was ashamed?"

"What'd he mean, he couldn't face what life's going to be now? What's going to happen?"

In the middle of the questions and the complaints, Lewis Motley Wommack silenced them all. He got up from his chair, far to the foot of the table beside Jewel's, and he walked right to the head and took the Master's chair.

"Law!" breathed Gilead in the sudden hush. "Law, that does look *strange!*"

"Makes no nevermind how it looks," said Granny Goodweather. "It's as your daddy ordered it, and no doubt he had his reasons. You got a few words to say to us, Lewis Motley, before we leave this room and turn properly to mourning your brother?"

"First," said Lewis Motley, "I'll settle the riddles for you—those as seem fit for settling, in my own judgment."

"You'd do that, would you?"

"Yes, Granny, I would and I will. Jacob Donahue Wommack saw that the end of the Confederation meant the beginning of chaos, and he couldn't face that. He's had order all his life—and there'll be no more order. That's one riddle answered. As for the shame, he knew it was his place to stand against that foolish ending set in motion by the Travellers and carried to its fruit and harvest by the Smiths. He was no young man to be carried away with the excitement of the moment, nor any fool like the Brightwater that was Chair and let the meeting be run away with and said not one word to stop it—he was a man in the wisdom of years, and a man that saw clear. He knew what it would be like, and he knew he should speak, and he said nary a word, just for fear of the fuss it would make. That's the shame he writes of, and a shame I share."

"You tried to speak up!" Jewel protested. "I saw you, from the balcony. You were hollering for them to let you speak."

"So I was," said Lewis Motley bitterly. "I stood there, and I hollered. The proper thing to do, once I saw nobody else was going to, would of been to snatch the crown off Delldon Mallard's fool head, take away his scepter, and use it to beat some sense into as many idiots as I could get to—starting with the Chair. I did *not* do that, you notice; as my sister tells you, I stood there hollering for somebody to listen to me, like a nanny goat. The only person at that meeting as did anything honorable—the one and only person—was Troublesome of Brightwater. A *woman!* We deserved every word she said, we deserved to be driven from Confederation Hall and have it locked against us, and we deserved the look of her back as she rode out of town."

"Accurate," said the Grannys together.

And Granny Goodweather checked her pocket. She'd taken the tall glass that sat on the table by Jacob Donahue's bed, rinsed it carefully to be sure certain every last dreg of the poison he'd used was gone, and smashed it to bits at the back of his fireplace. But she'd kept one shard for herself, a good-sized one with a trace of a berry vine etched on it, and given another like it to Granny Copperdell. It wouldn't do to lose that shard. Such things were very useful, and not often come by; and she had a feeling they might be needed more often in the days to come than they'd been in the past. The sharp bit was still where she'd put it, lying between a shammybag of herbs and her long scissors.

"Well? Is there more?"

That was the son-in-law again, and Lewis Motley gave him a long considering look, what was called a "withering glance" in that Castle, and much feared. Sophia cuaght her lower lip between her teeth, and moved closer to her husband, that'd made so bold as to challenge the heir.

"I'm still on the riddles," he said coldly. "When I've finished, I'll say so. That suit you?"

"It suits me."

"Consider our situation, then: say you don't worry, as my brother did, about lack of political order. I'm willing to grant that's not an issue likely to grip everybody's mind as it did his, and does mine. But we are the *Wommacks,* I remind you. We are alone, fourteen thousand-odd of us, in the middle of a wilderness barely cut back from its original state, surrounded by a great ocean known for its storms. And to comfort us? We have the Wommack Curse."

"Lewis Motley—"

"No more comsets to provide us easy company, tie us tight to the other eleven Families at a push of a button. No more freighters pulling in to our dock with the latest gewgaws from the cities. Not likely we'll have visitors flying in by Mule, anxious to see the beauties of our wilderness and our inhospitable coasts. We are going to be *alone* now, in a way that no Ozarker has ever been alone before. That, now, I reckon you can understand, whether you're interested in politics or not. And it's that that's got to be dealt with."

He looked at them all, long and hard, and rubbed at his beard with both hands, fiercely, like it tormented him.

"As for me being Master of this Castle," he went on, "that's a piece of foolishness, and brings me to the end of the riddles and the beginning of business. I told you I'd let you know—what I am about to say is the urgent business of this day."

"Now, Lewis Motley?" demanded Granny Goodweather. "You think that's fitting?"

"Now," said the young man. "Right now."

"Then I'll have the tadlings sent out of here, and the staff told to feed them and cosset them and put them to bed. This is no place for children."

"Fair enough, Granny Goodweather," he told her, "fair enough. I've no special desire to bore them, and nothing to say that would interest them. But anybody that's reached the age of twelve stays—that's no child. Not any longer, if ever they were. Jewel of Wommack, you'll stay. And you, Thomas Lincoln. And while you're sending the rest out, Granny, I'll say my say.

"I understand," he said, "all the fire and brimstone you Grannys are putting out about not crossing Jacob Donahue, and it strikes me very odd, seeing as how you never scrupled to cross him ten times a day and twice that on Sundys while he lived. But I'm not afraid of either one of you—let us have that straight and no question in your minds about it—and I'll *not* be Master of Castle Wommack. Master! The very thought turns me sick." He saw the Grannys' mouths open and he shouted at them, "Hear me out!"

"Very well," said Granny Copperdell, and Granny Goodweather nodded. "But what you say had best be carefully thought out aforehand, young man. Custom is, the Master of the Castle names the heir; you plan to go against that, you lay your reasons out mighty plain."

"This is no time," said Lewis Motley grimly, "for the people of Kintucky to be asked to accept me as Castle Master. Nineteen years old, known—as my brother pointed out—to be wild; and far less willing than he thinks to be any less so. That may be romantic, but it's not good sense. I'll have no part of it. But I'll compromise, for the sake of your sacred damned customs, and not to scandalize the countryside further, and because I care for the Wommack name. I'll not be Master; but I'll be Guardian."

"Explain yourself!"

"Granny, if you'd leave off interrupting me, I might be able to do that."

"Get on with it, then."

"The proper heir, and proper Master, sits there beside you—Thomas Lincoln Wommack the Ninth, my brother's elder son. He's his daddy all over again, and he'll make a fine Master; he just needs a little time. I propose to give him that time. I'll be Guardian for this Castle, and him at my side to learn what there is to do—precious little that is, by the way, in case you females think I haven't noticed. I'll do the tasks left to the Master, and do them with my whole heart and my whole strength—until the day Thomas Lincoln reaches an age and skill suitable to let him take it on, and *that* day, ah, that day, I shall be free of this particular set of fetters my dear brother saw fit to leave me."

"Shame on you," said Gilead. "Him not cold yet, and you speaking of him that way! You're a hardhearted man, Lewis Motley Wommack, and not a natural one. He was your brother, and he stood as father to you, as best as ever he could!"

"That does not oblige me to be grateful, Gilead, when he hands on to me a task he tells us he couldn't face his own self, and not only am I not grateful, I resent it. You hear me? I resent being *used,* and I resent years of my life being taken from me, and nothing but my loyalty to this Family keeps me from handing this over to Chandler over there, that's just chafing at the bit to have the job! Or Jareth Andrew Lewis, hiding behind Sophia, that's already challenged me twice!"

Granny Goodweather raised her finger beside her temple

for silence, and waited till she had it, and then she spoke straight to Thomas Lincoln.

"You understand, boy, what your uncle is saying?" she asked him. "You agree to it? It's your right to object, and your right to *insist* on Lewis Motley following your daddy's wishes right to the smallest letter. And though he claims he's not afraid of a Granny or two, I give you my word on it we have ways of making him take *that* back in a hurry! What's your feeling on this, Thomas Lincoln?"

The boy threw his head up and gave her a casual look that was so like Jacob Donahue it made Gilead catch her breath.

"I think it shows good sense," said Thomas Lincoln, "and I stand behind it. And if it'll make Lewis Motley feel any better, there won't be many years taken from him, as he puts it—the sooner the better, to my mind."

The Granny sighed, satisfied. "That's settled, then." And she pushed her chair back, and smoothed her skirts, ready to leave the room and be about her business.

"Please sit yourself down, Granny Goodweather," said Lewis Motley, "I'm not through yet. There's just one more thing. We have ahead of us a long time of hardship and lack and terrible loneliness. And through that time, our people will need something to rally round, something to look to as a stable center. The Travellers have their faith to carry *them;* we have nothing but our Curse, and it makes a poor companion. Delldon Mallard Smith's an idiot, and the day will come he'll wish he'd never heard the word 'King,' but he has one thing worth copying. What we need, all alone out here, is magnificence. Pomp and circumstance. Ritual and pageantry. And lots of it. And as it happens, we have a perfect excuse for it."

"Whatever in the world?" demanded Granny Copperdell. "Whatever in this wide world?"

"We have the problem, now there's no comset, of educating the children on this continent. No more sitting them down every morning to learn what the computers served up from Brightwater; and the Grannys and the Tutors can't be expected to take them on more than a year or two past the seven years old they are when they finish with them now. They don't have the time, nor the training. And we have Jewel of Wommack."

He rubbed his hands together, and nodded politely at his sister, who was staring at him, feeling a chill in her bones.

Whatever it was he had in mind, she could be sure certain it meant another burden for her.

"We'll have a Teaching Order," said Lewis Motley with satisfaction. "And Jewel will head it—whether she fancies it or not! She knows chemistry, she knows physics, she knows biology, she knows music theory, she knows painting, she knows history, she knows linguistics—what don't you know, my much-indulged little sister? Always at the comsets, and Jacob Donahue so proud of your learning, saying you were to be let alone and somebody else could peel the vegetables . . . The day's come to redeem that favor, Jewel! We'll need a suitable *habit* for you, something splendid and yet dignified, something that will draw attention and inspire respect; and we'll send you with two Senior Attendants and a serving-maid for escort, all round the towns, to find and bring back here other young females with qualifications like yours. We'll house all of you in the north wing of this Castle—not a room of it's in use, except for one library, and that fits neatly—and you will be Senior Teacher. Teacher Jewel, we'll call you, and we'll send the other Teachers you train out over this scratched patch of living for people to be in awe of. One in every town, to be their own bit of pomp and majesty. Gilead, you're clever with the needle—you'll help me gown her properly."

"Not today!" Gilead cried. "Not today, nor tomorrow!"

"No—but the day after. And you, Jewel, close your mouth. You have the skill, you have the knowledge, you have the beauty; you'll have the elegance once we've garbed you; and most important of all, you have the will. You can command, and you're not afraid to. You'll do it beautifully, sister mine! You hear me?"

Jewel of Wommack had planned on a husband and half a dozen babes for herself, to add to the ones already making the halls noisy at the Castle. She'd planned on a suite of rooms nobody else had seemed to care for, a corner suite with a window looking out into a tangle of huge old trees, where a tadling could step right from the windowseat onto a treelimb and back again. Three girls and three boys, she'd planned on, all raised loyal to the Confederation, fallen or not.

She set that aside, now. As she'd set aside the idea of being a child, when her parents had drowned, and taken up her post as the woman that'd have to do for her brother.

"I hear you, Lewis Motley," she said.

She had some idea what a habit would be like. There'd been little room on The Ship for pictures of such stuff, but there were a few in the library her brother had mentioned, and she felt the weight of the wimple on her forehead already. And that brought a thought.

"I'll not cut my hair," she announced to nobody in particular. "You put that out of your mind."

"Is that where your learning is?" asked Lewis Motley. "In your hair?"

The Grannys clucked their tongues, and Goodweather spoke up.

"Too much has happened for one day," she said, "and all of us are in a sorry state. You there, making jokes at a time like this; and Gilead, about to faint on us. I believe you have the right of it, young Wommack, with your Teaching Order, I do believe that is exactly what we need, and I can see it down the way—it'll be a thing that comes to matter. But for now, enough. Enough and a right smart piece left over. This meeting's closed."

And then she thought of one more thing.

"Lewis Motley?"

"Yes, ma'am?"

"I'll be expecting you in my room shortly, about that earache."

"Granny," said Jewel, "that's a waste of your time. I've been trying to send him to you about that for days now, and he takes my head off every time I mention it. He's *got* no earache, you care to listen to him, nor no headache either. You can tell him all you like how many times you've seen him, wincing like somebody stuck him with a pin again, rubbing at his head and scowling—it won't do you a scrap of good."

"Lewis Motley!" objected the Granny. "You've got your work cut out for you for a good time to come, and no quarter anywhere. This is no time to be distracted with a misery, you need to be the very best you can be! You come and see me and let me—"

He cut her off with a sudden chop of both hands in the air.

"Like you said, Granny," he told them, looking right through them all and biting the words off one by one, "this meeting's closed."

CHAPTER 14

AT CASTLE SMITH the sovereign was fretful, despite the fact that that very morning the new Granny'd flown in behind his Magician of Rank on his Mule and taken up residence in the Castle. She looked mean enough, and she talked the formspeech in a way that was a consolation to ears long used to hearing it, and having her there filled a hole that'd been gnawing at him. But he was not happy. He sat on the throne set up for him in the Castle Ballroom, now known as the Throne Room, and fidgeted, while his Queen watched him distractedly.

"She can't do it," said King Delldon Mallard Smith the 2nd. "I don't *believe* she can do it!"

"She's done it," answered Lincoln Parradyne.

"She's got no *right!*"

"On the contrary, Your Majesty—she has every right. Or, to be more accurate, Brightwater Kingdom has every right."

"There has *always* been the comset network on Ozark, Lincoln Parradyne. From the very . . . uh . . . first. The comsets supply our news. They carry our messages. They provide our education and our entertainment. They are everything that on Old Earth had to be done by a mail service, and a telephone service, and a television service, and a radio service, and a—"

"Your Majesty," interrupted the Magician of Rank, "I am familiar with the history of Earth. And I assure you that the comsets have done far more than all the services and media of that misbegotten planet combined. We will be greatly inconvenienced without them."

"Then—"

"But, Your Highness, Responsible of Brightwater is as much within her rights to restrict the range of the comsets to the Kingdom of Brightwater as she would be to keep its buildings there, or its Mule herds there, or anything else that belongs to it. Brightwater provided the comset service to the Confederation, not to the Kingdoms—and the Confederation is no more."

The King pulled at his lower lip, and blew out a long breath. "You didn't mention this point to me before the Jubilee," he said accusingly.

"On the contrary again, Your Majesty. I did."

"I remember no such thing."

"He did," put in the Queen. "I was there at the time, and for sure he did. You laughed at him. You said he was talking nonsense. You told him not to bother you with stories meant to scare tadlings, when you had important business to discuss. I remember *most* distinctly."

"Well, whatever happened—not that I'm admitting it, you . . . uh . . . understand, I tell you nobody mentioned it to me!—but isn't there a law? Can't she be stopped?"

Lincoln Parradyne raised his eyebrows.

"Your Majesty," he protested, "the comset stations, and the equipment, and all the transmitters and relays, *all* things, are the property of Castle Brightwater. The reply that was given to me yesterday by Jonathan Cardwell Brightwater—saying that to continue comset transmission would be an act of interference in the internal affairs of the sovereign Kingdoms—was absolutely right. Not to mention the expense, of course."

"Even if the sovereign Kingdoms desire to be interfered with?" demanded Delldon Mallard ignoring the part about expense. "In that one way only, of course."

"Really, Your Majesty!" said Lincoln Parradyne. "Think what you are saying. Either we are independent, or we are *not.*"

"Perhaps," ventured the King, "Responsible of Brightwater has a price."

"I doubt that," said Marygold flatly.

"Even if she did—where would you *get* that price? You have not yet established a Royal Treasury, and it's not because I haven't reminded you."

The point was a sore one with the King, who'd been putting off by every means possible the inevitable moment when he would have to inform his subjects of the new realities of taxation, and explain to them just what services they would be receiving from him in return for their funds. He did not have that worked out to his satisfaction as yet, and he was not so thick-headed that he did not realize it might take some fancy talking to bring it off. Taxes in the past had gone to Brightwater, and the services provided had been both obvious and welcome; things would be different now.

"Lincoln Parradyne?"

"Yes, Your Majesty?"

"How about our building . . . uh . . . our own comset rig? It's not secret how it's done, is it?"

"No, it's not secret. It was part of the information brought along when we landed here; it's available to anybody."

"Then let's do it!" It seemed very obvious to the King.

"All of the Kingdoms," said the Magician of Rank, "now that the Confederation has *finally* been dissolved, will have to consider that option. They might each build their own networks . . . they might go back to sending information by riders on Muleback . . . they might take up some of the devices of Earth. But it will take some time, Your Majesty. The decision must be made in each case, separately. The funds must be found. The necessary *technicians* must be found, or hired from elsewhere. A communication network requires experts, and money, and time."

"Do we have the people we need, here in this Kingdom?" asked Queen Marygold practically. "Seems to me that's the first question."

"No, Your Majesty."

"Then where do you reckon—"

"Marygold of Purdy!" said the King. "I have asked you, now that you are a Queen, to be more careful of your speech. If the Magicians of Rank can manage to talk without sounding like Grannys, surely you can do the same!"

Lincoln Parradyne forbore to mention the pitiful weakness of that argument, and answered his Queen directly.

"Madam," he said respectfully, "so far as I know they are all to be found on Marktwain—in Brightwater."

"Curse that female!" shouted the King of Smith. *"Curse* her!"

"Delldon, you have no way of knowing that Responsible of Brightwater is the one that ordered the comsets cut back," said his Queen. "It was Jonathan Cardwell Brightwater that spoke to Lincoln Parradyne when you sent him inquiring, not that girl."

The King sputtered helplessly about the ignorance of women, and his Magician of Rank moved to smooth the waters.

"I am much afraid, my dear Queen," he said, "that the King is correct. Whoever may *speak* for Brightwater, it is Responsible that holds the reins of power."

"That's very odd," commented Marygold of Purdy. "I don't understand it at all, and I don't see it as proper or fitting. How can a girl of fifteen be running a whole Kingdom?"

While Delldon Mallard was explaining that it wasn't that way at all, it was just that as was entirely suitable the Family at Brightwater saw fit to leave a lot of trivial detail work to the elder daughter, in the same way that he and Marygold left such stuff to Dorothy of Smith, the Magician of Rank mulled over the question. Not for the first, nor yet for the thousandth time. If he had the answer to that question, he would have the secret to all the mysteries. But seeing as how he didn't have, and no number of Formalisms & Transformations tried by him or any of the other Magicians of Rank would yield it up, there was little point in fretting over it. And so he smiled and spread his hands to indicate he was as puzzled by it all as Marygold was.

"There is always a Responsible—though not always of Brightwater," mused the Queen, leaning her chin on her hand. "And there always has been, so far as I know . . . and always she has had some special place. And yet she is not a Granny, and not a Magician, and not a Magician of Rank . . . And if you try to talk about it when you're little, the Grannys tell you it's not polite and shush you right up." She stared up at the ceiling, high above her head, and concluded: "I wonder how it *works?"*

"On Earth," grumbled the King, "people did not understand

science—and we know . . . uh . . . where that led. Here, we do not understand magic. And who's to say it won't lead to the same place?"

Lincoln Parradyne Smith was taken aback; it was a very perceptive thing to say, and sounded as odd in his sovereign's mouth as a bray would have. He hadn't thought the man had it in him.

"Nicely put, Sire," he said with great formality, bowing low. "Nicely put."

CHAPTER 15

SILVERWEB OF MCDANIELS found her refuge, finally, high up in the Castle, at the end of a tiny passage down which two people couldn't have walked side by side. It was a room smaller than the one in which the Castle linens were stored, but it was big enough for her purpose and clearly not wanted by anybody else; the dust and the cobwebs lay thick enough to show that it got no attention but the yearly spring cleaning, and the one window was so dirty that she could see nothing through it but a weak and murky light even at high noon.

She began by throwing out everything that was in the small space, carrying what was worth saving into the Castle attics—a simple task, since they opened on the passage, and there was no lugging up and down stairs to be done—and putting all the rest down the garbage chute on the floor below. There wasn't much to dispose of. A narrow bedstead with neither spring nor mattress nor hangings, not even a straw tick; a wardrobe that couldn't of held more than a half dozen garments, with a tarnished mirror on its single door that gave her back a crazed wavery image of herself; one low rocker, in need of polish but worth keeping; a threadbare rug the size of a bath towel and rank with mildew; and a pair of curtains that fell apart in her hands when she touched them—how long they had hung there she didn't know, but it had to of been many years.

When the room was empty she put on one of the coveralls the servingmaids used for heavy cleaning, and wrapped a kerchief round her hair. She scrubbed the floors first, till the boards had a soft gray gloss and were satiny to the hand; they had never been varnished. She scoured the walls and ceiling, stripping away from the wall where the bed had been an ancient paper that might of been roses once upon a time. And when she had the wood bare, broad boards vertical up the walls and then crossing the low ceiling, she rubbed into it a sweet oil made from the crushed fruit of a desert bush. It took days, but when she had it done the room had a faint delicate odor that was nothing you could put a name to; she liked it because it made her think of early morning, or high grasses after a soaking rain. The doors and moldings, inside and out, got the same treatment, and it was thorough. Silverweb was as strong as any average man her own age, and she put her sturdy muscles to good use with the rags and oil.

There was the window. She made it clean, till the old glass sparkled with an almost imperceptible tint of yellow, and looked out. If she looked down she could see all the way to the coast, and even make out the white curl of low breakers against the sand. But looking out, she saw only the Holy One's bright clear sky, and that was as she wished it to be. Trees, rooftops, mountains—any of those would have been a distraction, and Silverweb wanted no distractions.

Then came the very last thing. She worked on a table in the attics, finding her materials in broken vases and cracked or chipped glass things of all kinds. There were punchbowls there, and oval plates with nests for stuffed eggs, pitchers meant to hold tea for twenty or more, great glass trays for passing sandwiches, and as in any good Ozark household there was a bin of glass shards and chips kept for the principle of thrift and because the tadlings liked to use them for playing house. The leading was the only thing she lacked, and she found it easily enough in the town.

She cut and fit the pieces carefully, measuring and remeasuring, checking after each added bit to be certain there was no mistake; and when she was through she was flushed with pleasure. For her labors she had a pane of glass that fit into her single window, formed of every shade of yellow, from the palest lemon to a deep color that almost lapsed into orange. She set it firmly into the window frame, over the old glass, and made it secure, and she had perfection. In the early morning and all through the day till midafternoon the air in the room was golden, glorious yellow; then as the sun grew lower it took on a paler tint, the light of afternoons in winter when the lamps are on but the curtains are still open. Still a golden light, though it lacked the splendor of the morning.

"It is my place," she said when everything was ready and she stood looking round her. "*My* place." Her brothers would not think to come here, nor be interested if they did. There was nothing here for them.

Grateful, overwhelmed at the mercy the room offered her, Silverweb of McDaniels dropped to her knees on the bare gray-white floor, raised her eyes to the flood of golden light, and folded her hands—not in the prim steepling of the Reverend and the Grannys and the Solemn Service, but clasped together and round one another as if something beyond price were sheltering inside them.

Her lips moved, but she made no sound; the words were not intended for any human ear.

> *Holy One,*
> *Hail and all hail!*
> *Hosannah!*
> *Hosannah, glory in the highest!*
> *Allelulia!*
> *Amen.*

The prayer moved through her; as it was repeated again and again it was no longer Silverweb praying the words, but the words praying her. Love unbearable caught her up and surged in her, a touch that carried bliss for which no words would ever be adequate, and she became a part of the golden light. She was a crystal that rang to the touch of a Thing unseen but more real than the floor under her knees, a crystal burning in a constant fire that would one day—the Holy One grant her that grace!—burn away every last flaw and let the light pour through her as it poured through her window. And she, Silverweb, would disappear.

Oh, the flesh of her might move around, it would carry her through days and speak the necessary phrases and lie in a foolish bed at night and put food and drink into its mouth—but *she*, the real Silverweb of McDaniels, would not be there. She would be caught unto the One and radiating the glory of the universe; that would be her privilege and her life.

Soon there was only the one word left, and even her lips ceased to move. Looking at her, you might have thought she was not breathing, but she was. Her breath was the Allelulia! and all the rhythms of her blood and breath had set themselves to its measure, and she was aware of nothing else.

Anne of Brightwater knew that her daughter was occupied deeply by some project. Every day Silverweb ate breakfast with her family at Castle McDaniels, did the chores set her with her usual serene efficiency, reappeared again at supper—rarely at the noon dinner, but always at supper—read with them in the evenings, or sang for them in the clear strong voice that was the backbone of the Reverend's choir. Whatever was asked of her she did willingly, while the eight brothers tried in vain to shake her calm and she smiled at them. She would peel pan after pan of vegetables; given a basket, she'd go off and gather fruit or nuts; she would milk goats and bring the pails back brimming, not a drop spilled; hand the girl a pile of the most boring sort of stuff to mend—her brothers' stockings, or the heavy linen napkins and pillowslips—Silverweb took up her needle, found a chair, and shortly the work was done. She complained never, argued rarely, and spoke only when she was spoken to.

It was unnatural, and Anne knew it. No healthy young woman of sixteen, soon to be seventeen, behaved like that. She should have fussed, the way chores had been loaded on her in the last few weeks, testing for some response; she should of been complaining bitterly—and with justification. The Castle had servingmaids in abundance, and Silverweb had a mind glittering in its brilliance, a mind that had terrified the Grannys and impressed whatever crevice it was in the computers that set her lessons and graded them once she outgrew Granny School. Silverweb had finished every course offered, before her twelfth birthday; and someone—a human someone—had come to apologize. They were extremely sorry, he told Anne of Brightwater and Silverweb's father, Stewart Crain McDaniels the 6th, but there was nothing left to teach the girl.

"Youall could of course bring in a human teacher," the man had said, hesitantly, almost as if there were something impolite in the suggestion. "There are specialists that know many things we've never seen any need to include in the programs . . ."

Stewart Crain had been firm in his response; Silverweb knew far too much already to suit him. A young woman that'd turned down four young men he'd offered her for husband, one after another, with the same fool reason—she didn't "choose" to marry? A young woman that'd run away from home to try to join Responsible of Brightwater on her Quest, and had to be sent clear to Castle Airy for the three Grannys there to punish? He'd not have her taught more things she might use as warp or woof for her stubborn and always unexpected behavior; oh, no. He sent the man away, thanking him brusquely for his concern, and that was the end of it. Thereafter, Silverweb relied on the libraries.

But now she did not do even that. When she first began disappearing, slipping away as soon as the mountains of household and garden tasks set her were finished, showing up again only when her absence would be remarked upon, the libraries had been Anne's first thought. After all, through the brief days of the Jubilee, while the other young ones spent their time at the plays and the fairs, Silverweb had moved inflexible between their rooms and the libraries of Brightwater. But she had not found her daughter among the books. Not in the Castle's own very respectable room of volumes and microfiches; not in the town library with its banks of machines making available all the books of the world and facsimiles of some from Old Earth; not in the ample and specialized library of the Reverend.

And then she had had a thought that she almost dared not entertain: was it possible Silverweb was slipping away to meet some young man? Anne would of been obliged to make a show of stern disapproval for that, but in her heart she'd of been overjoyed. A girl not married at Silverweb's age, and showing no sign of any interest in the state, was a rare creature on Ozark. Anne didn't mind having a rare creature about, precisely, but she'd rather have had grandchildren, and the boys were still far too young to provide them.

She set the servingmaids, a few that she knew to be trustworthy, to watching, then. And they came back with just the news she'd feared. There was not, so far as any of them could find out, a young man in the picture.

At last, when she'd made up her mind to confront Silverweb and demand an explanation—an awkward thing at her age, and with her behavior so sickeningly perfect that it allowed no smallest chink for objection—the mystery was solved for her. Among the Castle staff there was a very old woman, well into her nineties, that'd been there all her life, born in the bedroom of her mother, also a McDaniels servingmaid. She was not expected to do anything now but sit and rock; though she insisted she could still outwork any woman in the Castle, she made no attempt to prove it.

Joan of Smith came to Anne's workroom to tell her, leaning on the cane she swore she didn't need—and would *not* have needed if she'd allowed modern magic to help her. She had an awesome stubbornness.

"I know where the young miss has been getting herself to, my lady," said Joan of Smith. "A long walk it was for me, but I checked before I came—and sure enough, there she was."

Anne stood up, heedless of the yarns slipping off her lap onto the rug, asking, "Well, *where?* Not in this Castle, surely!"

"Yes, indeed," said Joan. "Right here in this Castle. She's not a child to go gallivanting, not Miss Silverweb."

"But we looked everywhere—we even sent staff up to the attics, and they found her there once or twice fooling with bits of glass, but not after that . . . We looked this Castle up, down, and sideways!"

"Missus," said Joan of Smith, "there's a place you didn't look. I've been here all my life, and I've seen it only once or twice, and would of had no idea what it was intended for. But my mother'd heard of it from her mother . . . My lady, there's a room beyond the attics."

"Joan!" Anne of Brightwater settled the old lady into a chair and saw her comfortable, fussing over her till she was sure the pillows at her back were as she liked them, and talking the whole time. "I have not been here all my life, for sure, but I've been here a considerable number of years, and I have been over every inch of this Castle. There's no room beyond the attics—there's no 'beyond the attics' at all!"

"Oh, yes, Missus, there is. A few of the maids know of it, those as are truly honest about their work; they clean it once a year. But it never entered their heads the young miss'd go there, seeing as how they're scared to death of the place their own selves. Come cleaning time, they draw lots for who'll do the job, and it's always *two* of 'em, and garlic in both their pockets. Ninnies!"

"Well!" Anne sank down in a chair and pulled it close to Joan's, whose ears were no longer what they had been. "So there's a secret room in my Castle, and everybody knows about it but me, is there? You don't seem to be afraid of it, Joan of Smith . . . You know something the others don't?"

"As I said, Missus, *I* heard of it from my mother, that heard of it from hers. In my Grandmother's day—that'd be more than a hundred and fifty years back, mind—the Magicians were few and the Magicians of Rank even fewer. It wasn't like it is today, ma'am. Times there were when a Magician of Rank couldn't come when you sent for him, good will or not—even such a one can't be in two places at once, and it was a matter of choosing among the emergencies which was the worst. That left only the Grannys—and *they* were not so many in those days, either!—to do all the healing. And so it would sometimes come about that there'd be somebody taken sick as was *catching,* and it something the Granny couldn't manage, and might could be days before anyone from the higher ranks could come to the Castle. And a person like that, they put 'em up in the room back beyond the attics, with just a Granny to nurse them—or sometimes just a willing woman, if no Granny was to hand either. And there they stayed, for so long as was needful. It's a *tiny* bit of a room, Missus. Just a *tiny* one!"

"And you've been up there?" marveled Anne, staring at the aged woman with little but a quaver left for a voice, all bones and wrinkles, and a fine trembling to both her hands if she didn't keep them clutched tight on her cane. "Up to the *attics?*"

"I didn't care to disappoint you, Missus," said Joan. "If the room'd shown no signs of anybody being there, you see, I'd of said nothing. Hate to spoil the only thing that gives the young females on the staff any pleasure at spring cleaning. So I checked, first."

"Law!" said Anne of Brightwater. "Well, I thank you . . . And what's she got up there? A lovers' bower? A . . . I don't have any guesses, Joan; what is it? A place to get away from her brothers, that's clear, and nobody could fault her for *that*. But is there more to it?"

"You'd best go see for your own self, dear lady," said the old woman, giving a wave of the cane. "That'd be the way."

"I'm willing; tell me how to get there."

"Go all through the attics, to the furthest one, yonder on the east tower . . ."

"Yes?"

"There you'll find a old blanket tacked up on the wall. Looks like somebody just put it there to cover might could be a cracked place, or a stain where rain'd got in. Tacked just at the top corners, it is. You pull that aside, and back of it you'll find a kindly hall about wide enough for one person with her elbows pulled in real careful. And the room's at the end of that."

"I've seen that old blanket!" Anne declared. "I never thought . . . Isn't there a trunk pushed up against it?"

"Used to be. But not this moment. I expect Miss Silverweb shoves that trunk back there when she comes downstairs."

"Do the boys know about this room?"

The old lady chuckled. "Think the women as keep this Castle are pure fools, Missus?" she demanded. "*No* male person—less he was too sick to know where he was!—has ever known about that room. Bad enough that people have died in there, and people laid moaning while they waited for help. Bad enough with all the bedclothes having to be carried out and burned out behind the stables, right down to the mattress—*none* of us had ary interest, my lady, in little boys as would think it fearsome fun to wrap up in bedsheets and hide in the old wardrobe in there, and jump out at you when you went in to clear away the dust! No, no; the boys have no least notion."

"Then how did Silverweb find out, when even I don't know?"

"Ah, Missus," said Joan of Smith, "I'll not speak to that question. What a woman can do provided she's driven sufficiently—now that's been a wonder since the beginning of time. Every inch, as you put it, the youngun must of searched—just every inch! And not to be fooled by holes with a blanket hung over 'em, either. As I said—you'd best see for yourself."

Anne stood up and hesitated, half afraid to go see what her tall grave daughter was up to, wholly afraid not to, and Joan of Smith said, "The reason for that blanket and trunk, you see, that was so as nobody'd wander into there by mistake and catch whatever it was the person sick there had at the time. You see how that would be."

Anne saw. "You sit here and rest," she told Joan, "just as long as you fancy it. Up to the attics, at your age, and all those stairs! I'd fuss at you if I had the time, Joan of Smith, I declare I would—but I'm going up to see what's to be seen, before she comes down."

"That's wise," said the other. "And I can climb as many stairs as you can, or any other soul in this Castle, you keep that in mind, ma'am! I'm no invalid, and I'll be climbing stairs here when—"

Anne knew from experience that this would go on a long time before the old lady wound down at last and was satisfied with her disclaimers. She leaned over and patted the frail hands holding the battered cane—absolutely, she must be made to have a new one, if they had to send in the Grannys to make her give in to the change, this one was falling to pieces and would give her a broken hip one of these days!—and she slipped out and left her still at it, and headed for the eastmost attic.

The room was there; she found it easily enough. She found her daughter, too. Three knocks she made at the door, clucking her tongue at the sheen it had—she knew how many coats of polish that meant, and how much rubbing, and the servingmaids had never in a million years done *that,* or her name wasn't Anne of Brightwater—and there'd been no answer. She'd hesitated; a person of Silverweb's age had a right to her privacy, and clearly this was a very private place. Then her mother's concern had triumphed over her manners and she'd turned the knob and stepped inside, saying smartly, "Silverweb?" so the girl couldn't claim she'd been sneaking up on her.

It wouldn't have mattered if she'd come in with a brass band; she saw that at once. She went forward to where her daughter was kneeling, tiptoeing for no reason that she understood, and said the name again. Silverweb neither saw her nor heard her. Not at all.

Anne ran, then. Down the tiny hall, scraping her arm painfully on its walls in her panic, through all the attics one after another, down the flights of stairs—and came to a full stop. At the bottom of the first staircase, Joan of Smith stood waiting for her; that meant three flights the old lady had toiled up *again* this day. She would be weary and aching tonight, and Anne thought distractedly that she had to remember to have someone see to her.

"Found her, did you?"

"Yes, I did—and I don't like it!"

"Thought you wouldn't, child; that's why I'm here."

"What will I *do?*" She knew she looked foolish, wringing her hands and rubbing at her scraped arm—if she hadn't Joan would never have called her "child"—but she didn't care. She was frightened.

"Do? You can leave her be," said Joan. "You're Missus of this Castle, and a fine lady, as it's a privilege to serve under. You're mother of nine, and my womb never quickened—Aye, I'll go virgin to my grave, if you want to know the truth of it! Never could bear the idea of a man . . . doing as they do. But I have been walking this earth more years than you and all your babes combined, and I know a thing or two. Anne of Brightwater—leave her be."

Anne leaned against the wall, too weak suddenly to support herself.

"Oh, Joan," she wailed, "it's not natural! You know what it is, don't you? You saw her—you know what it is?"

"*Rap*ture, it's called," said Joan calmly. "And ecstasy, sometimes. I do believe rapture has a better sound to it, though I've always thought both were ugly words."

"And you say leave her be?"

"I do."

"I'll talk to the Reverend!"

"Do that, and he'll drive her away," came the warning. "She would be just as satisfied with a bare cave in the desert, or a hut out in the Wilderness Lands, as she is with that room up there. You care to keep her home, you say nothing at all to the Reverend. I've seen him, how he looks sharp at her when she sings in the choir on Sundys; he's suspicious already, and a word from you about this would be the last dot on the *i*. He wouldn't tolerate it."

"But what will become of her? What will she do, where will she go? On Earth she could have gone into what they called a convent, lived in a bare cell and prayed all the days of her life back of bars if she chose to—we've no such things here! She will be so terribly alone!"

Joan of Smith shook her head firmly, and then again.

"Oh, no!" she said. "There's nothing of this world as Miss Silverweb wants or needs, Missus, and nothing she lacks. She has the Love of Loves, beside which all else is no more, they say, than dry husks and ashes. Such things happen for a purpose, and hers will be clear in time—we will know, and the Twelve Gates grant these eyes live to see it!—we will know what that purpose is. Until then, there are two things to do."

"And they are?"

"Wait, in patience and in humility, if you'll pardon my using the word, as has no right. That's one. And give her hard work aplenty. Chores! To make a balance. Rapture's all very well, but madness lies just the other side of it. See to it she's in the kitchen and the garden and the orchards, make her *sweat,* to tie her safely to this earth in its *wholesome* parts. You've been doing that, I've had my eye on you; your woman's knowing, your mother's knowing, has been directing you as proper as you could be directed. See you don't stop that, now—I'd make it harder on 'er, were I you."

Anne nodded, numb to the core. It was right—every word of it—though how the old creature knew it she couldn't imagine. Perhaps it was the fabled wisdom of age, perhaps it was an experience Joan of Smith didn't care to speak of or had forgotten entirely . . . but it had the ring of rightness. Nevertheless, she was blind with anger. That this should happen to her daughter! All that blond ripeness, the heavy braids always wound in their figure eight like a crown! She had seen the pale down on Silverweb's breasts, and the way they strained at the fabric over them, and the long line of spine when she bent to weeding. And those good hips, meant for babies, designed for them! The waste of it, the utter heartbreaking waste . . . Anne could have cursed the deity that had stolen away her only daughter and denied the motherhood that daughter was fashioned for in every last detail.

Except the spirit. The spirit was—

"Warped!" she said aloud, defying the Powers to do their worst. And then, "Maybe she will grow out of it."

"That happens sometimes," said the old woman. "Might could be."

But Anne of Brightwater had seen her daughter's face, and she knew she spoke a lie, and that Joan of Smith humored her in it. Silverweb would not, would never, grow out of it, and the time would come when it would ripen to a terrible purpose that had nothing at all to do with the ripeness of the flesh, and there was no least thing she could do to stop it, or slow it, or turn it aside. It was like so many other things—it was to be endured.

CHAPTER 16

RESPONSIBLE'S LIST OF tasks had been reduced considerably by the turn of events. The project for spreading the Purdy girls round the Kingdoms to break the hold of the "you can't do anything right because you're a Purdy" idea would have to be postponed; at the moment, Brightwater had no kind of relationship with Castle Purdy to even suggest such a thing. She could also draw a firm line through the item that instructed her to see to the Arkansaw feuds; Farsons, Guthries, and Purdys could now go at one another with broadswords and bludgeons, free from all interference—the advantages of sovereignty. The matter of holding a day of celebration in honor of the alleged Skerry sighting had become irrelevant, even if there really had been a Skerry. The penalty for failing to celebrate was bad luck, and that had already arrived in ample measure. And the superstition at Castle Wommack?

Responsible thought about that one awhile. No question about it, she would of welcomed any sort of excuse to visit Castle Wommack, seeing as how that was where Lewis Motley

Wommack the 33rd was to be found. Her sleep was filled with dreams of him, far too vivid to be restful, and she woke from them drenched as she had risen from his arms. Once awake, she guarded her mind rigorously, stamping out any thought of him the same way she'd have stamped out fire in dry grass, but her nights were a scandal. The advantage, of course, was that they required no effort on his part and only she was troubled by them; she would heartily have enjoyed a chance to let him share the occasions.

But the Wommacks had done no more to save the Confederation than any of the other Families had, and had left Castle Brightwater as rapidly as everybody else, and they'd left no invitations behind them. While the Confederation stood, she'd felt comfortable touring the Castles; now, for all she knew, they'd bar their gates against her and shout Spells. She'd best leave Castle Wommack alone.

Some of the Families had been prompt in their actions, praise the Gates. Castles McDaniels, Clark, and Airy had sent bids for alliance, obviously written as fast as Family meetings could be held, votes taken, and Mules saddled to fly the documents to Brightwater. Castle Motley had sent its own Magician of Rank, Shawn Merryweather Lewis the 7th, to let Brightwater know that Castles Motley and Lewis would remain allied with Brightwater for so long as it was possible to do so.

She looked up at the map above her desk; the tiny continent of Mizzurah had all of Arkansaw between it and Brightwater, and looked more like an island off Arkansaw's coast than a nation of two Kingdoms. It was brave of Lewis and Motley to send the message, and a bit of good fortune for them that they had a Magician of Rank to SNAP it on to Brightwater; but they were very isolated now, just the same. When their supplies began to dwindle, which wouldn't be all that long a time off, she was reasonably sure they'd have no choice but to turn to Arkansaw for help—and that would be the end of their ties to Brightwater.

There'd been no word from Castle Smith, now surrounded by Brightwater allies but only a brief flight away from Castle Guthrie, just across the narrow channel between Oklahomah and Arkansaw. Presumably they were debating their options . . . or might could be Delldon Mallard Smith was really fool enough to think he could go it entirely alone.

She turned back to her list, it being pleasanter food for

thought than the blamed Smiths. There was the question of whether Una of Clark had acted alone in using magic against Brightwater to scuttle the Jubilee—she'd waste *no* time on that one! The Jubilee, and all that went with it, was over, and she intended to put it behind her, thought *and* deed, like any dead and dishonored thing.

But there was one task that had now become not just one more promise, one more duty postponed, but a matter of urgent necessity. She had given the Gentles her word. Whatever happened to the Confederation of Continents, stand or fall, they would not be involved in the results. For thirty thousand years of recorded history they had lived in the caves of Arkansaw; they had granted the surface of the land without stint or hesitation to the humans, by treaties that guaranteed them the right to go on with their own lives as they always had. And now they were smack in the middle of the feuds. Might could be the Farsons and the Guthries, and the Purdys following along, would hold to the treaties for the sake of simple decency; she would have liked to think so. Might could be, on the other hand, they'd take the position that the old treaties were Confederation agreements and no longer bound them. The Gentles would of been safer, all in all, at the hands of the Travellers, obsessed as they were with righteousness. No telling *what* the Arkansaw Families might do . . .

It was going to be a curious situation, grant that right off. The Granny had been discussing it that morning at the breakfast table, and Granny Hazelbide had laid it out for the rest of them with aboslute accuracy.

"It'd be one thing," she'd said, glaring over the top of her coffee cup, "if the very minute of First Landing we'd divided this world up twelve ways and sent everybody off to their own homeplaces and stayed that way since. That'd be *one* thing! As it is, that is *not* what we have on our platter, not in any degree whatsoever. We're all scrambled and mixed and conglomerated . . . why, there's not a place on Ozark that's not got folks all settled in from every one of the Twelve Families!"

"Travellers excepted, might could be," said Granny Gableframe. "I misdoubt there's anybody on Tinaseeh but Travellers, Farsons, and Purdys—maybe a Guthrie or two. No more."

"Tch!" went Ruth of Motley. "That's not even decent."

"If we'd gone the way Granny Hazelbide was mentioning," Jonathan Cardwell Brightwater pointed out, "we'd of been inbred worse than the goats long before this."

"Jonathan Cardwell! Such talk!"

"May not be elegant, m'dear, but it's accurate," he answered her, and bent to kiss her cheek. "It's a right good thing the Families had sense enough to mix it up, and plenty of other family lines represented among them at the beginning."

"So it is," said Granny Hazelbide, "so it is. But it leads to a pure *mess* now. Take Brightwater, seeing it's so handy—is there any Family we don't have among the folks living here, Responsible?"

"No Travellers," she said. "Nary a one."

"Well, they don't count anyway. If they lived here they'd have to worry all the time about their precious souls, what with our wicked electric lights and our evil lizzies and far on into the night. You can't count them."

"Everybody else, though," Responsible agreed, "we have passels of. I know what you mean, and I don't know precisely how they'll do. Say you're a family with Smiths in all directions, living here in Brightwater, then what? That make Delldon Mallard your King, or not?"

"It has always been true," said Patience of Clark gravely, "that a woman gone to live in the house of a man considered herself a part of *his* family, from that time on, or went back to her own place. And the same for a man."

"True," said Thorn of Guthrie. "But that was when it didn't matter, if you follow me. That was when we were all one Confederation. There might be squabbles among us, and some Families more annoying than others, the way one of the tadlings in a house'll be more bothersome than all the rest put together. But in the ways that mattered, we were all *one*."

"Bless my stars," muttered Granny Hazelbide, "if Thorn's not begun to learn politics in her old age! Never thought I'd see the day."

Thorn of Guthrie curled her perfect lips and looked scornful, and allowed as how a question that related to the real world was worth noticing and she wasn't such a poor stick she *couldn't* notice it, thank you very much.

"It's a skein that'll be a long time unwinding," observed Patience of Clark. "I'm not all that comfortable about it."

"*Nor* me, child," said Granny Gableframe. "I've got a feeling in my bones."

"People will have to make up their minds, I suppose," said

Jubal Brooks. "Do they go by lines drawn on a map, when it comes to their loyalties, or do they go by blood? And say you're a Farson man married to a McDaniels, and the both of you living in Kingdom Motley—if you *did* want to go back to your own kind, which one'd take precedence? Farson or McDaniels? And the children, would they want to go or would they consider theirselves Motleys by having been born there?"

"It's Old Earth all over again," said Granny Hazelbide grimly. "Next thing you know we'll have people starving one side of a line that doesn't exist, and people fat and sleek on the other, burning their garbage. I can just see it coming. Just see and *hear* it coming!"

"This world once more," Granny Gableframe declaimed, "and then there'll be fireworks." Whatever that might mean.

It had put something of a pall on breakfast.

And thinking now, musing over the Families, scrambled or not, Responsible felt a good deal less than comfortable herself. She was *worried* about the Gentles.

Nothing she knew of the Guthries, for all that they were her close kin, led her to be optimistic about their behavior; they were sharp of wit, but they were by and large outrageous. The Farsons had a kind of elegant devious charm that was more dangerous than any of the right out front stupidities the Smiths had carried through. And the Purdys! Prejudice or not, you could *not* trust the Purdys. They didn't even trust one another. And there sat the Gentles, relying on the sworn word of Responsible of Brightwater, completely surrounded on all sides by the three of them. And not knowing, might could be, that anything had changed.

Her mind was made up. Anything that might come up here at Brightwater for sure didn't require *her* attention; there was a Magician of Rank and two Grannys under this roof. Already, she was pleased to remember, the Grannys had settled the Bridgewraith, and with the two of them working together it had taken hardly any time at all. She would go this very night, no more excuses, soon as it was dark enough to travel easily, and she'd see the warding of the Gentles. The supplies she'd gathered that night Lewis Motley Wommack had made such a sorry showing trying to follow her were adequate for the task, if she was. It was near on nine o'clock this minute; if she planned to see to the matter tonight, and for sure she did, it would take her all the rest of the day and a hard push to get ready in time. Starting with locking her door and sending down word that she was to be left alone and not bothered even for meals. That would give the Family something else to talk about at the table, at least.

Two hours later, purged of her breakfast—and thank the Twelve Corners the conversation that morning hadn't been the kind that made for a good appetite—and as clean as the three ritual baths could make her, her skin sore from the crushed herbs, she sat in her blue rocker and considered the problem. It was a nice one, and the more she thought about it the more complicated it became.

How, precisely, did you accomplish a task that could only be done by magic, on behalf of a large population that considered magic to be not only barbarous and primitive but unspeakably evil? How did you go about keeping a promise that had been a lie to begin with, on behalf of a race that so far as anyone had been able to determine was not capable of lying? For she had sworn she'd use no magic, when the complaint was made to her. And no way did she dare call in anyone for advice; as Granny Hazelbide would have said, she had a funny feeling.

She went over and pushed the computer access numbers for POPULATIONS, INDIGENOUS, which produced three entries: SKERRYS, GENTLES, MULES. That always made her nervous, finding the MULES on the list, but the computers were very firm about it. From among the set she chose GENTLES, and requested a full data display. The comset made none of its usual crotchety noises; the reduction of the broadcast area to one small Kingdom had improved its performance enormously. It hummed softly, and gave her what she asked for:

GENTLES, INDIGENOUS POPULATION OF PLANET OZARK—HUMANOID
ESTIMATED NUMBER OF YEARS ON PLANET, FIFTY THOUSAND
ESTIMATED NUMBER OF INDIVIDUALS, ELEVEN THOUSAND (CAUTION, THIS FIGURE BASED ON INADEQUATE DATA)
LOCATION: CAVES UNDER WILDERNESS LANDS OF CONTINENT ARKANSAW, BOUNDED ON

NORTH BY KINGDOM PURDY, ON EAST BY KINGDOM GUTHRIE, ON WEST BY KINGDOM FARSON, ON SOUTH BY OCEAN OF STORMS (NOTE NO EVIDENCE AREA INHABITED BY GENTLES EXTENDS TO OCEAN, DATA INSUFFICIENT)
PHYSICAL DESCRIPTION: MALES AND FEMALES, APPROX THREE FEET TALL, WHITE FUR ON ALL BODY SURFACES, EYES DARK PURPLE ON YELLOW, FELINE PUPILS PRESUMABLY FOR SEEING IN DARKNESS OF CAVES
PHYSICAL STRENGTH ONE FOURTH HUMAN APPROX (CAUTION, DATA INADEQUATE)
INTELLIGENCE PRESUMED EQUAL TO HUMAN (CAUTION, DATA INADEQUATE)
PSIBILITIES UNKNOWN
GOVERNMENT: OLIGARCHY OF THREE ANCIENT FAMILIES
RELIGION UNKNOWN
CUSTOMS UNKNOWN
HISTORY: CEDED ARKANSAW SURFACE TO HUMANS BY TREATY ON SETTLEMENT
(CAUTION, REPEAT CAUTION—GENTLES CONSIDER ALL MAGIC SINFUL, HAVE BEEN KNOWN TO SUICIDE FOR "DISHONOR OF MAGIC"—APPROACH WITH CARE)
DATES OF CONTACT: NOVEMBER 11 2129; APRIL 4 . . .

The list went on, showing some sixty-odd contacts in one thousand years—those would be the reported ones, and there'd be twice as many unreported, she didn't doubt—and then there were a few names with a handful of data attached to each, and the display winked out.

It was a pitiful fragment of knowledge to have about a race you shared a planet with. On the other hand, it was a tribute, after a fashion, to the Ozarkers. They'd made no attempt to investigate the Gentles, as they'd made none to seek out the Skerrys, about whom far less was known. If there was one thing an Ozarker did understand, it was a request for privacy.

Responsible prayed rarely. She had an idea that she ought

to pray more often, but she kept forgetting. This, however, was a situation where prayer was indicated forcibly enough to override even her desire not to be beholden. She found herself faced with the fact that if she did not use magic to protect the Gentles they might well be destroyed by the misbehavior of the Families of Arkansaw—not that they'd harm them on purpose, she wasn't ready to consider any such thing as that, but that in the course of tearing around the continent disputing with one *another* they were almost guaranteed to grow careless of what they tore up and who got discommoded in the process. And if she did use magic, and the Gentles should discover that she had, the whole population might well feel obligated to ritual suicide. Talk of being between a rock and a hard place! She prayed, and she prayed from the heart, and she prayed at length, though she didn't kneel; the idea that the Holy One had any special admiration for one posture over another, so firmly held to by the Reverends, struck her as ridiculous. The point was the praying, not how your legs were bent, nor how uncomfortable you could manage to get.

When that was done, she sighed, wishing she felt more confident and all charged with divine fire or some such, and not feeling that way at all, and she began taking things from her magic-chest. She drew out the gown of fine lawn and pulled it through the golden ring that fit her little finger; it went through without hindrance or snag, and she slipped it over her head. Her hair went into a single long braid down her back, bound by a clasp handed down from one Responsible to another since First Landing; she was always terrified she'd lose the fool thing and bring on some unspecified catastrophe, but so far she'd hung on to it. Next there were the shammybags that held the holy sands, to be hung from the narrow white belt that went round her waist, and the flagons of sacred springwater, bound together on a cord braided of her own hair and fastened to that same belt. A pouch of gailherb hung round her neck and slipped between her breasts to be warmed. On her bare feet went low boots of Muleskin made soft as velvet; over all, a hooded cloak of the same supple stuff. And she was ready.

She went lightly equipped, by Granny standards. They'd of thrown in two saddlebags of herbs, and put amulets and talismans all over her, and hung strings of garlic and preserved lilac from one end of Sterling to the other; there'd of been feathers and asafetida and probably conjure poppets . . .

Responsible grinned. By Granny standards she was off to a war naked and barefoot and blindfolded. She'd make very sure neither one of them caught sight of her, prowling the Castle in the night as was their habit. The thing was, the less of that truck she had on her person, the less likely she was to be spotted and seen to be engaged in magic if she had the awful fortune to be seen by one of the Gentles. And she'd not have used it anyway; this was a task requiring Formalisms & Transformations, not dolls and herbs and doodads.

As the sun started going down she began to get hungry, but that was to be expected. She ignored her stomach, and watched the line of Troublesome's mountain out through her window. When the sun was tucked exactly in the notch that marked the highest ridge, it would be time for her to go.

And what, she wondered idly, would Lewis Motley Wommack the 33rd have had to say if he'd seen her SNAP from her own windowsill without benefit of a Mule?

Law, there she *was,* thinking of him again! She clicked her tongue like a Granny, disgusted with herself. Sure enough, it had been a kind of peace, a kind of wondrous *rest,* being with someone whose mind she could share as easily as she shared ordinary speech with everybody else. Like moving around in a place of columns and soft wind and— She brought herself up short. If there'd been words for what it was like, it wouldn't have been what it was; she was just translating perceptions that had no counterpart into perceptions there were names for, and a mighty poor job she was doing of it. Nothing in the dictionary, so far as she knew, would cover an endless space confined in a finite one, nor label for her tongue a corner that you could not go round because it came back upon itself... She rubbed absently at the aching place just above her right eyebrow, that spot back of which the Immensity began, a golden Immensity swept by—

"Responsible of Brightwater, *stop it! Now!*" she said aloud, sharp as she knew how. A fine shape she'd be in for what lay ahead of her if she went on like this! Think of Una of Clark, rotten to the soul with the sickness of Romantic Love, and how she'd despised her, taunted her, for that! Then think of *her,* Responsible of Brightwater, mooning here at her window over this man she'd lain with twice, and neither time blessed by either Reverend or custom... Was she any better than poor Una?

It was just that until he came she had thought there was nobody else like her in all the world. It was a kind of loneliness that was not eased by sharing mindspeech with a Mule, nor what the Magicians of Rank thought passed for mindspeech. And he had eased it, unbraided her mind for her where the knots were tightest and most tangled . . .

Nevertheless, Responsible, there was such a thing as seemliness.

She stepped to her window, set one foot on the sill, made certain the picture she held firmly in her mind's eye was the proper one, so she wouldn't end up in some Arkansaw goatbarn by mistake—and SNAPPED.

On Kintucky, where it was daytime, the Guardian of Castle Wommack sat at *his* desk, going over again the specifications for his Teaching Order. He was pleased with the habit the Grannys and Gilead had designed; a long gown, high-necked and full of sleeve, hem right to the ground, with no sewn waist. It was caught round by a cord, from which could hang a useful pouch or two with the things a Teacher might need to carry. The cut would be useful; when a Teacher raised her arm to point to a map or a drawing, or just to get the attention of her pupils, the sleeve, narrow at the top and tapering out the rest of its length, would be dramatic. It would form a triangle, with its point below the Teacher's knees.

Choosing the color had been difficult. The Wommack colors were sea-green and gold, but neither of those had the solemn dramatic quality he was after. Finding a color not taken by any of the other eleven Families, now that the Smiths had added purple to their traditional silver and gold and brown, had seemed impossible. Black was surely dramatic and solemn enough, and the drawings of nuns after which the Grannys had molded the costume showed that they had been black—but black was the mark of a Traveller. Lewis Motley would not have his Teachers in black. They had settled at last on a shade of blue; not the medium shade worn by the Guthries, nor yet the Lewis azure—but a deep, dark, vibrant blue that was exactly right, and belonged to no one.

The headdress, the wimple and coif that Jewel had dreaded the weight of, the Grannys had modified only a little from the drawings. They had made it one piece and all of the same blue;

it showed only the face, coming straight across the forehead just below the hairline, and falling to a point at the waist in back. And round the neck, the only ornament; a medallion with the Wommack crest, on a leather thong.

There was nobody cared to point out to him that the color of the habits was exactly the color of his eyes. And no one of the women would have mentioned to him how the cut of the gown was the same as a woman wore that achieved the rank of Magician; it was, after all, a very different cloth, and it was not subject to the requirement that it be possible to draw it without hindrance through a gold ring that fit the woman's smallest finger. The women held their peace.

Already the first habit had been sewn up. He had trusted that task only to Gilead, whose fingers were famous for their skill with the needle. A ceremony had been put together—not hastily, either, for he'd done it himself, and he'd weighed every syllable and every gesture—and Jewel had donned the habit and the headdress and dedicated her life forever to the service of the Order. She rode out on Kintucky now, with the Attendants and servingmaid, the Mules walking every inch of the journey so that the people could see them pass by in search of other learned virgins, and she would bring them back to him at Castle Wommack.

The plans for the wing where the Order would be housed were before him, and he meant them to have his full attention. Until a few moments ago they had had it. But now he shook his head in that gesture the Grannys and Jewel noticed more and more often lately, and cursed bitterly, lengthily, obscenely, pounding his fist upon the surface of his desk till the knuckles bled.

Damn her, *curse* her, oh, the devils all take her and torture her, why could she not have the decency to stay out of his *mind?* Within him, something squirmed, and he was sick with a more than physical nausea; he knew now what the price of a witch's virginity was, without asking. The question he could not answer was how long it had to go on being paid, and whether he would ever be free again.

He was an Ozarker; violence was something foreign to him. When he used his great physical strength he did it without violence, because it was a force that happened to be needed at that time and place. But so tortured was he now by this woman he had thought to make a pastime of . . . if he could have reached her at that moment, he would have killed her with his two bare hands.

If she could be killed. Could she? He did not know even that, and he laid his forehead on his arms and wept with rage and the despair of utter frustration. He might as well of wished to rid himself of his heart! No—that at least he could have torn from his breast. He did not know where the place that Responsible of Brightwater befouled within him *was*.

Responsible stood quietly in the darkness, alert for any sounds that might mean someone had seen her SNAP out of nowhere and would be coming along to demand an explanation.

It wasn't likely; she stood in a tangle of trees and briars so thick she could not see her hand when she held it up before her eyes, and in her dark cloak and boots she would be invisible unless somebody stood almost within touching distance. Still, this was no time to take chances.

Nothing but nightbirds, used to her now and gone back to their singing, and something making a soft croak in a tiny creek that was running behind her just within hearing. And that was as it should be; there was no honest reason for anybody to be lying out here in the Wilderness Lands of Arkansaw in the middle of the night. The only possibility was a party of hunters—not probable in a tangle like this, it'd make a poor campsite—or the one thing she really feared, a Gentle standing watch. Not that she knew whether they stood watch or not! Ethics, that eternal millstone round her neck; not to interfere, as promised by the treaties, meant not to observe, either; and so she knew almost nothing about the people whose peace and tranquility she had come to preserve. It was not an ideal situation in which to work, and she considered, briefly, the idea of using a Spell of Invisibility as a means of making certain that the ignorance stayed mutual.

No, she decided. Spells were not a part of Formalisms & Transformations; they fell into Granny Magic, and mixing levels was a sure way to get into a mess. She'd just be *powerfully* cautious.

Her eyes were getting used to the darkness now, as far as that was possible in this tomb of branches and thorns and roots, and she unrolled the pliofilm map, no bigger than her palm, that she was carrying in the left-hand pocket of her cloak. It showed all of Arkansaw, but that didn't concern her; the part that interested Responsible was the part that glowed dimly, barely above the level of darkness. A line, running round and bordering off the Wilderness Lands; and then eleven tiny *x*'s, marking each of the entrances to the territory that was the rightful domain of the Gentles. She must ward each and every one of those entrances.

Technically, she could of done it by Coreference alone, working with the tiny map. But equally technically, it shouldn't have been required at all. The Gentles should have been safe from the Families for all time, just because they were Ozarkers, and their word pledged. Just because of *privacy*. The Gentle T'an K'ib, coming to Responsible in the night to present her complaints, had not felt that to be any guarantee of the security of her people.

No, she would ward each entrance on the actual spot it held on the surface of the land, all eleven one at a time, SNAPPING from the first to the last. And it was time she began. The Twelve Gates grant she did not land right on top of some Gentle, out doing whatever it was that Gentles might do in the darkness, or find herself sharing a bedroll with an astonished hunter. Accuracy was not going to be a simple matter in this murk and with the limited information she had available.

Three hours it took her, moving from *x* to *x*, carefully, silently, until she had completed the circle and stood at the first one once again. Now each of the entrances was marked by the asterisk that means FORBIDDEN, laid in six overlapping lines of the holy sands. Three lines of white sand, three lines of ebony, alternating to form the six-pointed star, so: *. That should cause any ordinary citizen, happening to approach an entrance either accidentally or deliberately, to feel a sudden disinclination to move one step closer that could not be overcome by any effort of will.

And then, against not the ordinary citizen but some Magician or Magician of Rank bent upon mischief, or made curious by the repelling effect of the asterisk, she had set yet another ward at each—the double-barred arrow of the Transformations, slashed through with a diagonal line. Golden sand for the arrow; silver sand for the slash that said THE TRANSFORMATION DOES NOT APPLY and would keep anybody skilled in magic from removing her asterisks by a Deletion Transformation.

Over all the devices of sand she had poured sacred water from the flagons, so that they sank into the earth and could no longer be seen, but were bound there irrevocably by the power of the waters. Perhaps the Out-Cabal had ways of undoing such a warding—they claimed to have, bragging and threatening through the Mules, calling the Ozark magic bungling and primitive. But it was not against the Out-Cabal that she had promised to protect the Gentles, and no Ozarker, whatever his or her level or skill at magic, could undo what she had done. And nobody had seen or heard her, neither human nor Gentle. If the small people, down in their caves, had somehow heard her moving about and were to come up in the dawn to investigate the sound, they would find nothing; there would be nothing to see, nothing to sense. The wards were set *for* them; they would not be affected by their presence in the earth.

She tried to think; had she forgotten anything? There was a last step, but once it was done she would no longer have the power to make changes if anything had been neglected.

She checked it off on her fingers. Eleven entrances, eleven asterisks, eleven signs that said FORBIDDEN. Eleven entrances, eleven slashed arrows, eleven signs that said THE TRANSFORMATION DOES NOT APPLY. Twenty-two signs; water from the sacred desert spring poured over every sandgrain that formed them, the whole branded into the land. She could not see what else there could be to do, and she was tired; when she had first planned this, she had never considered that she'd have it all to do by herself alone. She'd thought a few of the Magicians of Rank would be with her, giving her aid, making it a minor effort.

That was before the discovery that a Magician of Rank could turn his magic against a Granny. It was natural that they should attack her, Responsible of Brightwater, they had reason to hate her—but harm a Granny? It was unthinkable, it was a tear in the fabric of magic, and she trusted them no longer. And she was weary, weary . . . which was no excuse for carelessness. Deliberately, she pinched the sensitive skin at the base of her thumb till she was certain beyond question that she was alert.

And then she moved to the final act that would complete her task and some left over. One flagon of water she still had, one small shammybag of sand all of silver. Carefully she prepared her Structural Index, using the little map with its glowing border and its eleven *x* points. Scrupulously, she prepared the Structural Change, specifying all eleven points of Coreference rigorously. The sharp point of her silver dagger cut it all into the earth at her feet, laid bare of its layer of thick leaves and protesting tiny crawlers and wigglers. In the glow of the map she made sure there was no character of the formal orthography not cut clean and clear and deep. The weariness moved over her in sluggish waves as she worked, and she knew there would be no SNAPPING back to her room until she had rested. She would be lucky if she had strength enough to get her over the water and onto Brightwater land, under some convenient bush that would hide her while she slept a little while.

Responsible of Brightwater stood then, and traced the double-barred arrow in the air, where it hung, quivering and golden, throbbing with its stored energy held back only by her skill, between her two hands.

"There!" she whispered, and released it.

It was a Movement Transformation; the arrow sped straight for the line that bordered the Gentles' holdings and raced round its perimeter in a blinding streak of gold, faster than the eye could follow it, out of her sight. She knew where it was going, though she could no longer watch its progress; a few seconds later she saw it again, coming back, and it plunged to the ground at her feet and winked out in the darkness.

Now, it was done. Well and truly done. Not only had she warded the entrances themselves, so that no Ozarker would be capable of passing them, but she had linked the wards one to another to make of them a *ring* of wards. If that was not invulnerable, if it did not represent a full keeping of her promise to T'an K'ib, then doing so was beyond any skill known to Ozark. It *should* be invulnerable, and no way for any Gentle ever to know that what guarded them was the magic they so abhorred. There was nothing left to give the secret away, and there was no living soul that knew what she had done, to tell them. It was done, over, accomplished.

If all her blood had been drawn from her veins she could not have been more weak, but she must get safely off Arkansaw before she let herself rest. She was aware that she shivered in the warm summer night and that she had bitten nearly through her lower lip, forcing herself not to fall, not to close her eyes.

She SNAPPED, sorry now she had not brought a Mule, clearing the coast of Marktwain but not reaching the borders of Brightwater, and fell unconscious in a patch of brush back of a goatbarn somewhere inside McDaniels Kingdom. She was past caring if the farmer found her there before she woke.

CHAPTER 17

THE MAGICIANS OF RANK SNAPPED in one by one on their Mules, even the four from Castle Traveller, not more than half a dozen minutes apart. They made a spectacle in the courtyard of Castle Wommack in their elaborate robes of office; and the nine Mules were not your average Mule. The stablemen that led the animals off to be rubbed down and watered and fed did so with a wary eye and a delicate touch. Feisty creatures these were, and accustomed to special treatment, *in*cluding a ration of dark ale with their grain. Treated with anything less than the respect they considered their due, they'd been known to kick an unwary staffer right out a stable door with one contemptuous stroke of a back hoof. The men circled them gingerly, doing their best to stay out of range while at the same time accomplishing all the necessary attentions. The fact that the Mules were obviously hugely amused by it all didn't make it any easier.

When it was all over, and everybody safely out of the stables, the men had much to say about animals getting above theirselves, and how a whack with a two-by-four right between the ears would of done this or that one a lot of good—but they waited till the Mules were safely stalled and the stable a hundred yards behind them before they let any such talk escape them.

"Howsomever," pointed out one of the men, "I'd rather deal with the Mules than with *that* lot." And he jerked his head toward the Castle entry, with its doors thrown wide, where the nine distinguished visitors were still standing in a huddle waiting for things to begin.

"Right you are," said another. "They give me the shivers, the whole nine of 'em. And the sooner we're out of their sight the better, I say. Unless there's one of youall as fancies getting changed into a billy goat, or SNAPPED off to Castle Purdy 'cause they don't like the look of him."

"What are they doing here anyway?"

The man that had expressed the strong preference for Mules over Magicians of Rank shrugged. "Can't say," he answered, "but Lewis Motley Wommack sent for 'em. Sent an Attendant off on a Mule to Mizzurah, that's got a Magician of Rank of its own, and got him to SNAP the invitation round to all the rest."

"And they came?"

"Well, you *see* 'em there, don't you? Like a pack of fancy birds, to my mind, more'n men."

"You'd be better off to watch your mouth," said the oldest. "You know if they can hear you out here? *I* don't."

"I just don't understand why they came," the first one muttered. "Who's Lewis Motley that they should come when he calls 'em? Now, I ask you, how do you explain *that?* He's not even Master of a Castle!"

The Magicians of Rank were a tad surprised their own selves, most of them having been convinced almost to the last minute that they would ignore the whole thing. They were busy men, important men, and they had images to maintain. But when it came down to the wire, not a one had been able to resist the invitation from the young Guardian; the wording had been irresistible. He needed their help, it had said, "in a matter involving Responsible of Brightwater, a matter that can only be attended to by Magicians of Rank, and that requires the utmost secrecy." And here, only slightly embarrassed, they were.

They saw one another rarely, but that didn't keep the four from Traveller from commenting that the rest looked like a passel of females, or the passel so addressed from replying that *they* looked like a quartet of carrionhawks.

Veritas Truebreed Motley made a slight change in an ancient hymn. "How many points do you *expect,* gentlemen," he asked them, "for darkening the corner where you are?"

Feebus Timothy Traveller the 11th didn't hesitate a heartbeat.

"One *dozen,* dear colleague!" he gave it back. "One dozen exactly!"

"Darkness," added Nathan Overholt Traveller the 101st gravely, "is a prerequisite for the perception of color. If we four weren't here, you five could not be seen at all."

The two Farson brothers, Sheridan Pike the 25th and Luke Nathaniel the 19th, smiled that very limited smile that Castle Traveller allowed its residents, and moved closer to the other two. They had the solidarity that comes of fanaticism, and would be formidable if they chose to be. The other five, lacking that useful characteristic, moved uneasily away from them and pretended to be very busy discussing matters of great importance.

So it was that when Gilead of Wommack came down the steps to invite them up to the Meeting Room, she was treated to the sight of two clusters of magnificently garbed males. The Traveller contingent in its deadly black relieved only by the silver clasps that caught the folds of their robes at the shoulder. And the other five bearing the colors of their Family lines—Smith, Motley, Lewis, Guthrie, and McDaniels. But Gilead of Wommack was not interested in their costumes, not even in the Farson brothers' strange acceptance of the Traveller black instead of the red, gold, and silver that was rightfully theirs by birth. She knew more about Magicians of Rank than that—it was their hands that you watched, their clever swift fingers and their supple wrists. That was where the danger lay, and where it would of stayed if you'd dressed them in feedbags and put milkpails on their heads.

"Welcome to Castle Wommack," said Gilead briskly, determined not to appear intimidated. She'd seen them all at the aborted Jubilee, and they hadn't eaten her alive; no reason to think they would do so here under her own roof.

"Thank you, Gilead of Wommack," said Shawn Merryweather Lewis the 7th of Castle Motley, him that'd been kind enough to carry the message to the others. "We are ready to see your . . . Guardian . . . when he is ready for us—but would you remind him that we are busy men? We'd like to get on with this."

"Follow me, please," Gilead replied. "He's waiting upstairs in the Meeting Room."

"We're your guests," put in Feebus Timothy Traveller, "but there's something that must be said. This innovation—this title of 'Guardian' rather than 'Master' as custom dictates—we don't approve of it, not one of us. A Castle without Master *or* Missus; that's not proper, Gilead. Granny Leeward has asked that we express her objections in the strongest terms, and we concur."

Gilead was not a formidable woman, and she still bore the silent displeasure of the two Grannys; but she was no coward, and she was a true Six—her loyalty to her Family and her devotion to its members were her ruling qualities. She faced the Travellers, all nodding their solemn agreement, and she spoke up clear and confident.

"At least," she said, looking them straight in the eyes, "this Kingdom will never have a *Pope!*"

They drew back from her, white and furious; that had struck home, and it told her a few things worth passing along to the Grannys later. Jacob Jeremiah Traveller, all alone at Booneville on Tinaseeh with nobody to challenge his authority for thousands of miles, and no comset to grant anybody an occasional peak at his doings, must be busy demonstrating to the people of his Kingdom what a heavy yoke a burning faith could be.

"And how are we to address this . . . youngster?" spat Feebus Timothy.

"Try 'Mister Wommack,'" she said pertly. "Or just 'Lewis Motley'—he doesn't suffer from delusions of grandeur, gentlemen."

And she turned her back on the two groups before the tension could grow any worse, or her traitorous knees fail her, and led them after her, feeling ice between her shoulder blades at the idea of what those nine pairs of hands might be doing that she could not see. Just as *well* she could not see, if they were in fact about their mysterious flickering business; she wouldn't see it coming, whatever it was, and she'd no desire to.

But nothing happened; and they were at the Meeting Room

door, where one Senior Attendant stood casually with folded arms, waiting. "Here," Gilead said to him, "are the nine Magicians of Rank of this planet, come to see Lewis Motley. Will you take them in, please?"

Lewis Motley Wommack sat at the head of the table, smiling at them as they came through the door. He wore the Wommack seagreen, a color that was as appropriate to his copper hair and beard as it was to the sands of the beach. The long narrow robe was of a soft woven stuff suitable for the summer heat; it had no collar and no cuffs, just the elegant sweep of a well-cut and well-sewn garment, and the Wommack crest on a heavy enameled pendant hung round his neck on a leather thong. On his right hand was a gold ring with the same crest, and his feet were clad in plain low boots of green-dyed leather, narrow-cuffed. He sat in a worn heavy chair at the head of a small round table, and that was all. And the sum of it was wholly regal.

It was not what the Magicians of Rank had expected.

"Should you lose your youthful figure, Lewis Motley Wommack," said Sheridan Pike Farson the 25th to break the speculative silence, "that garment you wear will become something of an embarrassment."

The young man gave him a long considering look, and Sheridan Pike was astonished to discover that he felt rebuked. He had not experienced those eyes before; Responsible of Brightwater could have told him something of the dangers they posed.

"Be seated, gentlemen," said the Guardian, as if the remark had not been made. "Anywhere you like, please. There is wine there, and ale for those who prefer it. I thank you for your courtesy in responding so promptly to my invitation, and for taking time from the pressure of your duties to come to my aid."

The Farsons glanced at each other, and Sheridan Pike touched his brother's hand with his fingertips, like moths lighting, spelling out in the ancient alphabet of bones and knuckles the single message—"Beware his eyes." And Luke Nathaniel Farson spelled back—"And his speech."

You could tell a person's station on Ozark by their speech. There was the formspeech of the Grannys, a carefully artificial register of exaggerated archaic vocabulary and intonation—

especially intonation. There was the speech of the ordinary citizen, that had undergone all the normal processes of language change, but whose speakers prided themselves on its roughness and its lack of pretension; they spoke as boones, however crowded they might live. There was the flowing mellifluity of the Reverends, required of them only in the performance of their duties, but often taken up for all purposes as a man grew older in the profession. And then there was the speech of the Magicians of Rank, restricted to those nine, laboriously learned along with the Formalisms & Transformations, intended to force respect by its elegance and elaborate usage, as artificial in its way as the mode of the Grannys. Lewis Motley Wommack the 33rd had spoken only a few dozen words, and they might indicate nothing more than his excellent brain and even more excellent education; on the other hand, there was a suspicious ring to them. The mode of the Magicians of Rank, unlike that of the Grannys, ought not to be easy to assume; most citizens had no contact with a Magician of Rank in all their lives.

"Gentlemen?" The Guardian of the Castle was waiting, and they took their chairs, with a mild scuffle over who should be at the dividing line between the Travellers and the others, and that dubious honor falling at last to Lincoln Parradyne Smith. Lincoln Parradyne was uncomfortable; the contrast between the self-made King he had at home and the utter elegance of this youth was striking. When he returned to Castle Smith he thought he might try some fine-tuning . . . perhaps convince Delldon Mallard to remove some of the gems from the crowns and settle for less sumptuous robes at least around the Castle and on non-state occasions.

"I will not waste your time," said Lewis Motley, "I am well aware that your duties call you, and that your leisure is limited. I call you here only because I have nowhere else to turn, and I have reached the outmost limits of my own endurance in this matter. The task of rendering assistance to me in my quandary is appropriate only to your group; therefore, I have called upon the nine of you for succor. You are the sovereign remedy, so to speak."

That settled it, if what came before had not; he *was* using their register, the speechmode of the Magicians of Rank. It was a subtle declaration—but of what?

"Your manner of speech, sir—" began Feebus Timothy

Traveller, ready to express the displeasure felt by all of them, but Lewis Motley cut them off.

"The 'sir' is not called for," he said. "Nor will it ever be—I have no interest in such things. As for my manner of speech"—he smiled again, and looked all round the table—"it is said that imitation is the sincerest form of flattery.

"And now," he went on, "if you are all comfortable, I would be pleased to present my problem. It is, as I told you in the invitations, a matter regarding a woman—Responsible of Brightwater."

That changed things. A moment before the only emotion in the room had been the chill of disapproval and angered pride; now the nine leaned forward as one man, their pique forgotten. If there was one thing that united them, other than their shared duties and privileges, it was their hatred of the woman he named; perhaps the most difficult task Veritas Truebreed Motley had to deal with, living as he did under her very nose, was hiding that hatred from everyone except her. He knew it was useless to try to fool Responsible, even if he had cared to. The Magicians of Rank were like preybeasts that have caught a scent; they had been nine, now they were one.

"You are not fond of the daughter of Brightwater," mused the Guardian, watching them. "That is indeed curious; except for you, Veritas Truebreed, I should have thought you would of had no dealings with her to arouse your emotions. I am astonished, gentlemen, at the way in which one mystery often lies behind another, only to reveal a third and a fourth beyond."

"You assume a great deal," said Michael Stepforth Guthrie the 11th, he of Castle Guthrie itself, known planetwide for his skill and for his delight in elaborate mischief. There was no mischief in his voice now.

"Where there is knowledge, one need not make assumptions," said Lewis Motley calmly. "Is that not a general maxim, gentlemen?"

He took the medallion bearing his crest in his fingers, stroking it lightly, smiling at them, that maddening constant smile, and waited; and Michael Stepforth Guthrie spoke again.

"What is your problem with Responsible of Brightwater?" he asked roughly. "She is Thorn of Guthrie's daughter. The Mistress of my Castle, Myrrh of Guthrie, is her grandmother. I know her better than anyone here except perhaps Veritas

Truebreed, who has the misfortune to share her roof—and I know no reason she should have drawn your notice. She is not even a pleasure to a man's eye, Lewis Motley . . . and less by far to a man's ear. What have you, an ocean and two continents away, to do with Responsible of Brightwater?"

The Guardian's face hardened, and for a moment they saw not a youth of nineteen but a glimpse of the man he would one day be, when he had more years to his credit.

"You have said she is no pleasure to the eye or ear of a man," he said grimly. "I am a good judge of women; I am in full accord with that judgment. She is an awkward, scrawny gawk of a girl; her face is too bony, and her breasts are too small. She runs when she should walk, interferes when she should refrain, and speaks when any decent female would keep silence. But I will take it a step farther than eyes and ears, gentlemen! A *large* step farther . . . Had I only the sight and sound of that accursed young woman to deal with, I would not have needed you. The distance of which Michael Stepforth speaks would of solved my problem."

"And it does not?"

"She is not bound by distances," said the Guardian flatly. "Not in space; not in time. So far as I know, unless you nine have the skill to restrain her, she is bound by nothing in this universe but her own whim. And her whim is to make of my life an unspeakable hell."

A stir went round the table; they were more than interested, they hung on his words.

"Explain yourself!" ordered Michael Desirard McDaniels the 17th, Magician of Rank in residence at Castle Farson. "We cannot help with riddles—save those for the Grannys, and do *us* the favor of plain speech."

"And promptly," said another. "Enough of this dawdling."

"Responsible of Brightwater," said Lewis Motley, "offends the eye and the ear; in my case, she does not scruple to offend the mind as well."

"The mind . . . *how* does she offend your mind?"

"I thought a long time before I called you," said Lewis Motley slowly. "It is not pleasant to be telling tales on a female not much more than a child—for a long time I was determined I would not. But she has gone far beyond that limit at which the scruples of ordinary decency and honor apply to her; she no longer merits any of those scruples, and my conscience is clear. To betray evil—monstrous evil—I owe her no hesitation. Not any longer."

"What in the world," breathed Veritas Truebreed, "has she *done* to you?"

"Done? Not only done, but *does!* Every day of my life."

"Lewis Motley—"

"She will not leave me in peace," he said simply. "As another female might tag after you day and night in the ordinary world, forever after your attention, always there wherever you look, her voice always in your ear, Responsible of Brightwater tags constantly after my mind. *I want it stopped.*"

The last four words fell like four stones into a pool of silence.

"Well?" demanded the Guardian. "Can you or can you not control her? Do you or do you not command this world of Ozark and all that moves upon it? Is this a simple matter for you, a mere child's trick—as I have been led to believe—or are you a pack of *frauds?*"

The Magicians of Rank were in a state that did not inspire confidence, all trying to speak at once, and their fingers flying under the table like frantic insects. It was a discomfiting sight, and Lewis Motley shoved back his chair from the table and stared at them with frank wonder.

"Answer me, gentlemen," he said, and still he did not raise his voice. "I am surprised—I admit that frankly. Your behavior is . . . bewildering." And he added, "If the people of the six continents could see you now, they would never be in awe of you again, not if you sailed a thousand golden ships with silver sails, not if you SNAPPED from here to the stars and back! They would laugh at you, as they laugh at Lincoln Parradyne's puppet of a King—and they would be fully justified in their disrespect. Be glad, gentlemen, that there is no one here to see you but myself!"

Nathan Overholt Traveller was the oldest of the nine; Lewis Motley's words brought him instantly out of his disarray. He had not been spoken to in that way since he donned the garments of his profession, and he didn't care for it.

"That will do!" he declared. "You may be of some importance in this backwater, you may be Guardian of this Castle—whatever that means—but know that we can make you a *dead* Guardian, without moving from these chairs! Guard your *tongue*,

Guardian; or you will find your tenure short, I promise you."

Lewis Motley sighed and pulled his chair back into its proper place.

"Now that," he said with satisfaction, "is the sort of thing I expected. Thank you, Nathan Overholt; you have restored some portion of my confidence."

Veritas Truebreed cleared his throat. "Lewis Motley Wommack," he said carefully, "do we understand you to mean that Responsible of Brightwater uses mindspeech with you? Is that your claim, or do we misunderstand? Be careful, now—you realize that it's a grave charge you are making. That goes beyond mere illegality, for a woman; you charge her with blasphemy. Be certain!"

"Mindspeech . . ."

"Well? Is that your claim?"

"Almost," said Lewis Motley. "Almost. It would be more accurate to say that she uses it *at* me than with me . . . I certainly have no means of making reply. And she does not confine herself to speech; she does not scruple to—" He caught himself, and a muscle twitched, suddenly, in his cheek. "I will not speak of that," he said, with a determination that had all the finality of a Castle gate swinging shut and its bars falling into place. "There are obscenities that a man keeps to himself. Just see that she respects the privacy of my mind; I ask nothing more than that. You can do that?"

"The problem," said Nathan Overholt, "was not whether we could; it was a question of whether it was permitted to us . . . whether it was justified. You have answered that question for us."

"Good," said Lewis Motley. "*Good!*"

It was clear to the Magicians of Rank that Lewis Motley had no idea what lay behind their temporary confusion, and there was no particular reason why he should have. Mindspeech on this planet was supposed to be confined to them, to a rare and exceptionally talented Magician, and—for some unknown and outrageous reason—to the Mules. A Magician not sufficiently skilled to be a Magician of Rank, but beyond the ordinary, could mindspeak in a clumsy fashion, one or two semantic units at a time, with great and exhausting effort—it was a rare thing. Leaving out those exceptions, the Grannys and the Magicians had empathy to spare, but could go no further. As for Responsible of Brightwater, the news that she could use mindspeech, and his hint that there was more to it even than that, went beyond revelation. It was the Twelve Towers crashing down about their learned heads. He could not know that, but they did, one and all.

"Perhaps," suggested Michael Stepforth Guthrie carefully, "it is only your imagination, Lewis Motley. You have been under a great strain lately, and the pressure of your new duties, isolated as you are here, and your brother only a short time in his grave, must be extreme. Please consider once again: are you *certain?"*

And then there were nine Magicians of Rank leaping with varying degress of nimbleness out of the way as the Guardian of Wommack threw the heavy table over into their laps.

"Months I have lived with that witch prying and poking about in my head!" he shouted. *"Months!* At first it was only a moment, only a nudge now and then . . . then it was every day . . . soon it will be every hour of every day! Why she leaves me in peace in the nights now I cannot imagine, but I know it will not last . . . And you dare ask me if it is my imagination! *Imagination!* I may be imagining *you,* gentlemen, I may be imagining of my own heart, I may be imagining this room and this chair and this table—but I do not imagine the liberties that Responsible of Brightwater takes with my mind!"

The Magicians of Rank, back against the walls and the door, began to feel almost warm toward this arrogant stripling, for all that he had shown them less deference than he had shown their Mules. If what he said was true, and by his words it surely must be—if he had been mad they would have known at once, his mind was harried and fretful and fractious, but it was sound—if it was *true,* then at last they had their chance to revenge themselves! Even with one another, whatever it was she used to bind their lips held; they could not speak of the experiences they had shared. But they knew, every one of them knew, and for the opportunity to pay her back as she should be paid there was almost nothing they would not have offered.

Lewis Motley was breathing hard, and staring round him like a Mule stallion with a threatened herd. When the Magicians of Rank began moving toward him, speaking to him with the voices they used for the ill and the frantic, he had only one thing to say to them.

"Can you make her stop it?"

He had no interest in anything else they might be able to do, to him or for him.

"Can you?"

They were grinning at one another in a way that lacked dignity, but had enough of malice and sheer unfettered glee to make up for it. For a man to use mindspeech, unless he were a Magician, was illegal. For a *woman* to do so . . .

It would take all of them, and for once in their lives they would have to work together. But it was allowed. Her offense was monstrous.

"Yes, Lewis Motley," they said, "we certainly can."

They were nine ecstatic Magicians of Rank, and they could already taste the sweetness of revenge in their mouths.

CHAPTER 18

SHANDRA OF CLARK was out of breath; first, there'd been dropping the eggshells into the batter for that morning's cornbread and having to make a whole new batch, and the cook down on her for that; and then there'd been tripping over somebody's small boy as had *no* business being in the staff hallway down the side of the Castle . . . and then going back for another pot of tea to replace the one she'd half spilled on Miss Responsible's tray, and the cook down on her for *that*. She was determined this time to get up the stairs and down the corridor, and the tea delivered with no further mishaps.

"Keep on as you've been, Shandra of Clark," she muttered to herself as she went along, "and you'll spend the rest of your life stuck in the back kitchen of this Castle peeling things and taking dressdowns from the rest of the staff, see if you don't." That wasn't her plan for her life; she intended to work her way out of the kitchen and into the affections of a certain young man with good prospects—but first she had to get out of the kitchen.

Responsible's door . . . there! She stopped, balancing the tray carefully on one hand, and smoothed her hair down, and then she knocked softly three times.

"Your tea, miss, and good morning with it," she said, hoping she sounded more agreeable than she felt. The cook had been *really* mad at her, and considering it was two dozen squawker eggs wasted, that was reasonable.

She waited for an answer, and passed her time admiring the door. If ever she did have a house of her own, she wanted just such a door. Boards of ironwood, set vertical, and the top arched to a high peak, and then the whole thing painted a proper blue. And the doorknob had set in its center a Brightwater crest—she wouldn't have that one, of course—in glorious bright colors you could near see in the dark. And the horseshoe nailed above the door was a dainty thing of silver, no rough and (admit it) rusty iron such as she had over her own door on the Castle's top floor. Time she polished *that,* for sure.

"Miss Responsible?"

She knocked again, and frowned. Miss Responsible was an early riser, saving always that day after the Granny'd potioned her, and lately she'd been up so early that several times she'd come down after her own tea and caught the staff just coming into the kitchen. Shandra fancied having her own house to run, but she didn't envy Responsible of Brightwater the managing of this great hulk of a Castle, thank you, not one bit she didn't.

She knocked sharper, and then clucked her tongue, irritated. Now she'd be getting it in the kitchen for being gone too long right in the middle of making breakfast!

If it'd been some doors, she'd of opened it—not looked in, of course, but just opened it a crack—and called right into the room. But nothing would have brought her to that at this door, or either of the Granny's, nor the Magician of Rank's either. Warded doors she'd keep her hands off of unless invited, now and forevermore, and she had no intentions of having Miss Responsible do . . . something. She wasn't sure just what Miss Responsible could do, but she gathered it wouldn't necessarily be pleasant, and she had no desire to test it out. It was said Miss Responsible was right clever with Charms and Spells.

There being nothing else to do, she took the tray back to the kitchen one more time, and told the others that Responsible of Brightwater wasn't answering her door this morning.

The cook set her arms akimbo and made a fuss like she'd

made over the eggs, only more so. "*Are* you for sure of that, Shandra?" she demanded. "Seems to me your mind's dead set this morning on seeing if you can't do the day backwards and hindside *too*. Did you knock? Loud enough so as you could tell somebody was knocking?"

"Three times three times, I did! And loud, the last time. *And* I called out. And it's cruel of you going on and on about the eggs like I did it on purpose—"

"I'll have none of your sass," said the cook, and Shandra closed her mouth abruptly. She stood a head taller than the cook, and likely outweighed her by twenty pounds, but Becca of McDaniels was a true Five, she'd as soon take your head off as look at you, and she ran the Brightwater kitchen the way her husband ran its stables. No sass, no slack, and no time to breathe from the minute you got there till you were through *by the clock*.

"Yes, ma'am," said Shandra of Clark. "Begging your pardon."

"You knocked, and you called, and no answer, you say?"

"Yes, ma'am."

"Then you take that tea, which is strong enough now for goatdip, I expect, and you go straight to one of the Grannys and you tell them what you just told me. They aren't as impressed by wards as we are."

"Nice having two Grannys in the Castle, don't you think, Becca of McDaniels? It makes a person feel safe."

"If you don't hightail it, and right this instant, it'll take a sight more than a couple of Grannys to keep you safe, young missy!"

Shandra gulped, and followed instructions. Down the hall again, up the stairs again—only one flight, praise the Gates, the Grannys were both on the second floor—down *that* hall, and she almost ran into Granny Hazelbide coming out to breakfast already.

"Oh, Granny Hazelbide, I'm glad to see you!" said Shandra. "You'll pardon me for holding you from your breakfast, I hope, but I've knocked and knocked and I can't rouse Miss Responsible, and the cook said as I was to come tell you and you'd see what was up."

"She did, did she?"

"She did. If you'd be so kind, Granny Hazelbide."

"Nothing that pleasures me more of a morning than traipsing

up and down the stairs with the servingmaids," said the Granny, "you tell Becca of McDaniels that. *I* have nothing better to do with my time."

"Yes, ma'am, Granny Hazelbide. And thank you kindly, ma'am."

"You were any more humble, you'd disappear altogether, you know that?"

"Yes, ma'am."

The old woman humphed, and gave the floor a good one with her cane, but she followed Shandra briskly enough, grannying at her all the way, and the girl managed to keep her face straight even though the part about the epizootics, till she stood once again at Responsible's bedroom door and gave it three knocks.

Back at her came the silence, and she turned to the Granny. "You see?"

"Where's that girl got to now?" grumbled Granny Hazelbide, and she reached right out and grabbed the doorknob that Shandra of Clark wouldn't of touched for ten dollers, nor for fifty either. And then Shandra did feel strange, for the Granny snatched back her fingers as she would have done from a live flame and cried out "Double Dozens!" like her voice was scorched, too.

"Granny Hazelbide? Is something the matter?" quavered Shandra of Clark.

"Girl, you set down that tray—right there on the floor'll do—and you go get Granny Gableframe, fast as you can hoof it, and send her here to me! Go!"

Shandra did, fast as she could as instructed, and then she fairly flew down to the kitchen to tell, stopping only to grab the tray as the two Grannys disappeared into Responsible's room.

"The Grannys sent me away!" she said, right out, before Becca of McDaniels could have at her again, and she set the tray of tea down on the big kitchen table so hard the teapot rattled. "They said for me to *scat!*"

"And?"

"And they both went into Miss Responsible's room . . . and they did *not* close her door behind them. Which means they were afraid to touch it, seeing as how it burned Granny Hazelbide the first time!" Shandra clutched herself tight with both arms and wailed, "Oh, Becca of McDaniels, I'm plain terrified!"

She had to tell it all, then, and everybody gathering round to hear, until the cook shushed her in no uncertain terms. "It's none of our business," she said, grim of eye and lip, "but the breakfast is. And if we're to know what's going on, we will; and if we're not, life'll go right along just the same. Now turn to, and no more nattering and lollygagging."

"But if—"

"Turn *to!"* thundered the cook, her hollering twice as big as anything else about her, and that was that. If they died of curiosity, they'd just die of it. And Shandra berated herself for an idiot; if she'd "forgotten" that tray she'd of had to go back up after it and she might of been able to find out something, and as much trouble as she was in already it wouldn't have made a scrap of difference. Trust her to make a mistake when all it got her was broad words, and then do a thing right when the mistake would of been worth it!

Up in Responsible's room, the two Grannys stood, one on each side of her bed, and pondered.

"She's breathing," said Granny Gableframe.

"Barely. *Just* barely. There's none to spare, Gableframe."

"The mirror clouded over."

"But see her bosom? Still as my own hand—not a move, not a flutter."

Granny Hazelbide laid her fingers to the girl's throat and pressed, hard, below the joint of the jaw.

"Pulse *there,*" she declared. "It's not thumping and pounding, but a pulse it surely is. She's breathing."

"Tsk!" went Granny Gableframe. "Now what*ever* do you suppose?"

"You? You're senior to me—what do *you* think?"

Granny Gableframe pinched her lips tight and shook her head.

"I don't know," she said slowly, "I surely don't. But the wards on that door weren't put there just to keep out the servingmaids, I can guarantee you that . . . see that mark on your palm where you gripped the knob? Looks like you'd gone and picked a handful of coals up out of a fire!"

"Coals," said Granny Hazelbide dryly, "don't have an asterisk when they burn," and she turned up her palm, where the little scarlet star glowed sullen and sore.

"Law!" breathed Granny Gableframe. "Will you just look at that!"

The two old women stared at Responsible, and they stared at each other; and then Granny Gableframe said, "Do you sup*pose?*" and pulled the pillow gently from beneath Responsible's head.

There was nothing gentle about the way she first ripped off the pillowslip and then tore the ticking right down the way she'd of made cleaning rags.

"It's there!" she cried. "You see that, Hazelbide?"

And she plunged her hand into the pillow and pulled it out, triumphant, holding the thing she found there gingerly with the tips of her fingers, and let the ruined pillow fall to the floor.

Granny Hazelbide whistled a little tune under her breath.

"More of 'em, I wonder?" she said, when she got to the end of it.

"I misdoubt that—one's more than enough."

Granny Hazelbide looked again at the asterisk branded into her palm, and then she took the other pillows and patted them all over, muttering that she'd never seen such a girl for pillows and how many times had she told Responsible she'd end up with a double chin, and then she got to the last of them, and said: "Sure enough. Sure enough, there's one in here or my birthname adds up to a minus Two and yours along with it. Look here, Gableframe, just look here!"

"Well, who the Gates'd want to put *two* feather crowns in the pillows of one scrawny girlchild?" demanded Granny Gableframe.

"More to the point, seeing as how it's this *particular* scrawny girlchild," said Granny Hazlebide, "who *could?*"

Who could put burning wards on the door, and feather crowns in the pillows, of Responsible of Brightwater? It was a nice question, and both Grannys pressed their fists to their top teeth, thinking on it.

"Well, she won't wake," observed Granny Gableframe in the silence. "We'd best brush out her hair and make her tidy."

"You're sure?"

"Not for us, nor for any Granny Magic, she won't. We'll get the Magician of Rank in here—maybe for him. But I'll have her neat first, afore he sees her."

"And these nasty pieces of work?"

Granny Gableframe looked with disgust at the feather crowns. They were squawker tailfeathers, tips together and fanning out from the center, making a circle big as a feast-day platter.

"Notice," said Granny Hazelbide, "how the feathers go? Widdershins, both of 'em."

And so they did. Counterclockwise.

"I'd burn them both," said Gableframe, "except that might could be they'll be needed later on to get to the bottom of this."

"Or pay for it."

"Ah, yes . . . there's that."

"Give me the one you have," said Granny Hazelbide decisively. "I've already crossed those wards, might as well go whole hog. I'll stand here and hold them, and keep my eye on that child—for all the good it'll do—while you get Veritas Truebreed Motley the Fourth in here, and then I'll give them into *his* keeping. This is a tad past me, I don't mind admitting."

"*And* me," said Granny Gableframe; and she handed the feather crown to Granny Hazelbide and set to brushing Responsible's hair and straightening her nightgown. "And it's good fortune you have a Magician of Rank here . . . I don't like the look of her."

"Will you hurry then, Gableframe? We've been standing here, gawking and gabbing, it'll be near half an hour."

"Peace, Granny Hazelbide," said the other. "You know as well as I do, there's no chance of her dying. They could of put a *dozen* feather crowns in her pillows, bad cess to 'em whosoever they may be, and she'd still be in no danger of dying. Not so long, Granny Hazelbide, as there's no little girl in a Granny School on this round world as is named Responsible—and there's none."

"One misnamed again, maybe?"

"*No*-sir!" Granny Gableframe shook her head. "I'd know, if there were—there's nobody senior to me expecting Golightly at Castle Clark—I'd know. My word on it. But I'll get Veritas Truebreed, because there's far too much here as I don't know anymore about than that servingmaid did—and I will hurry."

It was all over the town and out into the countryside before the day was over, and the ban that Jonathan Cardwell Brightwater had set on the comcrews as to how they'd be jailed for treason if they put one word out on the comsets hadn't slowed it down one bit. It was that sort of news.

Responsible of Brightwater, people were saying, lay on her bed like a poppet made of ivory wax, just barely breathing, her eyes closed and her lips sealed and making no response even when she was pinched and stuck with a sharp needle. And under her head, in her pillows, they said, there'd been two—not one, but two, and *that* never had happened before!—two feather crowns found, and both of them made widdershins! And they'd called in all the Magicians in the Kingdom, and the Magician of Rank as well, and not a one of them as could do anything for her, or even explain why not. And to send shivers up and down your backbone, if all that wasn't enough, it seemed that as Veritas Truebreed Motley the 4th marched out of Responsible of Brightwater's bedroom door, throwing up his hands and declaring himself helpless, the bright silver horseshoe nailed over the door flew off the nail that held it, all by its own self, and struck him right between his shoulder blades!

"It fair curdles the blood in the veins," they were saying. And "It's not natural." Mothers caught a suspiciously quiet clump of tadlings playing at making feather crowns and put an end to *that*—every one of them sent off to find a perfect willow switch, take off every leaf, peel it down to the lithe core, and bring it back for application where it would do their characters the most good. You didn't switch a child often, nor lay a hand to one in anger; but there were some things that had to be made so clear they'd never be forgotten. This was one of those things.

There were no places on Marktwain given over entirely to drinking, as there'd been on Old Earth. Whiskey, made powerful as gunpowder, was kept as a medicine, made from the tall red Ozark corn; beer and wine were served in the home on festive occasions, and that was the end of Ozark drinking. But there were three hotels in Capital City, where a man could get a glass of berry wine, or a strong dark ale, for a *private* occasion—be it feast or distress—and they did a heavy business in beverages that night.

The men discussed it logically, gathered at the long tables set in the hotel diningrooms. Gabriel Micah Clark the 40th had offered as opener that it was his opinion the ruckus at the Castle was an example of pride going before a fall.

"That Brightwater girl has called down the wrath of the Powers on herself," he announced. "That's how *I* see it." And he blew the head of froth off his ale. "Been tempting fate now fifteen years—"

"Oh, come off that, Gabriel Micah," snorted his left neighbor, a lawyer of the McDaniels line and given to nitpicking by trade. "You can't accuse a one-year-old babe of pride; a tadling's not even civilized till it gets to be three."

"You know what I mean," Gabriel Micah protested.

"Put it clear or don't put it at all," insisted the lawyer.

"Near on ten years at least, then, that split the hair fine enough for you? I mind her *very* well, I was working in the stables at the Castle then, and she but five years old, and you talk of *pride!* Why, she'd come right down to the stables and give us all what for about the tackle not being hung right, or the straw not clean enough on the stall floors. And ten minutes later you'd hear her in the Castle, like she was Queen of all the Shebas, ordering the servingmaids around and telling them where she'd found more dust than suited her fancy. You can't tell me *that's* natural!"

"Well, some of that should be laid to the account of Thorn of Guthrie," put in another. "If she'd been doing her job as mother—"

"Thorn of Guthrie?" Gabriel Micah was amazed. "All that woman needs do to fill her role in life is breathe in and breathe out and let the rest of us have the privilege of looking at her."

"That may well be, but it makes for sorry mothering."

"*For* example, let's consider Responsible's sister Troublesome!"

"For example, let's not." The Reverend was a tolerant man, considering, and he didn't scruple to spend an evening here with the male members of the flock, listening to what they had to say and getting a certain perspective on the turn of their minds at any given time—but he had his limits.

"Sorry, Reverend."

"I should hope."

"Like I said, Reverend, I beg your pardon for mentioning that one. But Responsible's another matter, and I say she's meddled and poked her nose where it wasn't wanted, and wasted good money on folderols till the time came when even the Holy One couldn't stand her any longer. And this is what it comes out to."

"There was that Quest of hers—talk of wasting money! Every Castle on this planet—always excepting those fool

Smiths, and I don't doubt they were up to something as wouldn't bear the light of day or they'd of been in on it too—every Castle put on some kind of to-do for the 'daughter of Brightwater'! I've heard it said it was the Grannys as ordered that, but I can't see it. Can youall?"

Everybody agreed that they couldn't; it didn't sound like the Grannys.

"And there was her traveling outfit—you recall that? Three hundred dollers, good Kingdom money, that all cost, or I mistake myself!"

The Reverend set his ale mug down with a thump, shaking his head.

"How much, then?"

"Excepting the whip and spurs, that have been in that Family now over three hundred years and didn't cost any of *us* a cent, though they may of been a strain on some of our grandfathers, that costume came to precisely sixty-three dollers and twenty-nine cents. I happen to know."

"Magic in it, then," said the lawyer.

"A needle goes a sight faster with a Granny pushing it," agreed the hotelkeeper, filling glasses and mugs all round.

"And then, there's all the money—Reverend, you can't tell us it wasn't enormous sums of money!—as was spent on that fool Jubilee!" Gabriel Micah snickered. "What's the opposite of 'Jubilee,' Reverend? A wake?"

The Reverend gave him a chilly look.

"You, Gabriel Micah—if I remember correctly, and I believe I do—you had a good time at the Jubilee such as you've not had since you were caught that time down by the creek, with—"

"I recollect that, Reverend," said the man hastily. "No need to review."

"Well? Are you trying to tell me that all the people in this Kingdom, and many a dozen more that were our guests, didn't have a fine time at the Jubilee? Didn't enjoy the fairs, and the picnics, and the competitions, and the plays, and even—one or two of you—the sermons, and all the rest of it? I'll grant you Responsible didn't have much fun out of it, but I didn't hear any of the rest of you complaining as it was going on."

"No," said another, "it was a right fine celebration. Fair's fair, Gabriel Micah—and the rest of you, too. Not to mention, long as we're talking her up, that it was Responsible of Brightwater as ordered five days' wages paid to every last one of us out of the Castle funds so we wouldn't have to work during the Jubilee."

"That was our own money—tax money!"

"Howsomever; there's a lot of other things it could of been spent on that we'd never of had any good from. And there was nothing to make her do that, you know. They could just as well of said work as usual and find time for celebrating after, if you've any energy left—and spent the tax money on theirselves. And you know it very well."

"Well, if she's such a fine lady," demanded Gabriel Micah, determined now to be spokesman for his position if he died trying, "then how *come* she's lying up there now, as near dead as makes *no* nevermind, and nothing any of the Magicians can do to bring her out of it? That sound like some mark of heavenly favor to *you?*"

The Reverend listened to them grumble and fuss for a while, and then left, clapping each one in his reach on the shoulder. He was satisfied that the doings at the Castle weren't worrying the men much; if anything, they were pleased to have something new to talk about. The fall of the Confederation had made no difference in their lives up to now, since they were of Brightwater Kingdom and enjoyed every privilege they ever had, with the added advantage of not having to put up with the Continental Delegations coming in one month in four and filling up the hotels.

The men of Brightwater were in no way worried; curious, distracted at worst, uneasy perhaps that the Magicians and Magicians of Rank seemed not to know what was going on. But not worried.

It was the women that worried. At home in their houses, they were white-faced and tight-lipped, and they had just one question: what was going to happen now?

The Grannys and the Family had asked Veritas Truebreed Motley the same question.

"Now what, you hifalutin fraud?" Thorn of Guthrie'd thrown at him, speaking for a number of them that wouldn't have dared say the words. "You and your high-and-mighty magic! What's going to happen now to my daughter?"

The Magician of Rank had smiled and expressed his approval of the first concern for her child he'd ever heard from her lips, and Thorn of Guthrie had come near spitting at him. "I'm *not* concerned for my child," she said, tossing that Guthrie hair, "not so much as my little finger-end's worth! My child, from what I can determine and from what you tell me, is resting comfortably. I am talking about the effect of her condition on all the rest of us!"

Veritas Truebreed raised his eyebrows, and then he bowed his head, ever so slightly, and clasped his hands behind him.

"My dear Thorn of Guthrie," he answered her. "I think 'all the rest' of you have no cause for concern. Responsible attended to a thing or two in this Kingdom, and meddled a good deal more than was appropriate in things elsewhere, but there's nothing she did that can't be handled by others. Your Economist can see to the accounts she kept, the staff can—"

"Veritas Truebreed!"

"Yes, Thorn of Guthrie! I am not deaf, you know!"

"I am not referring to the things Responsible did that could be handled by the servingmaids! You'll push me too far, even for a Magician of Rank! I am referring to her *other* duties!"

He looked her right in the eye and assured her that there was nothing—*nothing*—that Responsible of Brightwater ordinarily saw to that couldn't be handled just as well by the nine Ozark Magicians of Rank.

"You're sure of that?"

He was sure of it, and so were his colleagues. In the time it had taken them to accomplish the task of putting Responsible into pseudocoma—and that had turned out to be somewhat more of a project than they'd anticipated—they'd come to an agreement on that. The idea that the existence of a female, duly named and designated Responsible, in every generation—the idea that that was somehow essential to the well-being of Ozark—had been thoroughly discussed and set aside for what it was. Mere superstition.

EPILOGUE

It was eight o'clock in the morning on Tinaseeh. Morning prayer, morning chores, and the essentials of the body were out of the way; now it was time for teaching. The Tutors, though they came from the ranks of the Magicians, wore nothing to distinguish them from any other Traveller male. Their charges—exactly twelve per Tutor—were miniature versions of themselves. Black trousers, black shirts, black jackets, black shoes, black hats; the only concession made to childhood was the absence of the tie. In Booneville there were six little boys that didn't have to go to Tutorials, because they were waiting for six more little boys to reach the age of three and bring their group up to the required dozen. The boys in the Tutorials hated them, because they were still free to play; the boys left out hated and envied the others, and felt deprived because they could not attend and would be late starting.

There were no problems of cirrculum on Tinaseeh. Each

Tutor had a heavy book he carried with him, laying out the content of each of the twelve hundred teaching days he would have with his pupils. Four years, from the third birthday to the seventh, he would have them, for three hundred days of the year. And there would never be a day in that twelve hundred when he thought to himself, "Now what shall I do today?" That's not how it was done on Tinaseeh.

On this particular day, the subject was "Governments of Our World."

"Boys?"

Tutor Ethan Daniel Traveller the 30th tapped his ironwood pointer once, for order, and was rewarded with instant silence. He was an experienced Tutor—weary of it, if the truth were known, and hoping this year's examiniations in magic would free him of the role—and his charges gave him no problems. They wouldn't have dared.

"You'll look at the map now," he said, and raised the pointer to touch each continent as he spoke.

"Kintucky!" he said first. "Up here in the left-hand corner, with the Ocean of Storms all around it. Kintucky, settled in—" He waited, with the ironwood poised.

"Twenty-three thirty-nine!" they shouted, and he nodded approval.

"Kintucky is held by the Wommack Family, and it is a mite different from the other Kingdoms. It's governed, right now, by a man called a Guardian, the uncle of the rightful Master of Castle Wommack, just until the boy is old enough to take his place. The name for such a government is a *regency*. You will remember that."

"Yes, Tutor Ethan Daniel."

"Mizzurah, across the Ocean of Storms and off the coast of Arkansaw, was settled in twenty-three thirty-two. It's a very small place, as you can see, but it belongs to two Families—the Lewises and the Wommacks. They are both democratic republics—as Kintucky will be, one of these days—and that means their government is a kind of council, that elects its leaders. But it has never happened on Ozark that that leader was not also Master of the Castle in that Kingdom. And so the government of Mizzurah is led by the Masters of Castles Lewis and Motley. Is that clear?"

"Yes, sir," chorused the boys. Those old enough to write

made notes with their styluses, and the three and four year olds said it over and over under their breath to help themselves remember.

"Moving on, we have the continent—a continent, boys, is a large body of land completely surrounded by water; you will remember that—we have the continent of Arkansaw. Cletus Frederick Farson? Are you paying attention? Look at the map, Cletus Frederick, not the ceiling; there is nothing written on the ceiling!"

The other eleven boys laughed and nudged each other; and Cletus Frederick, supremely uninterested in the topic of "Governments of Our World" but not so stupid as to let it be known, fixed his eyes firmly on the point of the stick and stared at the map.

"The continent of Arkansaw, with the Queen of Storms on the west and the Ocean of Remembrances on the east, was settled in—"

"Twenty-one twenty-seven!"

"Twenty-one twenty-seven, quite right. It is held by three Families: the Farsons, the Guthries, and the Purdys. The Farsons and the Guthries have Kings, and are called—*monarchies*. You will remember that. Now Kingdom Purdy is a little different; it does not have a King, but it is not a democratic republic. It has a group of three men ruling it, that are called Senators; they rule together. This kind of government is called an *ol*igarchy. Say it after me."

"*Ol*igarchy!"

"Again!"

"*Ol*igarchy!"

"That's it. Now, crossing the ocean, still going clockwise, we come to Marktwain, the continent where First Landing happened in the year twenty twenty-one. For six years all of the families lived together on Marktwain, which—as you can see—is small, almost as small as Mizzurah. It is shared by two Families—the Brightwaters and the McDaniels—both Kingdoms are democratic republics."

"That's where the comsets are!" piped one very small boy.

"That's true, James Thomas," agreed the Tutor. "But we don't want the comsets, do we, boys?"

"No, sir!"

"And why don't we?"

"Because they are evil!"

"So they are, so they are. And what else is there on Marktwain, in the Kingdom of Brightwater, that is evil?"

The boys looked at each other, not quite sure what he wanted. There was so much evil everywhere.

"James Thomas?" said the Tutor sharply. "You brought up the comsets—how about you telling us the answer to my question?"

"Responsible and Troublesome," mumbled the little boy very fast, looking at his feet and hoping.

"That is *exactly* right!" the Tutor thundered. "Exactly! Two evil women. Troublesome of Brightwater, exiled now for years to the top of a far mountain also called Troublesome, where decent people will not have to be around her! And Responsible of Brightwater?"

"She's asleep!"

"Yes; she's asleep. She was so wicked that the Holy One struck her down, putting her into a sleep like unto death—and she has been that way now for ten months, two weeks, and three days. You *see* where evil leads?"

They assured him that they did, until he was satisfied.

"Now," he said, "you see the Outward Deeps there, off to the east of Marktwain? We don't know anything much about the Outward Deeps. But to the south of Marktwain is the continent of Oklahomah, settled in twenty-one twenty-seven jointly with Arkansaw. That is, an expedition moved from Marktwain in two parties; one to Arkansaw, one to Oklahomah, at the same time. That is called a *joint expedition*. You will remember that.

"On Oklahomah," he went on, "there are three Families. Two of them are democratic republics—the Kingdoms of Clark and Airy. One, Smith Kingdom, is a monarchy, which means that it has—"

"A King! A King!"

"Good. A King. And finally, we come to"—he swept the pointer around to the bottom left-hand corner of the map with a flourish, and the boys cried—"*Tinaseeh!*"

"Settled in—"

"Twenty-three forty-nine!"

"Good boys! Tinaseeh is the largest of all the continents, and it is the only one to have an inland body of water large enough to be called a sea. That is our *Midland* Sea. And its government is?"

"A *Holy* Republic!"

"So it is. And do we have a King?"

"No!"

"Why not? Why don't we have a King?"

"The Holy One is our leader!"

"And the Holy One's representative on this continent, that interprets the laws and says how we must behave?"

"Jacob Jeremiah Traveller, Master of Castle Traveller! Hurrah!"

Cheers from all directions; the Tutor allowed that for a minute or two. They were, after all, very young. And enthusiasm for Jacob Jeremiah Traveller was a sentiment to be encouraged.

"Now, we are through?" he asked finally, quieting them.

"Yes!"

"No; no, we are not. First, there is a very important question. Remember that there are six"—he held up six fingers—"*six* Kingdoms on Ozark that call themselves democratic republics. Those six—Brightwater, McDaniels, Clark, Airy, Lewis, and Motley—are joined as the Alliance of Democratic Republics. You will remember that. Now—does anybody know what the important question is?"

He didn't expect them to know, so he did not wait, but went right on. "What," he asked, "is the difference between a *democratic* republic and a *Holy* republic? Well?"

Silence. The Tutor tapped the pointer. Tap. Tap. Tap.

"Think!" he said. "Think how they are ruled; isn't that what we've been talking about all morning? How the Kingdoms are ruled? Now, *repeat after me*. A democratic republic is ruled by a man, but the Holy Republic is ruled by the Holy One! All together, now . . ."

He made them say it three times.

It didn't matter how many girls there were to a Granny School; a Granny took as many as happened to be there. And since, on all of Tinaseeh, the only Granny was Granny Leeward, it was a large group of little girls she faced that same day. But she had no more concern about what they must be taught than the Tutors did for the boys, and she needed no book to keep it straight in her head.

"Men," she was saying, "are of but two kinds: splendid, and pitiful. The splendid ones are rare, and if you chance on one you'll know it. What I tell you now has to do with the *rest* of 'em—as my Granny told me, and her Granny told her before that, and so back as far as time will take you . . ."

END OF BOOK TWO

GLOSSARY

ATTENDANT—An Ozark male in domestic service at one of the Twelve Castles. Attendants are reviewed each twelve years for merit of service, and may then be promoted to the rank of Senior Attendant, which carries with it administrative responsibility for lower-ranking staff.

BENISONWEED—A small green herb with white flowers used extensively in magic; it is not a plant brought from Earth by the Ozarkers, but is indigenous to the planet. The strength and efficacy of benisonweed is much enhanced if it is gathered by a virgin.

BESTOWING—One of the three means by which the Kingdoms could grant land on Ozark to individuals. A Bestowing is a grant of land as a mark of special honor, or a reward, and is infrequent. The other two types of land grants are *Landholdings* (grants of one hundred forty-four acres or more), made only to relatives by birth or marriage; and *Farmholdings*, grants of forty-eight acres made to friends or close associates—ordinarily for business reasons.

CAPTAIN, THE—Captain Aaron Dunn McDaniels, who brought the Twelve Families from Earth on The Ship originally.

COMSETS—A computerized television network established to provide communication for all of Ozark, with central facilities (including the computers themselves) at Castle Brightwater. The comsets are the individual units, ranging all the way from very simple portable equipment to the most elaborate. Comsets can be used not only for reception but also for the projection of information.

DOZENS!—One of a long list of oaths and exclamations based upon the all-pervasive number twelve. Other examples include: By the Twelve Gates! By the Twelve Towers! Bloody Dozens! Oh, Twelve Times Twelve!

FIRST GRANNY—The very first of the Ozark Grannys, who accompanied the Families on The Ship when they left Old Earth. Only after the Families were established on Ozark and there began to be a number of Grannys did the system for naming them individually become necessary; thus, First Granny had no "granny name."

FORMALISMS & TRANSFORMATIONS—The very highest and most intricate level of magic, restricted to the Magicians of Rank and (without their knowledge) to Responsible. There are four types of Transformations: Insertion, Deletion, Substitution, and Movement. Formalisms are the symbols, gestures, and other symbolic mechanisms for carrying out the Transformations.

FORMSPEECH—A mode of speech, or speech register, used only by the Ozark Grannys. It is marked by archaic vocabulary and grammar, and by a certain ritualistic nagging, but more important than any of these is its unmistakable intonation (the melody of the speech). Unfortunately, no method exists for reproducing this intonation in writing.

GAILHERB—A healing herb, indigenous to Ozark, prized for its property of closing wounds and stopping bleeding almost instantaneously. It takes a practiced eye to distinguish gailherb from ordinary grass; the best method for the beginner is to hold it up to the light, since it is completely transparent and grass is not.

GARNET RING—A group of politically allied planets sharing the same universe as the planet Ozark; their exact number is unknown. All planets of the Garnet Ring base their cultures upon magic rather than upon technology, and their systems of magic are said to be highly advanced. They are aggressive and imperialistic, and are anxious to add new planets to their membership; however, the conditions under which their laws permit this are severely limited. They have had their eye on Ozark for some time.

GENTLES—One of the indigenous races of Ozark, already long established on the planet when the Ozarkers arrived. Because both the Gentles and the Ozarkers share a fanatical respect for privacy, and because the Gentles live entirely beneath the ground, almost nothing is known about them. For the limited data that are available, see Chapter 16 in this book.

GRANNY—A Granny is an elderly woman skilled in that level of magic known as Granny Magic; it pertains to matters of healing (for simple illnesses), household and garden affairs, and the meting out of elementary punishments such as rashes and warts. The Grannys are also responsible for providing the crucial Proper Names for female infants on Ozark. To become a Granny, a woman must be celibate—by reason of either virginity or widowhood—and must pass rigorous examinations in Granny Magic administered by the already established Grannys.

GRANNY SCHOOL—A system of schooling for all Ozark girl-children from the age of three to seven, during which a Granny passes on to them a body of oral knowledge necessary to any Ozark woman's welfare. This information is not taught to Ozark males.

HOLY ONE—The Supreme Deity of the Ozark religion; there are no denominations in this religion, although observance may vary slightly from one Family to another.

IMPROPER NAMING—Giving a name to a female infant which is not the one intended for her by destiny. This is a serious matter, and will bring bad luck upon the entire Family in which it happens.

LIZZIES—Twelve-passenger ground vehicles, much like the automobiles on Earth, operating on solar power with backup storage batteries. Lizzies are the most usual method of ground transportation on Ozark, since the Mules can carry no more than two individuals and do well to manage ten miles a day on the ground. (Furthermore, they intensely dislike serving as beasts of burden in this manner, and have no reluctance about making their objections clear in the form of bites, kicks, and unceremonious dumpings of their riders.)

MAGICIAN—Professionals highly skilled in magic, and but one degree below the Magicians of Rank. A woman may become a Magician, but this is extremely rare; ordinarily, boys with a potential talent for the profession are spotted in early childhood and are apprenticed to a Magician for training, a system which does not lend itself to encouraging females for the role.

MAGICIAN OF RANK—The highest level of the profession of magic, and restricted to males without exception. Both the Magicians and the Magicians of Rank are able to make use of Formalisms & Transformations: however, while the Magicians work for the most part with the individuals or groups of two or three, the Magicians of Rank exercise their powers for the planet and the population as a whole. Only the Magicians of Rank have the skill of fluent mindspeech, or the ability to SNAP a Mule across any distance almost instantaneously. (The fact that Responsible also shares these abilities is not something that they are fully aware of.)

MULES—One of the indigenous races of Ozark. The original Mules were much smaller and had far less physical strength than the animals of today. Unlike Earth mules, they are not sterile, and the Ozarkers have managed to breed them selectively to their present state—large, strong, handsome animals of great intelligence. A highbred Mule is not only telepathic, but flies at a speed of sixty miles an hour as a result of an arcane mechanism maintained by the Magicians of Rank. The telepathy was there to begin with; the property of flight is entirely the result of Ozark magic. Just why the Mules are willing to cooperate with the Ozarkers to the extent they do, and to serve as domestic animals, is not known, and is a matter about which the Ozarkers feel a certain amount of nervousness; thus, the Mules are much indulged. They are the only form of genuinely rapid transportation available on Ozark.

Although they *could* communicate in mindspeech with the Magicians of Rank, the Mules will not do so, and the immediate result of any attempt by an Ozarker to force the issue is a blinding three-day headache. They can sometimes be induced to provide ground transportation, or to participate in a race rather than in flight; but this is entirely up to them, always. An Attendant who shows unusual talent for dealing with Mules can be absolutely certain of rapid advancement, large bonuses, and high rank.

OUT-CABAL—The representatives of the planets known as the Garnet Ring who communicate periodically with Responsible. Their physical characteristics are entirely unknown.

PLIOFILM—The usual substance upon which Ozarkers write; it is much stronger, more durable, and less bulky than paper, and is made from an Ozark seaweed. Because it is pressure-sensitive, one writes on it with a stylus rather than a pen or pencil.

PROPER NAMING—The system used by the Grannys of Ozark to ensure that a female infant will have the name intended for her by destiny. The mechanism is simple: a name is chosen, by use of the grid below, so that the sum of its letters will be one of the numbers from one to nine. That is not complicated. (For example: Joan = 1 + 6 + 1 + 5 = 13 = 1 + 3 = 4.) What requires skill is knowing which of those numbers is the proper one for a particular girlchild, since each has its own set of distinct characteristics. That knowledge is part of Granny Magic, and is one of the few parts of magic known to them alone. Here is the grid:

1	2	3	4	5	6	7	8	9
A	B	C	D	E	F	G	H	I
J	K	L	M	N	O	P	Q	R
S	T	U	V	W	X	Y	Z	’

(Note: The last symbol beneath the number nine is the *glottal stop*, which does not appear in the names of Ozarkers and is not part of their language. It was added to the grid by First Granny upon contact with the Gentles, who *do* have it as part of their language, not only as a neighborly gesture but because it pleased her to be able to bring the grid to an orderly three times nine items.)

Male infants, by the way, are named by their parents, and the name is chosen primarily for the pleasing quality of its sound. A record is kept of the number of times a name is used, and there is no rule restricting that number. Thus, there may be several dozen men at any one time on Ozark bearing identical names differentiated only by the numbers that follow them. Quite a lot of ingenuity is necessary if a family wants the number following a boychild's name to have the significance it had on Earth—that is, to indicate that the child is a "junior." The only real requirement is that a boy receive a first name and a middle name; it has no other significance.

PSEUDOCOMA—A physical state which can be induced in human beings (or other organisms) only by the Magicians of Rank. It is accomplished by reducing all bodily processes to a level just above that absolutely necessary to sustain life.

REVEREND—A very ancient term, originating on Earth and still maintained on Ozark. It designates the chief official of an Ozark church, all of whom are male. There have been no attempts by Ozark women to assume this function.

SERVINGMAID—The female equivalent of an Attendant (which see above).

SHAMMYBAGS—Small pouches made of tanned goatskin, used for storing and carrying substances required for the practice of magic.

SKERRYS—The third indigenous race of Ozark. They are very tall and thin, eight feet being an average beight, and are extraordinarily beautiful. Their skin is the color of copper, they have long silver hair below their waists—but no body hair whatever—and their eyes are the color of turquoise. They live somewhere in the strange desert on Marktwain, and are almost never seen. They are magnificent, and they are left alone; by tradition, if a Skerry is sighted a day of celebration must be held in honor of the sighting as rapidly as arrangements can be made to do so, and no one is allowed to work on that day. Even less is known about the Skerrys than about the Gentles—no one even knows what their own name for themselves might be, for example. It most assuredly is not "Skerrys."

SQUAWKER—An indigenous domestic fowl of Ozark, much like Earth chickens and used for the same purpose. An extremely stupid bird.

TADLING—Term used for an Ozark child older than two but not yet twelve.

TIME CORNER—A poorly understood sort of "tangle" in time

that causes a specific timelocation to be beyond the reach of any of the mechanisms for prophecy or foreseeing used in Ozark magic.

TIME CORNER PROPHECY—The famous prophecy regarding Responsible of Brightwater and Lewis Motley Wommack the 33rd, which goes like this:

FIRST: For a Destroyer shall come out of the West; and he will know you, and you will know him, and we cannot see how that knowledge passes between you, but it is not of the body.

SECOND: And if you stand against him, there will be great Trouble. And if you cannot stand against him, there will be great Trouble. But the two Troubles will be of different kinds. And we cannot see what either Trouble is, nor which course you should or will take, but only that both will be terrible and perhaps more than you can bear.

THIRD: And if you fail, Responsible of Brightwater, the penalty for your failure falls on the Twelve Families; and if you stand, it is the Twelve Families that you spare.

FOURTH: And no matter what happens, it will be a long, hard time.

This prophecy came to a Granny of Ozark in a dream, and became part of the knowledge taught in Granny Schools.

TUTORIALS—The equivalent of Granny School, for boys from age three to seven. The Tutorials are taught by Tutors recruited from among the Magicians, and the curriculum—unlike that of the Granny Schools—is primarily written rather than oral.

WARDS—Any one of a variety of mechanisms from magic, used to shield an area of an individual, or to prevent access or entry.

WILDERNESS LANDS—All territory on a continent outside of the original boundaries of the Kingdom staked out by the settling Family. Such territories are to be maintained as wilderness in perpetuity, and cannot be owned by any individual or group.

WOMMACK CURSE—In every generation, one girlbaby must be named Responsible and must assume the special duties that go with that name. A very long time ago, an inexperienced Granny at Castle Wommack made a mistake and named an infant Responsible in error. The ill fortune resulting from the error, which has persisted over the centuries, is known as the Wommack Curse.

For information about joining the Ozark Offworld Auxiliary, the official organization for the Ozark Fantasy Trilogy, write to Suzette Haden Elgin, Route 4, Box 192-E, Huntsville, AR 72740. She'll be grateful if you send a stamped self-addressed return envelope when you write.